ROLLS

Keith Weaver

IGUANA

Publisher: Meghan Behse
Editor: Holly Warren
Cover Image: "Gottengen Street Halifax NS" by Barb MacLeod, www.barbmacleodpeiartist.ca (Reprinted with permission.)
Cover design: Daniella Postavsky
Interior Designer: Toby Keymer

ISBN 978-1-77180-349-6 (paperback)
ISBN 978-1-77180-350-2 (epub)
ISBN 978-1-77180-351-9 (Kindle)

This is an original print edition of *Rolls*.

ROLLS

Écrit tout en pensant à mon très bon ami, Jean Forest

Chapter One

Each year, there comes a time in spring when I reflect on past and future while unlocking the door to my spot here on Queen Street in Leslieville, the restaurant known as M&B Resto. Dressing the place in springtime garb is an annual chore, but it varies from year to year, and each year brings new challenges. The problems are always somewhat different, requiring a different approach each year, but they always seem to bring a positive outcome: an increase in the dollar value of business, a larger base of steady clientele, or some new label of culinary recognition — which never hurts. So every year on December 22, I have an anniversary celebration. Right here. At my restaurant.

I bought this place six years ago, on December 22. It was a dark and stormy night. No, really! We were in the middle of one of those warm winter storms. Lightning flickered behind the heavy overcast, and it did this in silence — the big speakers must have been out of service that night. It was raining. The rain was cold and being driven almost horizontally, along with leaves, newspapers, and who knew what else. Nobody was making offers on pieces of real estate that night. Except me. And I got the place for $65 000. Just about what it was worth as a going concern.

Going concern! More like a concern with a failed main bearing. This humble little property had passed through several incarnations. It had been an artist's studio, worthy of an Alain Dégoût, of the — alas — short-lived TV series *Paris*. For a time it was a shop that had hopes of recycling old office furniture. It had been a coffee spot that aimed at fashionably shabby — it managed the shabby, but the coffee was terrible, and fashion had given it a wide berth. In fact, the place, I guess I should say *my* place, as purchased, was a study in atmospheric dilapidation, a characteristic that all three previous tenants had hoped to capitalize on — hopes that were drastically, fatally, misplaced.

Apart from the general down-at-heel appearance, closer examination brought other features to the surface. The wiring and the plumbing were just about all right. The interior woodwork had been painted over so many times that the paint had become a structural element. The basement smelled of rotting potatoes but was dry. The second floor hadn't been used, apparently, for about ten years and had that musty smell of a long-closed space. But the place had a large bay window, the quality and potential of which were evident to a careful eye and a good imagination. Disappointingly, the real estate agent provided no answer to my question "Is it haunted?"

In short, what I had acquired was basically a mess. And to bring it to some sort of operational state took a lot of planning, elbow grease, and a determination not to lose hope. Slowly, the place went from something nobody would set foot in, to a venue best described as a large snug that people were reluctant to leave. We went from rueful ruin to heady hotspot in stages something like this: removing rubbish; aerating and deodorizing; rebuilding walls and replacing old wiring and piping; adding new paint, pictures, and quirky murals, putting down the rustic floor and fittings; and bringing the back patio to a state that, although not usable, was at least fit to be seen through the back door.

"Hey, Rolls! Got any banana bread?"

"No, Gypsy, you ate the last two pieces about ten minutes ago. But I can make more. How long you plan to be here?"

"How long will it take to make?"

"About forty-five minutes."

"Then I plan to stay here about another fifty minutes."

"What a coincidence, Gypsy!"

Banana bread was the current favourite. No idea why. Food fads come and go quickly here at M&B Resto.

I did have a vision. First, I wanted a place where a quirky clientele could be encouraged to meet. So, once I had brought the place to skeletal respectability, I found a half-dozen candidate customers, invited them round for an open house, and offered really cheap food and drink in exchange for their insights and suggestions, then asked them all to go forth and talk to their friends. Second, I wanted to try my hand at cooking for people who are unassumingly discriminating. So, I put together an initial menu, the entries in which most people would never have heard of, but, nevertheless, I hoped would look intriguing.

By *quirky* clientele, I mean widely varied, eccentric, having interests and backgrounds that are collectively unlikely. *Quirky* also means curious, loving discussion, well-read either in fact or by intention, and having an intense hatred of bullshit.

Unassumingly discriminating refers to people who have a very clear idea of what they want and don't want but aren't interested in expressing it in terms of polysyllabic fine distinctions, and above all would cringe at hearing it all discussed in earnest symposium format. So, when I had their attention, I offered to let the clientele choose the menu, in advance and based on general consensus. Once they realized that the menu board would remain either depressingly spare or obstinately constant until some consensus was reached, consensus followed promptly.

The first problem was to determine the *required* characteristics for the appropriate quirky clientele. That was the easy part. The second problem was how to make a place like that pay for itself. That was the hard part. The third problem was the uncertainty over whether this would provide me the escape I craved. But we'll get to that.

What? Oh, yes. What induced me to become the proprietor of something called M&B Resto? I'll explain that to you while I prepare a batch of banana bread. On second thought, let me come back to it later.

"Rory? Is that you? Another pint of Flying Monkey? Coming up."

Now, when I say *coming up*, that's what I mean literally. In just about the middle of the building there is a set of twin dumb waiters. Inexplicably, they came as part of the *as purchased* structure. When one waiter goes up, the other comes down. So, those people who want to sit upstairs, which is where a lot of the higher level (sic) discussion occurs, have to agree to pick up their own food and drink from the dumb waiter, and to deliver empty plates and glasses back to it. After some initial teething problems, it all worked swimmingly.

There were, shall we say, challenges. One of these involved the back patio.

The area out back had basically been a refuse tip when I bought the place. I remember thinking it could have made a superb setting for a scene in *Trainspotting*. The contents of the tip included quite a few large black plastic bags, the contents of which were unknown and would remain so, since they appeared to be squirming on their own. There was a suspicion that somewhere in the heaps of stuff lurked the dead bodies of several animals, and we hoped that none of them had been human. There were pieces of bent corrugated aluminum, a pile of rotting lumber that appeared to have been destined for a fence, before a previous tenant's enthusiasm for carpentry waned, two bicycle frames, and (something that would have warmed the hearts of Michael Flanders and Donald Swann) an old bedstead. It didn't take us long to clear all this away, but it was at the cost of several pairs of jeans, a few T-shirts, and quite a few sneakers, all of which had reached a stunning level of permanent olfactory compromise and had to be committed to the flames. Sophistry and illusion made good their escape on that occasion, thumbing their noses at David Hume in passing.

It was a Wednesday, early evening. The place was, as usual, about two-thirds full. It seems always to be about two-thirds full, which is ideal both for me and for the clientele. For me, because it means that I'm busy but not run ragged. For them, because there's elbow room and the decibel level is comfortable. The place seats sixty people at capacity, so there were about forty customers present. They are almost all very local, although I have noticed, to my satisfaction, that increasingly there are people who come from somewhat further afield but still within a twenty-minute walk.

Who are *they*?

Well, they're a self-selected, eclectic group who came together over the course of a few weeks. I think Huff was the first to become a regular, and he invited about four of the others to give the place a try. The location of the Resto, its physical appearance once I had renovated, my own mad desire to cook and bake, I guess these all played roles. But I think it was really just one of those things that was meant to be. From a personality point of view, Wib is probably the most varied and unpredictable, and he was one of Huff's early invitees. The last one to turn up, The Colonel, is the quietest, and although he is pleasant, someone else always has to break the ice first. Most of the time he just sits in one of the booths, on his own, reading stuff the intellectual aridity of which would make most people shiver.

Gypsy likes to call himself unemployed, although he packaged out, very lucratively, of an accounting firm two years ago, and is formally "between situations". I think he is actually beyond hope for, and out of reach of, any *next* situation, although he's still under fifty. Rory is a real estate lawyer, and even though he comes around about every second evening, he always complains about having more work than he can handle.

Huff, whose real name is van 't Hoff, is a housebuilder, one of the best there is, but before he became that he was a professor of physical chemistry. He had given up his professorship, he said, in a huff (!!) when he realized that he would never catch up to his namesake, J. T. van 't Hoff. We scolded the old fart roundly until the truth came out: "It was the undergraduates", he seethed. "Swine before pearls", he hissed.

"Have another pint, Huff, for Chrissake", we brayed. And then it all settled down again.

Ginger is a small-animal veterinarian, and her practice is around the corner, but miraculously not round the bend. Wib is a full-time poet who works part-time as a patent attorney, and figures that by now he has probably added a year and a half of useful time to his life by refusing to state or respond to his full name, which is Wilberforce Abercrombie. Everyone is convinced that his father was a victim of undetected parricide. And then there is a whole gang of others — equally eccentric, equally appealing.

On this occasion, there was a noisy gang downstairs, publicly disputing something, and privately curious about The Colonel, who was reading The *Critique of Pure Reason*, something he'd been doing for almost a month. A more cerebral crowd was at work upstairs putting together a devastating response to an unfavourable review of M&B Resto that had appeared in *Goodeats*. The arrogant little clod who penned the review was evidently someone suffering from a near-lethal combination of Internet intoxication and narcissistic self-abuse. When our commando squad of review responders had finished, he wouldn't know what had hit him.

It was a warm Wednesday evening in April (did I mention this already?), probably the first really warm day of the year. The back patio would be opened that weekend. My former business partner had spent quite a bit of time with me getting it ready. The three large trees had been pruned. The passage from winter to spring revealed, as it does each year, the assorted debris (dead leaves, bits of newspaper, disposable coffee cups, and those nauseating clumps of grey sludge) that collects, God knows how, in all the corners, and remains undetected beneath its snow covering. All that had been removed. The first of the plantings were offering tentative smiles as their feet took a grip in planters and fence boxes. The outdoor grill had been reinstalled after being brought out of its winter storage, the outdoor beer taps were hooked up again, and all that remained was to sweep the flagstones, pull the heavy plastic off the stacked tables, place tables and chairs, and set up the umbrellas. The back patio went into operation our second year, and business spiked by twenty per cent.

I will be the first to admit, and I was the first to admit at the time, that I wasn't at all sure we could make the place work. Okay, it is a very comfortable space — *now*, that is. We got exactly the clientele I was hoping for, but it was far from clear at the time that we would — or could. The number of patrons was there pretty much from the get-go — likewise a pleasant surprise. And one never knows whether these things will flare up once but then die off permanently or settle into being a feature of people's lives, something those people quickly find that they can't do without. Looking back on it all later, from a plateau of success, was hugely satisfying, and it was pleasing to recall my conversation with Huff.

"What are you talking about, Rolls? I was convinced this place was a winner as soon as I saw what you had in mind. It's not just a restaurant, not just a pub, not just a place to gather, not just a clearing house for local news, and not just a meeting ground. You've hit exactly the right combination of food for mind and body, just as the name suggests. Come on, man! Get a grip!"

Well, okay, it wasn't really a conversation. It was a Huff harangue.

But he was right.

"Anybody seen Jimmy?"

We all looked around. There were puzzled expressions, puzzled more at not realizing before now that Jimmy wasn't here. Jimmy was always here, but Jimmy is a big boy, and, as always, the focus of attention quickly shifted to something else.

It was at that point that my cellphone buzzed, and, dragging it from my pocket, I realized that my capitalist expectation of a laid-back and rose-coloured future was premature. Merely having Rice as a partner was not enough to put me on easy street. I hadn't escaped. My reality, being a struggling bookshop owner no matter how much I enjoyed the place, was still dogging me like a Jungian snake. Well, perhaps *dogging* isn't quite right.

Why me? I had sold a quarter share of the bookshop — wait for it! The tale of the bookshop is coming — to Rice, so nicknamed because his given and family names are Ben and Burroughs, and despite his calloused touch, the place was humming like a top. Having brought him into the business, I thought I could just slope off, steal into the night bearing my folded tents, sink into a new obscurity, and forever after just cash my quarterly dividend. No more problems. Fat chance!

That epiphanic moment, that return of the bookish curse (or rather the realization that I had never escaped it), that was the beginning of the story I'm about to share.

Chapter Two

"Hello, Rice. What's up? Shop didn't burn down, did it?"

Rice is my partner in the bookshop, having bought into the business. He loves the place. And since the bookshop business is somewhat less seasonal than seems to be the case for the restaurant, Rice labours away happily all year. He had called me at the restaurant because he was worried about an odd email that had come in. Not something he should have spent time fretting over, since the email that isn't odd is generally the one to worry about in the used book business. I managed to calm him down, and he was soon back at work in the bowels of our emporium.

The bookshop.

The place Rice had bought into.

In common with a lot of, and perhaps all of, such ventures, it would never have been started had I known beforehand what was involved.

The short statement is that I already had history before M&B Resto came on the scene. The basic tale is that in my pre-eatery days I was a book–barrow boy of rising fortunes, hard on the heels of which I became the owner of a reasonably successful bookshop.

The whole-nine-yards experience of getting into the book business involved a huge amount of work, but there was fun as well. Until one morning I found something unusual in Crime Fiction. But let's hold off on that for a moment. We'll get to it in a few pages. I simply must tell you how this whole bookshop lark came to life.

I studied English literature at university. Went in all starry-eyed, eager, expectant, and (I thought) well-versed for someone who'd just turned seventeen. The ringing words of a former university bigwig named Bissell, repeated from that earlier time, echoed in my head: *an assemblage of students surrounding a library, a group of scholars known collectively as the University of Toronto.* I suppose I expected that the liquid light slanting in from a September sun, as I turned up on campus to start my first year, was just the initial enticing prelude. I expected that, at any moment, someone would appear and lead me away to the Forum, where I would join all those other worthies discussing their way unerringly into some Heideggerian clearing of light and understanding. Of course, this would all be achieved through close scrutiny of the finest literature the world had to offer. Guided by the sure hands of these redoubtable teachers, I would be led to that golden state where wisdom would leap from the pages before me and force its way painlessly through my forehead, in a subtle reversal of the Jovian miracle.

It didn't happen that way. In fact, whatever I expected *it* to be, *it* didn't happen at all.

Labouring dutifully in my student cell, becoming increasingly impatient at 2 am, and gradually realizing that wisdom clung stubbornly to the pages, that the hoped-for enlightenment had missed its appointment with me and was sipping wine elsewhere, I was forced to consider other, more unkempt and down-market metaphors. The appealing metaphor, the sophisticated *fin de siècle* daguerrotypical portrait of effortlessly imbibing and enthusiastically nibbling the associated literary delicacies was soon transformed darkly into the tough doggerel slog of hewing and quarrying, and its attendant complement of blisters and sweat.

The notion of intellectual virginity thrust itself at me — er, rather, rose up before me; no, that's not it either — *shimmered* (choosing a safer verb) in my field of vision. But even that went badly wrong. I expected a palm-lined avenue leading to a garden of the classically erotic. Instead, I traversed a darkened lane dead-ending in a rubbish-strewn stub courtyard. This desolate urban blind canyon was overlooked by rooms, cheerless rooms, in which scarred and depressing flock wallpaper invited Wildean one-liners.

Virginity was indeed the central notion. Somehow, my intellectual virginity had flown. But in my case, in this metaphorical context, it was neither *given up* nor *snatched away*, in contrast to the prissy *lost*. (I have yet to hear anyone asking plaintively, 'Have you seen my virginity? I seem to have lost it. I know I had it a moment ago'.) But alas, my induction into that vestibule of reproductive awareness could be described by none of these. My intellectual virginity had simply vanished at the hands of some unknown mechanism. Mine was the clear and certain knowledge of having visited a brothel but remembering absolutely nothing of what had happened in it.

These thoughts plagued me the following day, when a sleepy and bored lecturer threw pearls from the day's study of irony to his porcine charges. He pulled out a crusty handkerchief to protect his notes from any debris dislodged during the pulmonary excavations currently in progress. "Expressing something which is the opposite of what one thinks and wants the reader to think" ... "might or might not use humour" ... "need always to be alive to gradations, such as litotes, hyperbole, antiphrasis, puns, parody, and others, which you will find in Preminger".

No doubt, thought I, *this will be invaluable in the Forum.*

By the end of the first month, I began wondering about all those things in life that fall into second place well behind enlightenment — things like food, shelter, clothing. My initial doubts increased when I visited my erstwhile high school classmates, those who remained chained to their anvils, rather than taking flight. They had learned how to do *things*, but my disdain for their lowly status lost its footing when I saw money changing hands — that is, leaving *other* hands and entering *theirs*.

As you can see, no doubt, my four years spent wandering hopefully in the halls of academe, waiting to be led out (i.e., "*e-duc*-ated"), were not a complete waste. I did learn to cover my lamentation of disillusion by a nice pellicle of wordational integument.

In due course, there was a funny hat, a long black gown, I was given a rolled-up piece of paper and entreated to go forth into the world, pen in hand.

And, of course, I did.

There soon followed a long and nightmarish round of interviews:

Me: Business letter?
He: Yes. A letter to transact business.
Me: You mean something like "In response to yours of the twenty-first inst"?
He: Next please.

I recall a Miltonian cascade down through the levels of exaltation, eventually descending into the catacombs of the socially encrusted. It took little time to realize that those possible employers sporting three days of facial hair and dirty fingernails would wince at the suggestion of even minimum wage, and my interviews tapered to nothing. Soon I was enjoying the summer by lying on the grass in Queen's Park, reading works that the sad man at Smiley's Used Books allowed me to borrow.

The idea occurred to me while reading a battered copy of *The Moving Toyshop*. Here we had Edmund Crispin dedicating a work to Philip Larkin, both of whom had been successfully *led out*, as I had come to understand the term. The book's humour distracted me from my own grim reality for a while. My copy was missing pages 59 and 60, an omen to be taken seriously, I thought, since 59 is a prime number.

A few hours later, I knew the familiar dilemma one senses when finishing a good text; i.e., the post-perusal sadness on draining the last dregs of intellectual entertainment from the pages before one, but the delight at having got one's mind around a good story, perchance even to have learned something. Returning the book to Smiley's, I decided to continue wandering the streets, having little else to do. But Edmund Crispin had made an impression on me. Rather than just moping and gazing through fly-blown shop windows, why not spend my time in structured reading? Time would pass in either case, but reading to some purpose was better than nibbling at passing images of life on a random walk basis, and both were far less boring than just contemplating the universal hourglass. Circling back to Smiley's, I noticed behind his shop a broken-down book barrow. Given a bit of oil and some duct tape, it could be salvaged. And in a further leap, I reasoned that if I were to be reading books, I might as well have a store of them available and try to interest passersby into buying the odd one or two. Smiley proffered a fatalistic invitation to take what I wanted from the "crap shelf" and try to sell them. He would take a penny for each book. So, I loaded up the cart, which my sweat and duct tape had pulled back a short distance from the lip of its death-abyss, and trundled off. By the end of that day, I had read two books and sold twelve. Total income for the day: eighty-five cents. Smiley told me to keep his twelve cents share.

I carried on for a week, by which time I had grossed four dollars and eighteen cents. After two more weeks, I had sold a total of one hundred eighty-five books. I began keeping track of the books I had read, and what kinds of books sold most readily. At the end of a month, I had a growing database and became more systematic and more discriminating about the used bookshops I browsed and the kinds of books I was looking for. By the end of August, I was working more than twelve hours a day, and I had saved a total of just under eight hundred dollars.

Three doors along from Smiley's was a grim cubbyhole called Acme Books, run by an eighty-something gent who was spry of body and mind but much preferred talking to selling. I browsed his stock, a lot of which looked like it hadn't moved physically in decades. It was easy to kindle a conversation with him about books. I use "to kindle" in the old sense, of course, since I wouldn't know how to use an e-reader to initiate a conversation.

"A book barrow! How absolutely charming! Yes, of course! Feel free to select from my stock. Just let me know which ones you take, and which you manage to sell." On the selling part, he sounded less than convinced that success was in the air.

We struck a deal. He was cagey on what he wanted as his share. "At my age..." he said, through a cackle, an utterance which, as a collective package of sound, defied interpretation.

Well. The next day, I cleared more than seven hundred dollars. In a week, my receipts from the little barrow topped four thousand dollars. Near the end of September, I splashed out seventy-three dollars to buy a drill, two giant locks and all the associated tackle, plus eight massive bolts. The door to my humble room would soon be the envy of the entrance to NORAD headquarters. That's because by that time the large jar behind my bed contained over eighteen thousand dollars. On the way home from the jumble hardware store, I was struck by three realizations: (1) I knew a lot about books; (2) I knew a lot about readers; and (3) I could sell.

Buoyed by my experience thus far, I began scanning more distant horizons. This was a cinch, I said to myself, sensing imperial bookselling ambitions, but having no glimmer of complications such as property ownership, lighting, heating, taxes, and a hundred and one other evils sent to trammel the ideals of valiant youth. But it did appear that the stars were aligned.

I noticed the property in passing. It was in Kirkcaldy Street, just south of the university, part of an urban backwater that had been lying forlornly in the moonlight for decades, awaiting a gentrification lover. The buildings flanking the property, and extending four or five doors to either side, displayed a similar status of tottering moribund that wouldn't have been out of place in a seventeenth-century London rookery. The irrational draw of the place for me, however, was its number: 59 Kirkcaldy Street. Standing before that perennially disappointed candidate for renovation, whispering "and now, me proud beauty", I took a fateful decision. Convinced that destiny was calling to me, through the intermediary of my guardian prime number, I sought out the owner.

My shoes were unmatched, and the toecap on my left shoe was all but gone. My shirt and trousers were clean, but it was evident that they were afflicted by "mortal coil" thoughts. The owner, when he finally answered the door to his own dwelling five streets from Kirkcaldy, read "kindred spirit" from my clothes. We had a long chat over warm, flat beer. Two hours later, I had a purchase agreement for 59 Kirkcaldy.

It took a year to turn the ruin into a working bookshop. My skills in carpentry, plumbing, and wiring all went from zero to adequate during that time.

But other capabilities also arose. There were some rather sophisticated effects, nodes of personal development, that I could attribute only to having a vast range of books as constant companions. These effects were as surprising as they were unexpected and gratifying. Apart from gaining a vast store of general knowledge tidbits, randomly accreted and extending across the full range of human endeavour, there were specific areas of personal interest that germinated and grew, apparently of their own accord. One of these was history. The great wardrobe of history, in all its varied raiment, became a staple of my intellectual clothing. Ancient history was one area of note, involving Greece and Rome, and a great many of the dramatis personae who walked the boards of that theatre. Archimedes was one of my heroes, as was Empedocles, but a full range of philosophers and authors alike worked their appeal. At one stage, I devoured the big three ancient dramatists, but found contrasting diversion in the works of Aristophanes, Juvenal, Terence, and Catullus.

For some reason, not closely examined, I also became enamoured of the centuries-long struggle between those ancestral enemies, England and France, and its definitive conclusion in the Seven Years War. There were curious spinoffs from this.

One of these spinoffs, the development of my spoken French to a satisfying level, seemed to be driven by an accompanying interest in French literature and culture.

A second was the story of the Acadians, which was linked into large European historical themes but at the same time involved a backwater that was almost forgotten by most people.

It was probably natural that I also developed what seemed to me, in comparison to many of my competitors, to be a reasonably refined instinct for selling.

Although my sales experience to that point covered all sorts of books, my preference inclined toward mysteries. Any kind of mystery found a buyer, since there seems to be an inexhaustible demand for them. Out of all the various genres of books that I stocked, it was most fun hunting down copies of classics, and looking for new talent, even though almost three-quarters of total income came from non-fiction and textbooks. Proximity to the university was offered cynically as the reason for this, but I knew that slick salesmanship was really behind it all.

I kept odd hours at the bookshop. There was a regular scan to be made of my usual sources for new used books, and it had to be done at surprisingly high frequency — in fact, at least twice a week. The main reason for this was to try to stay ahead of the pack of unscrupulous vultures that infested the market; i.e., the owners of other used bookshops. There was also the need to be on the lookout, always, for new sources of books. The whole business became a bit like doing a high-end crossword puzzle. There were standard approaches (anagrams, hints based on alliteration, references to obscure synonyms, creative use of absurdity, trolling through broad and deep general knowledge, and sometimes just blind luck). Then there were the usual feints and parries of the book trade, where everyone is your best friend and your most implacable enemy, it being hard sometimes to tell them apart.

But although the hours were odd, they were predictable. They had to be. Customers needed to know that I would be there during specific hours. During off-hours, I was sometimes there as well, but working in the back, reviewing and updating the large and quite sophisticated electronic database I kept. This was the main thing that distinguished my business from those of others in the used book trade, who kept, or tried to keep, all their records in their heads.

I remember the day clearly. Tuesday. April 23. During the previous two days, I had finally got the restaurant into full spring operation, and it was time to turn my attention to the bookshop.

It had been a good morning. I had been out snooping about since six thirty and had found four caches of books. Not only did these include items that, together, would probably fetch in excess of a thousand dollars, there were over two hundred classic mysteries, all in good to excellent condition, the real value of which was that they would expand the scope of my stock to include titles that I knew many of my competitors didn't have. And I had noticed long ago that the more items of interest that caught the eyes of browsers in the shop, the more likely it would be that any given book in my stock would sell. This was one of the insights that I managed to tease out of my database.

Returning from my foraging, dragging a huge load of discoveries, I was back in the shop at about nine thirty, a half-hour or so before walk-in trade would begin. I noticed someone sleeping on the floor of the shop. Crime fiction evidently had appealed to him. His suit had been good quality but now was shiny in places. He looked very peaceful lying there, and I hesitated to wake him. At one end, the head end, was Sara Paretsky. At the other end, the foot end, was Louise Penny. But I quickly realized that the main feature about him was that he wasn't asleep; he was very dead.

Chapter Three

He looked to be about fifty-five, but he could have been anywhere in that prematurely old to perennially young no man's land that can extend from about thirty to about seventy. Although somewhat dumpy, he wasn't really overweight. His slightly curly hair was streaked in grey. A high forehead and a square but rather flabby chin. His cheeks were both permanently pink, making him look like someone who had just come off a ski hill and into the chalet, or had pressed a little too hard onto a new razor while shaving that morning. At the same time, he seemed to have no real facial hair at all, the need to shave perhaps being driven by a desire not to look like a peach. He had a ski-jump nose that sat uneasily above Cupid's-bow lips and steel-grey eyes that were neither flat nor penetrating.

He'd arrived at the bookshop only a short time after I had called the police. "Detective Sergeant Barnett." A diffident introduction, accompanied by an extended small, puffy hand.

"Henry Royce. People call me Rolls."

Barnett's facial expression remained impassive, but there was a slight flicker in his eyes. "And if your name had been Charles Rolls?"

"I guess we'll never know."

Barnett nodded in faint acknowledgement.

"I understand there's a body. Could you relate to me the events that led to you finding it, before we go and look?"

I walked him through the past few hours. He had pulled a notebook and pen from his pocket and was taking what seemed to be very careful and elaborate notes, not the more common sort of runic avian scratches other policemen seemed always to generate. At least he wouldn't have to deal with the discomfort that faced those other policemen when they were asked by a superior, weeks later, what their verbless spaghetti of nouns and adjectives actually meant.

"Did you know this man?"

"No."

"Do you recognize him as a customer?"

"No. But from the way he's lying I can see only half his face."

"So when you saw him lying in your shop this morning, that was the first time you had laid eyes on him?"

"To the best of my knowledge, yes."

"To the best of your knowledge?"

I sighed inwardly.

"Someone like me who deals with the public sees hundreds, maybe thousands of people each year. They fall into three groups. There are the people I know I know: friends, regular customers, other bookshop owners. There are the people who might look familiar, and who I have seen and might know or might have known at one time. Then there are the people I have actually never seen or met and could not possibly know. There's no way for me to separate the people I know or might know from the people I definitely don't know, because the information I do have is in an imperfect memory. That memory might mislead me. I might think I know someone I've actually never met or seen, because he or she looks like someone I have indeed met or seen. Or I might claim that I don't know someone when I have indeed met or seen them but just have forgotten completely. It's all something like the standard conundrum of the two important properties for a test to determine whether someone has a given disease."

The air around us was now laden by the haze of my Rumsfeldian philosophy on facial recognition, and I waited smugly for what I expected to be his stuttering response.

"Ah yes", he said smoothly, without missing a beat. "The old binary classification test. Very good."

I stood there, in stunned surprise, for a period of time long enough to put me into conversational default. "Would you like to look at the body now?" I managed finally.

"Yes. That seems to be the next step", he said, and I led him into Crime Fiction, trying to adopt a shop-owner-in-control approach to my dealings with this odd detective.

Once the body came into view, I stood back and let him do his thing. He stopped about five feet from the body and spent almost five minutes taking in the entire scene. He then retrieved a cellphone from his shirt pocket and made a call. The call seemed to be to the medical examiner, based on what I was able to hear.

"You haven't moved anything, touched anything? Have you?" he asked.

"No", I replied.

"Has anyone else been through here who might have disturbed the scene in any way?"

"No. There's some reason to believe that I have a business partner, but he hasn't appeared today. I have no employees, and once I discovered the body, I put off opening the shop." Right on cue, there was another round of indignant knocking at the door. My customers are important to me, and I respect and am constantly surprised by their wide range of knowledge and tastes, but they are the most irritatingly hidebound creatures of habit and routine. A surprising number arrive at the shop at specific times on specific days, stay for a precisely determined interval, then leave, and these people will turn grumpy instantly at any obstacle or delay that threatens the preplanned unfolding of their literary universe.

Barnett quartered the entire area carefully, apparently looking for anything that might have tweaked his antennae. He then drew a camera from his jacket pocket and began photographing the body, its surroundings, and several areas over which he had lingered in his study of the area. After he had taken about two dozen pictures, he put the camera away and turned back to me.

Acknowledging that he was the officer in charge but detecting that to this point our discourse had been following a decidedly corrugated road, I made a comment about the weather in a bid to ease things forward. Our conversational Red River cart squeaked but refused to budge.

I gave up and tried a different tack. "Well, then, when will I be able to open the shop for business?"

Barnett made one final, excruciatingly precise note in his notebook, looked up as though seeing me for the first time, and said "when the medical examiner has finished".

I looked at him closely. "Surely you mean 'when the medical examiner has removed the body'. Presumably he will be occupied for some time with it at the morgue."

Looking at the body again, I asked, "Do you have any ideas on why this man died?"

Barnett offered another deer-in-the-headlights blink, but before he could wheel out the elusive medical examiner once more to hide behind, I carried on.

"It's just that there's no blood, I see no wounds anywhere, and there are no signs of a struggle. In fact, it looks as though he just settled in here and passed away in his sleep. Should we try to find out who he is?"

Barnett eyed me closely.

"You seem very undisturbed for someone who's just found a cadaver in his workplace."

I waved an arm at my shelves of product.

"Compared to the mayhem that lurks within these covers, our scene here is as innocent as a lemonade stand." Short delay. "But contrary to appearance, I'm not relaxed and I'm not pleased."

Just then there was another knock at the door. You get to know customer knocks, and this wasn't one of them. This knock was one of official insistence, not that rapid tapping pout, reflecting outraged but unspoken questions, such as *Are you unaware that it's past opening time?*, or *I hope you realize that my time is valuable*, or just simply a pleasant *What the fuck?*

"That will be your M.E.", I said, and went off to open the door, leaving Barnett standing there wearing a very odd expression, as though suddenly he was aware that M.E. means Migrant Eurythmics, or that he'd remembered, without warning, that he had been married just the day before yesterday.

The M.E. made a brisk entry and strode unerringly to the scene, while his assistant showed remarkable skill in wheeling the gurney around various tight corners in the shop.

"Morning, Jason", the M.E. said, nodding a smile at Barnett.

"Doctor", Barnett replied coldly. It was clear that these two had a history and some choppy social dynamics. The day was looking up already.

"Time of death, doctor?"

The M.E. turned to me and introduced himself. "James Simpson. Don't mind Jason here. Probably wants to get home and have his Wheaties." Pleasant smile to me, eyes rolled toward Barnett.

"Henry Royce." We nodded to each other, then Simpson bent to his task.

"What have we here now?" He looked over the body carefully before touching it, then reached out and grabbed the hand the body wasn't resting on, lifted it slightly, and squeezed. "Rigor setting in."

Simpson rolled the body on its back, raised one of its eyelids, then searched all the pockets. "Nothing." He nodded to his assistant, and, in practised efficiency, they placed the body into a body bag, lifted it onto the gurney, and the assistant then wheeled it back through the shop.

Pulling off his latex gloves, Simpson gave Barnett an owlish look and said, "I think we can rule out drowning, but you'll have my full report late this afternoon." He nodded his pleasant smile again to me and left.

"Seems like the M.E. knows his stuff", I offered casually.

Barnett's sigh sounded like that of the Creator at the end of day six. "Yes. But I prefer them younger, before they have the chance to become omniscient."

We talked a little more about the dead man and who he might be. Barnett probed me once again about the possibility that I might recall who he was if I considered it more seriously, and he took more pictures of the space where the body had lain, muttering something I couldn't hear as his gaze moved at random over the bookshelves. I wondered idly about Wheaties.

"What will be your next step?" I asked, half-curiously.

"Normal police procedure", he replied, apparently thinking that the explanatory power of this would stun me into silence.

"There is a chance", I essayed, "that the victim could have frequented bookshops, even though I don't recall him coming here to mine. You might want to consider circulating a photo of the man to other bookshop owners, see if they recognize him."

"Good idea", he said brightly, taking the next few minutes to make yet another elaborate entry in his notebook.

"If you wouldn't mind, though, please don't mention that the body was found here, in my bookshop. Unwholesome publicity, you know."

He nodded what I took to be agreement. What I hadn't said was that I wanted to deprive other bookshop owners of the chance to find ways of using this information to denigrate my own operation. I also didn't say that I could use an event like this to my own huge advantage. After all, finding a *real body*? In the *crime* section of *my* bookshop?

The books on the lowest shelf, next to where the body had lain, looked innocent enough, the usual range of authors in the Ps. But when I looked more closely, I saw it. The books sat loosely — *too loosely* — next to one another. Shelf space in Crime Fiction is at a premium, and I was sure that I hadn't sold anything from among the P authors recently.

But it definitely was missing. *Stylus of Death* by Nondas Parmenides was missing.

I began to realize then that I had no inkling of what might be happening. But, in fact, it was worse than that.

Chapter Four

I didn't expect to hear from Barnett again.

He had very little to say after the body had been removed, but he hung around all the same, like some ghoul at the scene of a fatal traffic accident. He walked through the entire crime fiction area, stopped to ponder a few books, and on three or four occasions just stood there, his head cocked at an odd angle, eyes toward the ceiling, as though listening for a summons from King Alfred's blowing stone.

After about fifteen minutes of these histrionics, he nodded to me and walked out.

I then had to devote almost a half day to smoothing the ruffled feathers of customers who had been left stranded in the street, cut off from their daily fix of literary ambrosia, and feeling themselves helpless in the enclosing grip of a Marxian panic, seeing, or thinking they were seeing, all that was solid melting into air. But these people are my bread and butter, and I had sympathy. Because addiction to the written word is a Janus blessing and curse that could visit any of us. And because one person's addiction is another person's (i.e., my) income.

Some people reading this will react in dismay — scoff even — when I say that one missing book could hold the key to my body-in-a-bookshop puzzle. A title and an author's name containing all that's needed to unravel a set of totally unrelated real-world events? It's worse than that irritating essay "Right and Wrong as a Clue to the Meaning of the Universe". The scoffers will have none of this! Readers have to be discriminating, they say, not ingenuous suckers led about by the nose. Don't just fall for any old situation an author tries to pawn off, they warn. If something appears to be a camel taking a run at the eye of a needle, then it doesn't pass the basic sniff test that should be applied to every text by any self-made reader, waving the banners *Realist*, *No Bullshit*, *Feet on the Ground*. If any text fails this test, then the most it warrants is some spot well beyond The Pale.

But they just don't know the work of Nondas Parmenides.

Nondas Parmenides is the pen name adopted by one Harold Tinker, not related to the baseball player. He wrote a short series of novels about the life of an investigator in ancient Kroton.

For those who have forgotten, Kroton (modern Crotone) was a city in the instep of the Italian peninsula and was part of that large Greek diaspora known as Magna Graecia. It reached its height some centuries before the Common Era — as we're inclined to refer to our current system of dates — began. Magna Graecia included cities elsewhere in the peninsula, Paestum being a good example, and in many locations in Sicily, notably Akragas, and Ortigia, now part of modern Syracuse, and which was home to the great Archimedes.

Nondas' work was competent, and although it prefigured the writing of Steven Saylor and Margaret Doody, it didn't rise to their levels. But that's a separate matter.

Stylus of Death tried for the gravitas of Sophocles, but in the eyes of many it attained something more like the hilarity of Aristophanes. It was a good yarn, and the main elements of the story came through well. The thing that intrigues and puzzles so many is that the text displays, simultaneously, all the elements of farce and sublime drama, and that, most likely because of this, the book became a critical success but a popular failure.

Now, by all that is true and honest, I should have been devastated by the loss of this book. There was no doubt that it was missing. In the days following the incident, I searched our entire stock, with great care. *Stylus of Death* was nowhere in the shop. The date I had acquired it was logged in my database, but no entry recorded its sale. And I took such care over my database that I was prepared to place overwhelming, practically absolute weight on its reliability in reflecting what resided on our shelves. These are my books. Something about which I'm inspired to rhapsodize: *Those many. Those nominally happy many. That band of generally unrelated...*

And then, as happens often to me, being overcome without warning while in my bookshop, I was suddenly reminded again of the multifarious existence of my charges, the books ranged on my shelves.

Bound but not gagged. Long since trindled. Colophoned. Petrichored. Chainlined.

Musty (often). Mephitic (rarely).

For some reason, I thought of the fourth wall just then, likely a stray memory from my brief flirtation in university with matters thespian.

What are you doing Rolls, wheeling out all these mummified terms? Showing off, are we? It was the Inner Voice cutting in, droning in exasperation. *Do you think everyone's buried as deeply in the book world as you are?*

I invited the Voice to go and urinate somewhere, preferably off-stage. Because the situation before me needed to be rechecked carefully, and that required my undeflected attention.

But no. My copy of *Stylus of Death*, previously dozing here among its unlikely shelf-fellows, assigned its place through the insensitive whim of alphabetic imperative, had now become an *introuvable*.

The bell at the front of the shop signalled the entry of another customer, and I felt the sudden urge to relieve them of all the cash they possessed. Not for the first time, I wondered whether I was on the road to, or already ensconced in, some place of Bedlam, recalling that first infamous hospital for the deranged. How had I got to where I was? Facing this Hobson's choice? Having to deal with this Scylla and Charybdis? The insane delight of a bookshop versus being willing victim to the daily Promethean round of a restaurant!

But. This is not fair. I must come clean with you, dear reader.

Under these circumstances, I ought to have been crushed. Stricken. Disconsolate.

I wasn't.

And the reason for that flowed from what I now recognized as the bibliophile's seventh sense, that whispered premonition of ineluctable need, that undeniable and almost sexual urge for the safe bolthole of redundancy.

In other words, I had taken the precaution of finding a second copy of *Stylus of Death*, and that copy slept now in my bibliographic Holy of Holies. To come clean, this was true of my full set of Nondas' works. My intense interest in history is easily aroused. I had taken a serious shine to his writing and had acquired duplicate copies of all of them. But coming back to *Stylus of Death* specifically, that meant...

Yes, alas. *Redundancy* and all its charms now had been replaced by *at risk* and all its fears.

His *excuse me* was like an emergency hammer striking the glass in a railway carriage.

"Yes", I said brightly, looking up at an embodiment of the nondescript, but nevertheless potential bearer of some of my flow of lucre, and most likely a decent sort. After all, anyone who enters a bookshop...

"Do you have any copies of works by Parmenides?"

The question entered my ears, but then flowed throughout my body like a tide of liquid nitrogen.

"Par— Parm—" I essayed then stumbled to a halt.

"Yes. The Greek philosopher."

The liquid nitrogen evaporated instantly, replaced by a floral-laden surge of warm Alpine air.

"As you probably know, only fragments of his works survive. But yes. We have books that include those fragments. Second floor. Near the back of the shop. Philosophy and Ancient Classics."

His *thank you* betrayed the imminent gratification he'd obviously expected.

My previous train of absurd contributions from the literary somewhere we all know well had now been derailed, resulting in a sudden pileup along the normal lines of thought. A disordered heap of bent and twisted mental boxcars ... Yes. Okay. This sort of image is a fecund source of crossbred metaphors.

Come along, Rolls, I said to myself. *There's work to be done.*

And indeed there was. Without real hope of success, I now had to go in search of a replacement shelf copy of *Stylus of Death*. Not only that; I also had to do some sleuthing of my own, come up with possible explanations for the presence of Mr. Slumber among the Crime Fiction Ps. The police would be interested only in determining who did it and why. They would have no concern for impacts on my business. And it was my job to make sure that those impacts were positive ones only. Cross though it might seem, my P body represented a rare business opportunity, a gift from Apollo.

On a piece of brown wrapper, I began to make notes.

1. Body found in Crime Fiction P. Implication: None evident.

2. Existence of body at all. Implication: Indicates something so important that no trail could be left. Example of honour among thieves? Body of someone who was unwilling participant? Last-minute action to deal with attempted double-cross by victim? (Unlikely, since that would mean the perpetrator had come prepared to do this deed.) Further implication: Victim's death had been planned all along, and it was victim who had been double-crossed.

3. Copy of Stylus of Death *missing. Implication: Possible connection between missing book and location of body.*

4. Mere presence of body is significant. Implication: Body could not be removed. No time? No perceived need? Not possible?

Implications of 1 and 2: Location of body significant. Body not moved because of weight involved. Indicates not a strong man or perhaps a woman?

Further implication: More than one person, but at most two people had been involved in whatever happened in my shop.

5. No outward signs of violence on body. Implications: Natural death? Murder by sophisticated and quick-acting means?

6. No identification found on body. In fact, nothing at all found in pockets. Implication: Normal criminal precaution?

I felt I was getting somewhere now.

Chapter Five

I couldn't expect Rice to do what I had in mind. Guile, you see — something needed by the bucketful — was thinly stocked on Rice's shelves.

For several years, I've sponsored a crime reading group. An odd but interesting and dedicated group. And the sponsorship involves a modest subsidy on the price of the books they buy and read, books they all buy through me, of course. There's a payback, naturally, i.e., their willingness to acknowledge at every opportunity how much my involvement improves the variety and pleasure of their reading. There's also a regular acknowledgement on their website, and I've noticed over the past year that this route to public visibility has begun to pay off. My estimate is that an annual income stream of about four hundred dollars can be attributed to the nudges this website has delivered over three years.

A quick email missive to my tame book club was in order. Keyboarded and dispatched to the twenty permanent members of the club, my item of breaking bibliophilic news recounted the basic event, recorded my sadness at the fate of the unknown gentleman, whose identity, no doubt, would be revealed by the police in the fullness of time. I ended the first portion of my note by expressing the hope that this dreadful occurrence would not put our relationship under any strain. Then came the change in pace.

Although shocked by this sombre event, I wrote, *I was reminded at the same time of all those novels involving a body turning up in a bookshop or library*. I then produced a list of about thirty such works. *Should you be interested*, I concluded, *I would be more than willing to make a brief presentation to your group on the body-in-a-bookshop theme*. After sending out the missive, I experienced a slight pang of concern. Had I been clear and accurate in all the details? Might it be possible, heaven forfend, that an incautious phrase in my letter might encourage the suspicion among these armchair sleuths that the events resulting in my P body had been copied from one of the classic works?

My prediction was that there would be a delay of about an hour. But the bush telegraph connecting aficionados and booksellers is ever poised and is slick and productive once activated. An hour turned out to be a gross overestimate. The word was out, and the message rang throughout the bush.

Within fifteen minutes, there were two calls from other bookshops. One delivered little more than a torrent of abuse, the intemperate outrage of a blindsided business rival. The second, also from a bookshop owner, was looking for some joint operation, an attempt to cash in on what evidently was seen as a massive advertising windfall that had landed solely, and therefore unfairly, in my lap. I knew that there were others out there, considering, manoeuvring, scheming, seeking advantage, and most likely trying to turn the matter to my disadvantage.

But no disadvantage would be forthcoming, of that I was fairly sure. A quick check revealed that the website of my tame reading group had already posted two items on the happening, and comments had begun to roll in. As effective as a scientist publishing first, priority had been established.

Having leaked my news, a socially doubtful but commercially exigent move, I abandoned all other activities, save the servicing of customers, to go in search of another copy of *Stylus of Death*. I spent a few moments pondering the downside of such a search. There was a mystery associated with my copy of *Stylus of Death* and why it had gone missing in this particularly bizarre way. I had thought my way into some of this mystery, and was reasonably sure that the downside was, if anything, a gentle grade rather than a cliff.

Over the next few days, the universe unfolded in its own way. Barnett called to say that Mr. Slumber had now been identified, and that he was a minor villain, connections currently being traced. Contacts having links to my book group point person rattled my cage, one of them coming straight out and asking about "my body". I sanded his gears by saying "it's not for sale", then feigned misunderstanding, reporting eventually that there was no news yet. I was still working out how to spin the fact that the body had belonged to someone who was genuinely shady. My queries on *Stylus of Death* brought back all sorts of responses, but most expressed the belief that all copies had been hoovered up long ago, and sent wishes, sincere at first glance, for good luck on my search.

I had handed day-to-day bookshop operations back to Rice, asking him to forward to me any further responses on the Parmenides book, and I had returned full time to M&B Resto, where I had met a deluge of welcome. Well, okay, it was more chaff than welcome — Had I finally had that anal lobotomy? Was I drawn back to my kitchen despite the heat? Had I really cleaned out my accounts and made ready to bolt to my pad in Menton? It took a day to bring matters to heel at the Resto. Bread was made, wine was restocked, my suggestion for an M&B Resto version of lamb biryani brought thunderous approval. The list of things to do was massive. It is always thus in a restaurant, and on any given day I kept chipping away at what seemed most important.

I had been back physically at the Resto five days, but each day brought multiple intrusions via my cellphone, all somehow related either to the body or to the Parmenides book. This necessarily involved some juggling. It's surprisingly difficult to keep two balls in the air when they're as large as a restaurant and a bookshop. Difficult without a cellphone. Impossible without my trusty kitchen help, who likes to go by the name Hinge for some reason. Some people speculate that the prefix *un-* has gone missing. But Hinge is okay. Works best alone in the kitchen, something that suits everybody.

The Resto was a miasma of rumours. Word had crept in, beneath the door and through fenestral cracks, fragmentary and afloat on a froth of speculative invention, concerning recent events in the bookshop. Occasional customers swept in, early embers of curiosity sticking to their clothes, begging to be fanned into flames. Word spread to the normal clientele, the *Stammkunde*, and beyond. As a result, business boomed. More covers were served than is usual, by quite a factor.

But it was at the bookshop where the afterburners really kicked in. The ghouls were easily identified by their leading request, *show me where the body was found*, which resulted in them being shown nothing but the door. Sales of murder mysteries supernovated. Rice scoured the city every day just to replenish stock. This shop owner's wet dream was not hurt by a breathless story in the generally trashy booksellers' newsletter *Gut and Garotte* describing the new and feverish drumbeat of excitement felt by anyone reading a murder mystery from Rolls' bookshop. "Essence of real dead body", the writer gasped, "now imbued the pages of all the books from that shop".

It was on the sixth day that I sensed something unusual.

A copy of *Stylus of Death* became available. It was offered to me at the extortionate price of $12.99. (To a bookseller, all offer prices, except his or her own, of course, are extortionate.) Everybody knew of the body in my bookshop. But nobody knew of the discovery that my copy of this book was missing. Consequently nobody was aware of the potentially dynamite role this little book might play in the whole affair. But I had been conscientious in scouring the trade for a copy, and everyone knew that I would pay a reasonable price for a book that no shop possessing a copy had been able to sell for years.

I went myself to the bookseller who had the copy, a small, neat spot run by a gentle fifty-year-old who had made his money in the wine retail business and now just wished to relax amid a genteel collection of favourites.

"It came in yesterday", he said.

"Came in?" I asked. This made it sound improbably like a lost literary soul that had staggered in on its own.

"Yes. Someone dropped it off, saying they didn't enjoy it and didn't want it. I noted your interest, and so…"

We chatted a while. Nice guy. No unpleasant commercial agenda. Might as well make a good impression. One never knows.

Then I left. With a replacement copy of *Stylus of Death*. Redundancy restored.

I went straight back to the delightful chaos of M&B Resto, saw that everything was humming along splendidly, spoke to a few diners, then repaired to that corner of my kitchen where a seat from an old high-end Deux Chevaux has been incorporated tastefully into a pair of wine barrels to serve as my *coin d'inspiration.* I settled down to an examination of my $13 book purchase.

Reading a few pages revealed nothing more than an affirmation that I had overpaid. But I continued flipping through the volume, until something caught my eye.

On page 106, all the letters *o* had been filled in using a pencil. Well, the distribution of readers does have its freaky extremes. *And thank heavens for that,* I thought. *Otherwise my bookshop would be crammed full of the kinds of books I dislike,* and the names of some detested authors rose up in my mind against my will...

Now, Rolls, the familiar voice said. *Stop this hypocrisy. You have copies of books by all those authors on your shelves. If you feel that way, get rid of them.*

Both of us, me and the voice, knew that wasn't about to happen. Commercial cupidity meets pristine principle, bearing pistols in the swirling dawn mist.

Pristine is a poor shot.

I looked through the volume a bit more closely, and it appeared that only page 106 had been tagged. But something else was nagging at the edges of my mind. The book had someone's name on the inside of the front cover. Very common, if somewhat barbaric practice. *Samuel Barrington 1979.* Pulling out my tablet, I consulted my database.

When I say that I am careful in updating and maintaining my database, I'm not kidding. Every book — note, this means every *individual* book, not just every title — has its own story. It is bought new by someone, given as a gift, possibly never opened (save to enter the defacing signature), read, cherished or abandoned, and, displaying the same frailty as all flesh, eventually crumbles to dust. Or perhaps ashes. I have great deference for this individuality. I record and track evidence of it.

I stared at the screen on my phone for a long, long time. Wondering.

Samuel Barrington.

The book I was holding was the very book that had vanished a week earlier from my shop.

Chapter Six

Now is probably as good a time as any to talk about that group of people who are my colleagues, my competitors, my great friends, my sworn enemies, my blood-brother allies, my vicious battlefield foes…

Yes, all right. They're the owners of other used bookshops. It's love–hate, Jekyll–Hyde, neurosis–hysteria, whatever. I go along with this line because it's the path of least resistance. Most people think they know what these terms mean, and disagreeing is just a waste of time. Secretly, however, I've worked out our situation — I mean, the situation of any group of owners of used bookshops.

The violent dynamism implied by all the dualities just listed doesn't really happen. In fact, we're all just bibliophilic icebergs. We're majestic, physically and temporally stable (or at least we want to give that impression), but most of our existence, our mental lives, our commercial striving, is out of sight. And this green and pleasant prospect is what you see if you look closely: most of the time, even under some of the most extraordinary circumstances, we all get along fine. And we do that because we have no other choice.

There are people who believe that owners of used bookshops, and owners of restaurants as well, swing continuously in financial agony, ever at risk of being dropped into the great meat grinder of bankruptcy immediately below them.

Perhaps some really are chronically in this situation. I've never felt that to be the case for my businesses. But then I have a highly polished, friction-free, stainless steel business model that I'm always fine-tuning. Part of this involves, necessarily, a positive and interactive outreach, recognizing that the world won't come to me spontaneously. But in addition to that, I watch every cent, the result of which is that the dollars look after themselves. I have no trouble saving money nor making necessary investments. But the price of all this is eternal and ruthless vigilance. The fact that a lot of used bookshops continue to exist indicates that they're doing something similar. But, and to switch to a different metaphor involving dangling, appearing to be at the mercy of a great Damoclean sword can be protective coloration for the owner of a used bookshop. Crying the financial blues can help to disguise hefty price markups.

Now it's true that the owner of an average used bookshop will not suddenly transform into a Bill Gates or a Jeff Bezos. Not ever. But that doesn't mean that they can't live comfortably, that they can't build up a decent financial cushion over time. This is what I've been able to do. Without that, the story I've begun to tell would have followed a very different path, and I'd now be dodging the receiver.

Even for a successful owner of a used bookshop, the commercial reality he or she faces can be quite stressful. And that can bring out the petty and mean-spirited side of people. It's important to be able to detect signs, to take hints. The look on a customer's face, any dubious suggestion betrayed by the body language of someone who wants to sell you something, and a whole range of other tells — these can all be used to your advantage, but only if they are interpreted correctly. The big risk here, and it's something that simply comes with the territory, is seeing slights, suggestions, hidden agendas, implications, traps, and subterfuges where none really exist. This is where virtually all the problems among owners of used bookshops arise. As sophisticated readers of fiction learn to do, owners of used bookshops must learn to suspend judgment until just the right moment. The infuriating thing here is that there are no rules whatever for deciding on when that moment has arrived.

Most of the used bookshop owners I know are aware that everyone plays essentially the same game, so beyond a point no purpose is served in trying to hoodwink or mislead, and attempts to do this are just a frustrating waste of time. Everyone has to earn their crust. This standard formula is true for, and followed by, all the used bookshop owners I know.

All but one, that is.

That one is Marielle Demetrios.

Marielle owns Paestum and You, a successful shop on Harbord Street.

She has her critics, of course.

At the age of twenty-two, newly out of university, she received an inheritance from a doting uncle, which allowed her to buy the building her shop is located in, load in quite a lot of good stock, and have enough left over to get the place on its feet and to live comfortably.

It didn't take long for the whining and moaning to turn up.

Unfair!

Cheating!

She should have had to struggle for years in a Euripidean cave, without food or running water, just like the rest of us!

Now, I know of no bookshop owner who has ever had to live in a cave. But that's the nature of the beast: the fervent wish to have competition limited by an impossible entry requirement and an unavoidable need to struggle through some apprenticeship period under the maximum weight of adversity. That's the prevailing mantra upheld by some of us.

It's all bullshit, of course, but in the spirit of some puritanical ideal of fairness, of an equal allocation of misery to all, some people find it fun to swing this hyperbolic sword.

Marielle and I have a good working relationship.

Well, actually, dear reader, let me come clean: Marielle and I have a massively complex relationship.

In her shop, she stocks and sells mostly Greek material. Of course, there's the full gamut of stuff from ancient Greece. She has it all. Well, most of it. The stuff that I don't have. But she also has the most intriguing and fascinating collection of modern Greek material. You wouldn't think that there were so many philhellenes in Toronto. There are tens of thousands of them. And Marielle knows them all.

Her shop is open seven days a week. Every Sunday, she has a large sign in the window that says *Always on Sunday!* The shop seems perpetually to be busy, Greek music always is playing quietly. Whenever a Greek author is in town, you can be sure that he, or more often she, will give a reading in her shop. Marielle often gives readings herself. She organizes seminars on Greek literature. Essentially, she works like a horse.

The material she has from ancient Greek authors and philosophers is better and more complete than anything I've seen. My collection is good but is not a patch on hers. A lot of my customers like Greek texts, so I make an effort to locate them. When I'm able to pull a coup, relations between Marielle and me can be stormy for a while, but the bad weather never lasts.

Her modern Greek material is unrivalled. Ever heard of Jeffrey Siger? Petros Márkaris? Christopher Bollen? Paul Johnson? And that's just for openers.

And Marielle has read them all. She travels to Greece every year. She hunts out new talent. She can be seen regularly on the Danforth, handing out cards and flyers. And she's hard to avoid. Not because she's obnoxiously in your face. For quite other reasons.

She has classic looks.

She has a rich beautiful voice.

She's tall and willowy.

Her garments make sure that you know her gorgeous olive skin is olive everywhere.

She speaks Greek, English, and French, each in a distinctive modulation.

I can say without hesitation that she's delightfully, naturally, and unpretentiously voluptuous.

As a result of all this she extracts longing looks from most men and frigid glares from more than a few women.

And me?

Well, Marielle and I are fire and ice. Guess which one is fire. But it's amazing how well fire and ice can get along in bed.

But I need to stop thinking about Marielle now.

Otherwise I'll never get back to the thread of this story.

And I'll lose the ability to think straight, to add, to chew gum, to … well … never mind…

Chapter Seven

Practically from the morning I found Mr. Slumber, now unmasked by the police as Rod McGrath, I had begun analysing the possible reasons for my copy of *Stylus of Death* presenting such allure. My ponderings revealed five possibilities.

1. It was just an opportunistic grab and the thief had been impressed by the title.
   Assessment: inane

   It was an attempt at diversion. Leave a body, take a book.
   Assessment: unlikely

   It was only part of the result, and one or more other books were missing as well.
   Assessment: possible, but logic not evident

   The book contained something that, given the right piece of additional information, would lead one to unravel the mystery.
   Assessment: possible, but distant

   The book had been the only target all along.
   Assessment: possible and probable

Then there was the body itself. Why was it there? The feasible responses to this were few. All of them required the additional assumption that there was a second felon:

1. Rod had tried a fast one on his partner, some blackmail or a double-cross at the last minute and had to be neutralized.
   Assessment: possible, but implied that the partner had come prepared to do the heavy

   Rod had been the only one who knew which book to nick, but after he shared that information, he became expendable.
   Assessment: possible, but unlikely

Rod had died of natural causes, e.g., a sudden and massive heart attack.

Assessment: possible and probable

The post-mortem would help here.

How many of them were there, other than Rod? Probably just one; otherwise, they likely would have been able to do their own body removal.

And then there was the *big one*.

What was special about *Stylus of Death*, and why was my particular copy singled out?

This was a problem of the head-butting variety.

There is nothing inherently significant about *Stylus of Death*. It unfolds a decent plot about wealth, jealousy, business rivalry, and death in ancient Kroton. The story is set at the time of one of the several outbreaks of skirmishing between Kroton and its neighbouring city Sybaris. In these dust-ups, Kroton always won. There is a love interest, a wild romance between a Krotonite, Spiros, and a beautiful Sybarite, Agariste. A *Romeo and Juliet* prequel, the story lurches toward its conclusion through a series of *grands pas de chat*. Spiros is killed by the ugly and deformed villain, who yearns for but has no chance with Agariste, but then responds credulously to Agariste's advances only to end up being poisoned by her. Agariste then kills herself.

But wait…

Agariste's family are not happy just to accept what happened and swallow the explanation for it, so they hire the dashing and brilliant private investigator Dimitriou to find out what things are out there and to get to the bottom of them. This he does, and he concludes that Agariste, although ready to commit suicide, didn't get the chance. She was actually poisoned, the means of doing this being a stylus, a result achieved through a devious scheme and aimed at far more than just the death of Agariste. The fortunes of her family were also in the game and in the sights of the man who turns out to be the arch-villain. Dimitriou identifies the three youths involved in this jape, and the evil and despotic Krotonite who was behind the scheme and who directed and funded it. Our fearless PI collaborates with a famous rhetorician and hems the three actual perpetrators within a logical argument so tight that they realize their best way out is to poison themselves. At the same time, he has outflanked the main demon and is about to deliver him to Agariste's family, but alas, the miscreant slips while trying to escape along the beach, drowns, and becomes fish bait. Well, at least some of him does. Some seriously gnawed remains wash ashore a few days later. This outcome is fortunate because Dimitriou has discovered that the *bad man* had some shady commercial connections to Agariste's family, the explanation of which would have been delicate.

Bad guys dealt with. Potential for threat of smears to the family honour sidestepped. Dimitriou walks off with his fee and gets pissed on limoncello.

The story moves along at a good clip and is full of asides about life in Kroton and Sybaris, but it's a bit too staged.

So, whatever the reason for my copy of the book being such a draw for the charlies who had lifted it, that reason had nothing to do with the book's tale.

That left only a couple of other possibilities.

But first, some background that I managed to unearth. Hold on a second — *background*? If it was *unearthed*, wouldn't it have had to have been *under*ground rather than *back*ground?

Never mind.

Stylus of Death was published in 2002. The original, and only, print run for *Stylus of Death* was 1200 copies. About three hundred and seventy copies were sold. There was no paperback version produced. The publisher remaindered a hundred copies, and the rest were pulped. This all happened between 2002 and 2009. So, ultimately, there had been about four hundred and seventy copies that were sold or could have been sold. I did a check among booksellers and public libraries, and managed to find out a few things after quite a bit of digging. Public libraries had purchased eighty copies, of which twenty-eight were still in library collections. This was all before the days of Amazon's rise to pre-eminence, so the libraries almost certainly sent the missing fifty-two copies to the pulper. All the copies held by booksellers were second-hand, and there were fifty-five of these in 2009. By 2017, that number was down to nine. Books like *Stylus of Death* are quite ephemeral and tend not to stay in private collections for more than a few years. The best estimate among those who know is that books in private collections are discarded at a rate similar to that experienced in public libraries. So, by 2009, there were about three hundred and twenty-five copies that might have gone originally to private hands, but this number would likely have fallen to two hundred and seventy (subtracting the number of books shifted to second-hand sellers) and again to forty-four (accounting for books in private hands being lost or sent to paper waste). As of 2017, my estimate was that there were nine books in second-hand shops, four copies (my estimate based on quick and dirty research) in public libraries, and only twelve copies in private hands. So, twenty-five copies altogether. Of these, I was prepared to wager that half the private owners of these books wouldn't know they had them. After all, the best place to hide a book is in a library.

Where did this leave me? Well, with a large time deficit for research, and with a result — i.e., an estimate of perhaps twenty copies — that wouldn't help me much, even if it didn't have large error bands. Scratching my head, I longed for the simplicity of a restaurant food inventory.

But the result was not entirely useless. It did indicate that finding a replacement copy would not have been necessarily all that simple. What about the nine copies in used bookshops? Just an estimate, I reminded myself, resting on plenty of assumptions, and the actual number might well be zero. Probably was zero, in fact, given that my offer to buy a copy brought no response.

It indicated much more clearly one other thing: given the limited number of other copies out there, the decision by someone to send my purloined copy back into the fray had not been a casual one. Whatever my thief had been looking for in the book, it appeared that he had not found it. That didn't mean that what he wanted wasn't there, just that he hadn't found it. Under these circumstances, one might think that the best course would be just to destroy the copy. But then if he had missed what he had hoped to find, he would have lost it for good.

No. Better to put the book back into circulation and hope that any resulting excitement might pry loose a clue. This meant that, on the basis of what we both knew, my thief and I now were almost on equal terms. Almost, because I still had no idea how he determined that what he wanted was in my particular copy of *Stylus of Death*.

But hark, what light through...

Booksellers are a mad combination of relationship omnivores and social chameleons. We have to be able to appeal to a vast number of different types of customers (the chameleon part) and then, having done the appealing, we need to be able to deal with all those types (the omnivore part).

This is not easy, since everyone is predisposed to certain likes and dislikes. While conversing with someone I find detestable, it is necessary for me to display a smile that beams out spontaneous sincerity but offers no trace of reptilian predation or the spasmodic contortion of forced bonhomie that comes across as a rictus.

These traits of omnivore and chameleon became primal for me now. Having looked through my newly reacquired copy of *Stylus of Death*, and keeping clearly in mind that every book has things imparted by its owner(s) that make it unique, different from all other copies of the same book, I went out into the world.

No. That's not right. I'm getting ahead of myself.

I did something else first. I made two calls.

The first was to Dr. Simpson, the medical examiner. He was helpfulness personified. He explained to me that Mr. McGrath had indeed died of a heart attack. "Would have been fatal within minutes, at most." He gave me a few more unimportant details, I thanked him, and we ended the call.

The second was to Barnett. He feigned not remembering me at first, but then he experienced full recall in what sounded over the telephone like a flash flood of recollection.

"Well", he began eventually, "I can't comment on an investigation in progress."

"So, apart from knowing that the body belonged to Rod McGrath, I take that to mean that you don't yet know who the other guy was, the real perpetrator?" I had a good idea what was coming next.

There was a short pause.

"Have you learned something new since we spoke last, Mister ... er ... Rolls?"

"No."

I had decided that he was going to have to work for it.

"Then you're assuming that two people were involved?"

"Yes."

"And that's because…?"

"Well, Mr. McGrath didn't steal the book."

"Hmmm", Barnett responded. "I'm treating that as an assumption, since you claim that a book was stolen but there's nothing to support that claim."

"You can treat it as an assumption if you like. But the body wasn't something I assumed. And the body became dead for what appear to be natural reasons, but in a place and at a time that was not at all natural. So that still needs to be explained. A good way to do that is to suppose that someone else might have played some part in making the body dead. Meaning that there was someone else there. Which brings us to the question of *why*? Given that they were in a bookshop, theft of a book is at least a good possibility. A random unexplained occurrence doesn't cut it. So, for example, it's unlikely that McGrath offered some enthusiastic suggestion, like 'I know! Let's find a bookshop, break in, and you can kill me! It will be such fun!' Or have you learned something new since the last time we conversed?"

"I see you've spoken to Simpson."

"Yes", I replied. "I'm trying to run a business. People are asking me questions. I'd like to be able to give them answers."

It was also the case, of course, that the odd juicy morsel of information might help the business run quite a bit faster.

Then I went out into the world.

Well, actually…

I called a guy named James Hazlitt, known commonly as Jocko, someone whose capabilities in competitive intelligence I've taken advantage of more than once, but more importantly in this case the man who can find out almost anything about almost anything or anybody.

Then I went out into the world.

Chapter Eight

Now, when I say *go out into the world*, I could mean various things. There can be the exercise of leaving one's present location (home, office, pub — but in this last-mentioned case, only after serious reflection) and walk the streets. Then there is the other sense.

The physical world can be boring, but mostly it's just puzzling. Without the parallel mental world each of us carries in his or her head, the physical world can be meaningless. I think a lot about these two worlds, but now isn't the time to go into details. So, I went out into my physical world, meaning I left the bookshop, and into my mental world, which was where I would try to figure out what was going on.

The first thing I had to do was check on M&B Resto. The place was hopping when I got there. A few exuberant cries of "*Salve!*" greeted me; The Colonel looked like he had reached a gripping part of his *Critique of Pure Reason*, something that seemed to me impossible; and Hinge's owlish presence filled the kitchen. In short, God was in his heaven; the world continued to turn.

I left to do the first of my tasks, which was to walk around and think. After forty-five minutes of that, I let myself into my residence, sat at my desk, fired up both my computers, grabbed a notepad and pen, and wrote *why* and *how*. Then, at the bottom of the page, I wrote *Samuel Barrington 1979*.

It seemed to me that this could be a clue, or rather two clues — the name and the number.

I spent some time thinking about this. Who was Samuel Barrington and why did someone consider him important enough that his name should grace the inside cover of a book? Did the book owner consider him a friend? Was he a relative? Or was the book owner himself named Samuel Barrington? Was the inscription linked somehow to the drama that appeared to surround this particular copy — the drama of a dead body, the theft of the book, and then its puzzling return?

Or was Samuel Barrington someone prominent, linked via this book to some quite different situation or event? And what about 1979? The first presumption is that it refers to a year. I checked the legal page in the book. Hmmm. Couldn't refer to the year the book was acquired, since it wasn't published until 2002. So, a year having some other significance? Or maybe not a year at all? A safety deposit box? A coded reference of some sort? The speculative possibilities were potentially endless, and it was clear that I would need to try to tackle this systematically.

Could I just ignore the whole thing? That might end up being what would happen eventually. The body in my bookshop was a police matter, out of my hands. A book, apparently stolen and then returned, might be just one of those strange puzzles. It's certainly the case that my curiosity was aroused, and on that basis alone it wasn't a natural option just to forget the matter. In addition, there was probably scope for commercial advantage to be reaped, and the owner of a used bookshop has to pursue every opportunity, no matter how slender. I had not yet got to the point of thinking whether a dark side might be involved. After all, a body…

This was how I started on the first of what would become many online searches. My first search turned up at least one American football player, several people in the health care business, two insurance salesmen, and quite a few other private individuals. There were at least fifteen people by that name in Toronto alone. Was I going to start looking into every one of them?

No.

I went back to the book. It was a quirky mystery story. Would probably appeal to someone having a taste for history. And from the state of the book itself, published by a small local press almost twenty years earlier, there were a few things to note. It was in very good condition: no water damage, the spine in excellent shape, had not been left lying in the sun for long periods, no pages folded down as bookmarks (something that always incenses me). A book that had been cared for, either deliberately or by lucky neglect. Leafing through the pages, I found no underlining or notes; in fact, there was no defacement at all.

Except.

All the letters *o* on page 106 had been filled in by pencil. Someone distracted on a slow day?

So. Probably one careful owner. A book that had seen little if any use, and certainly had not been dragged through the used-book mill.

Where did this get me?

Nowhere.

Come on, Rolls. Stop pissing about.

But there was something coming out of the search that hit me right between the eyes.

There was one really significant Samuel Barrington, and in fact he was Google's first hit.

Samuel Barrington, Rear-Admiral of the White. Born 1729, died 1800. Remains lie in the family vault in St. Andrew's parish church in Shrivenham. This brought back recollections of many visits to a nearby village, Chiseldon, in Wiltshire, and very pleasant evenings spent there with friends. But this trail, despite its initial and perhaps even budding promise, soon felt as though it also was leading nowhere, despite what appeared to be some intriguing real links to local Canadian history: Barrington at Louisbourg, Barrington at la baie des Chaleurs — victories against the French. All estimable stuff, and worth pursuing on its own merits.

But what could this have to do with a mystery penned in modern times and set in old Magna Graecia?

Sorry, Admiral. This is all too distant, and I'm going to resist being sucked in.

So, Samuel Barrington was just one of those odd mysteries, one of the *vêtements* acquired by this particular copy of *Stylus of Death* during its unique passage through time. Other garments might be provided by my database.

In my database, I record everything that might be of use in the future. I keep all this secret, since booksellers are at least as unprincipled as bankers. I even go to the extent of storing my database on a computer that never has been, and never will be, connected to the Internet. I also keep a copy on a tablet that I carry with me on occasion. This arrangement means carrying home each evening or at regular intervals the notebook where I record sales, acquisitions, etc. That was the other computer I now turned to. Retrieving the file on *Stylus of Death*, I read:

Entry Number 16-31168
Stylus of Death
Nondas Parmenides
Sundown Reach Publications
Toronto
Published 2002
Acquired May 18 2016
Purchased from Raymond Lansdell, Good Home Used Books
Price $8
Condition Very good. Spine firm. Covers good. No internal notes or annotations (see Markings).
Markings "Samuel Barrington 1979" Inside Front Cover
Markings All letters o filled in by pencil, page 106

Entry Modified

First things first. I modified the entry, recording the dates for the disappearance (theft) of the book and its reacquisition.

Leaning back in my chair, I reflected, not for the first time, that there exists a slice of that population who prowl the used book world, a slice whose behaviour I can't explain. Not to myself. Not in any way. They do odd things. They display sudden enthusiasms that they could acquire only from those enthusiasms being teleported to them from an as yet undiscovered planet.

I reflected also on the fact that my time in the bookshop had offered far more puzzles and unanswered questions, per unit time, than had arisen from any other quarter of my life. And now another one sat before me.

What was I going to do? I decided that some investigating was in order. If I traced back through the history of my copy, would anything interesting result? Start with where I got the book in the first place.

Raymond Lansdell, Good Home Used Books. A quick visit was needed. But I didn't have high hopes.

Raymond is nice enough, even though I have no idea how he can possibly make any money from his shop. He's one of the keep-it-in-your-head crowd, and when asked whether he has a given book, he will tap his right temple suggestively, wink at you in a way that defies interpretation, then head off into his book warrens. If there were ever a shelf collapse, he would be like a coal miner deep underground after a cave-in. I once kept a check on him. If asked whether he had a book, he would adopt one of three courses: (1) to reply "No, I don't have a copy"; (2) to reply "Yes, let me get it"; and (3) to reply "Good question. Let me check". Out of fifty requests that I put to him to plumb his collection for something, on thirty-eight occasions he had to go and check (third course of action), and on thirty-five of those occasions he came back empty handed. For nine of the fifty requests, he said immediately that he didn't have a copy. On the other three occasions, he said confidently that he had a copy, but on only one such occasion was he able to come back book in hand. A mathematician would conclude that Raymond's stock was randomly ordered.

"Morning, Raymond."

"Ah! Good morning, Rolls. What brings you here?"

"I'm hoping for some information. It relates to something we transacted quite some time ago, so I won't be surprised if you can't help me."

"Well, let's give it a go."

"Excellent, Raymond. In 2016, I bought a book from you, *Stylus of Death* by Nondas Parmenides."

"Yes. I recall that vaguely. What would you like to know?"

"Well, Raymond, basically I would like to know if you remember the book, but particularly if you remember anything about the name written on the inside front cover. The name is Samuel Barrington."

"Barrington ... yes ... that does ring a bell."

There was a pause here while we both gazed at the ceiling.

"Ah! I believe ... yes. It was part of a consignment. A lot of naval stuff. Yes. It was an estate sale. Most of the stuff I off-loaded eventually to two bookshops in Halifax."

"Did you keep an inventory of what you shipped to Halifax?" Alas, I knew the answer to this already.

"No. There was nothing in it of real value."

Even if Raymond did have a list, and even if, somehow, I could have looked at the books consigned to Halifax, it was a very long shot.

"Do you happen to remember who the books belonged to? Whose estate it was that was liquidated?"

"Hmmm. Let me see. Yes … I think the name was Graham. Yes. Or … maybe Gorley? Greeley? It was something like that."

I made a show of jotting a note in the small notebook I always carry, then looked up and smiled. But it was as I expected. No real advance. Nothing solid to grab hold of. It had been worth a try.

"Thanks, Raymond. Good memory."

And then we chatted for a while. Never miss an opportunity to peer into a competitor's knickers.

On the way back to my own establishment, the various loose ends rolled around in my head like tumblers in a broken combination lock. Just as I turned the last corner, my phone vibrated.

"Jocko! How are things?"

"Terrible! Too much work. Questions all difficult. Rates too low. I'm thinking of jacking in the whole thing."

This was classic Jocko. If he ever stopped moaning, one would be sure that either he was on death's door, in the grip of a terminal depression, or irredeemably sad. A complaining Jocko is a happy Jocko.

I reminded him of the questions I had asked him to answer. He rumbled and spluttered, cursed his life as a cross between Sisyphus and an indentured Delphic oracle, and then settled into giving me my answer, punctuated by periodic aftershocks.

"A weakness for cream puffs?" I exclaimed.

"Am I laryngitic? That's what I said! If you don't believe me, get someone else to fossick in your shit heaps!"

"No, Jocko, you're fine. Always have been. But what else was that you said? Something about our Mr. McGrath being involved in fencing some Royal Navy gear?"

"Too long to explain over the phone. I've sent you a package. The invoice is in it. I'll be looking for my cheque." And then I was alone on the line.

As always, Jocko was as good as his word. Just a few minutes later, I received an email from him. It had two attachments, a large one containing a lot of information scanned to PDF, and a smaller but far more important one: Jocko's invoice. I sent Jocko his money by Interac e-Transfer right away. Keep Jocko happy; keep the info flowing.

It took me more than an hour to read the package Jocko had sent. Thorough. Complete. Two decisions presented themselves right away.

The information contained the names of sixteen people who had been associates of McGrath at one time or another. There was a short description of each of them. Three of them were known wheelmen, so I could safely discard their names. Two were in prison. One was released from prison having served his term, and appeared to have decided to go straight. Four were out on parole, and there was no indication that they had broken any of their parole rules, such as consorting with the wrong people, and all four were seeing their parole officers at the specified intervals. From this information, it looked as though the list of sixteen could be pared down to six. Still quite a few.

I went back to Jocko's package and looked at the files of these six more closely.

Jocko presents information in its most trimmed-down form. These six characters each warranted two paragraphs at most. Three of the six had been arrested at some point, and brought to trial, but in all cases the charges had been dropped due to lack of evidence. One of the remaining three had gone underground, or had left the country, and had reappeared only eight months previously. Of the last two, one appeared to be something of an enforcer. And then there was the last individual. He had been investigated for involvement in a rare-book heist, but the police never managed to bring charges.

None of this proved anything, except the probability of being able to rule out the enforcer and the wheelmen, species not known for their cerebral acuity. But looking at the whole sorry bunch, the man who had relevant experience seemed the best bet. This was progress.

Working assumption: Mr. Rare Book, whose name, from Jocko's file, was Tim Reynolds, looked like he was my man. And so, given the events that had transpired, it looked like I was his man. Meaning that he and McGrath had gone to a lot of trouble to steal the book, implying that there was something about it that was important for them. So what had happened? Why was the book now back in my hands?

Did they not find what they wanted? If they had been mistaken, if there really was nothing important about that book after all, wouldn't they just have thrown it away? Why go to all the trouble of putting it back into circulation, and in fact doing this in a way that pretty much guaranteed its coming back to me? It occurred to me that they, whoever *they* were, would be operating within their own perceived set of opportunities and constraints.

I leaned back and thought about this, thought about the whole unlikely situation. A few things came to mind eventually.

First, it's no secret in the book world out there that I'm a fan of Nondas Parmenides. He's generally good on plots, his writing is reasonably fluid, and he does spend time on detail. He appeals to my historical bent. And so I have all his Kroton books. In fact I have duplicates of all of them, and I keep the better copies in my own inner sanctum. People in the business know this, and I don't try to keep it a secret. We all have our enthusiasms.

Second, since I have some quite valuable items in my collection, all my books are tagged with magnetic markers, and sensors at the exit from the shop prevent casual or even determined daytime theft. This precaution is also not common in used bookshops, and my use of it is also generally known. So neither McGrath nor Reynolds could simply have walked in during business hours and made off with the book. But—

They could have come into the shop any time and checked first that a copy of *Stylus of Death* was on my shelves, and that it was the copy they wanted. And would that be because of the Samuel Barrington inscription? Had they actually done that?

Disturbing, to say the least.

Park that one for now.

Third, my obsession with history is well known. This is principally what draws me to the Kroton books. Nondas handles the history well. My history obsession is reflected in my collection. It's also reflected in what I purchase for my collection. There seemed to be a thread here that I couldn't quite catch hold of.

Finally, everyone knew about my database. Publicly, it was a topic for mild hilarity, an expression of my own brand of eccentricity. Privately, I knew that other dealers found it interesting. They didn't know what was in it, but they seemed to believe that it conferred some kind of magical power onto its user, a sort of used bookshop owner's Excalibur. I had had two requests to sell the basic format for the database. My answer was always, "You can't afford it".

Just the fact of enumerating these points was making me feel uneasy. And that was because a picture was emerging, one that I didn't want to emerge.

If just any copy of *Stylus of Death* would have been okay, I knew that three other bookshops in Toronto had copies, and one of them had two copies, in fact. Nobody had sold a copy for many years. Reynolds and McGrath could have bought any one of those. Hell! They could have stolen any one, since the security in those places was so poor.

Apparently it had been my copy they wanted. What was special about my copy? Despite wanting to look for other rationales for what had happened, I kept coming back, unwillingly, to the Barrington inscription as the thing that was driving all this.

Okay. If my copy was the target…?

They knew they couldn't steal my copy during opening hours, but why didn't they just buy it?

This one stopped me for quite a while. There seemed to be no obvious answer here. Except, perhaps, for two things…

First, it's surprising how much the owners of used bookshops know about their competitors' businesses and what stock they have moved recently. Would the sudden sale of what appeared to be an unsaleable book raise eyebrows? Would this be something that would concern Reynolds and McGrath, cause them to think twice about making a purchase?

Second thing? My database.

I don't record customers' names, but nobody really knows what information I do record. Did their game really have such high stakes, was it really so important, that even my database and its possible partial record of their activities could scare them off, and so they decided on a nighttime break-in?

Shit, Rolls! You're going paranoid on me!

The Voice.

I invited him to come up with a better theory.

Silence.

Just as I thought, Voice.

Supposing then that Reynolds hadn't found what he wanted or expected from the book. Suppose he then deliberately put it back into circulation, expecting that it would wind up once again in my shop. What did he hope would be the result of my reacquisition of the book? Did he hope that I would wonder, just as I was doing, about these events? Did he hope that I knew something about the book that was, for him, a missing clue? Did he hope that all this might lead to behaviour on my part that would put him back on the scent?

A story had been forming in my mind, and I could see now the outlines of it. The outline was this:

Rod McGrath and Tim Reynolds had broken into my shop to retrieve my copy of *Stylus of Death*.

There was something about that book, or something in it, that they felt pointed to something important.

It seemed that McGrath had been the only one who knew exactly (or maybe approximately) what that something was, and he kept that information to himself. Until he could be sure that he would get something out of it all? To prevent Reynolds from pushing him out of the picture, perhaps permanently?

Reynolds must have had some other evidence convincing him that there was something important out there. Had he decided to play along with McGrath until he, Reynolds, had learned what he wanted?

But then the wheels came off. They broke into my shop, managing not to activate the alarm, and found the book, but then McGrath collapsed unexpectedly, and died right before Reynolds' eyes. Reynolds removed all ID from the body and left it where it was.

Reynolds then made off with the book, apparently hoping that the information he needed would become evident if he examined the book closely enough. But it appears that that didn't work out for him.

Reynolds put the book back into circulation, and it was very likely that he knew I now had it. Although this was just a theory, and it seemed to fit the facts, it was far from watertight. But it wasn't a great theory, because it indicated no way forward.

So. What now?

I thought about this for quite some time, and it gradually opened onto a disturbing panorama.

Most probably Reynolds had me under surveillance. How else would he get any sign that I knew something or what that something was? Plus, he had nothing to lose from putting me under surveillance except time. If he learned what he needed, he was home and dry. If he didn't, he could just walk away.

BUT. There was this big but. If Reynolds became reasonably certain that I knew what it was that he wanted to know, or at least had information that might give him what he needed, then in the extreme he could always try to get that information out of me by common criminal means, i.e., beat it out of me.

It was clear that countermeasures were needed.

Urgently.

That meant going back to Jocko.

Chapter Nine

"Jocko. I need someone to check whether I'm under surveillance."

There was mumbling, grumbling, and bubbling.

"I'll send you a list of three names."

"No time for that Jocko. Give them to me now, over the phone."

"What am I? A supermarket?"

"Two hundred and fifty dollar bonus, Jocko. Right off the top. Names."

Now, Jocko likes his loot as much as the next guy, maybe more. So the grumbling stopped, there was a bit of sniffing, and something that sounded like an expert tasting generous portions of prize truffles.

"Okay", Jocko said. "Here are three names. Get your pen ready."

I took down the three names and their contact information.

"Do you recommend any one of them particularly, Jocko?"

"They're all good", Jocko said testily, but holding back any outburst out of respect for his bonus. "Ronnie Klein might be busy just now. But ask him. Dan Fairley just started a job, but this kind of work … well, what can I say? A natural fit. Mark Whelan is very good but more expensive than the others."

"Whelan", I said. "Isn't he the guy who had some trouble at his place up north last year? Balsam Lake?"

"That's the guy."

"Don't know much about what happened", I said, "but it sounded like a real zinger." Thinking of the bookshop, as always, I asked Jocko whether anyone had written it up as a story. "Would probably sell like hotcakes", I mused hopefully.

"Wouldn't know. Not a literary agent. Have to go now. My invoice will be in your inbox in a few minutes." And then, once again, I had only the telephonic aether as company.

I phoned all three. In the end. No, not quite true. I emailed Fairley, on Jocko's suggestion, and in the end it was Fairley I opted for. Whelan was unable to start for a couple of days. Klein had just accepted two other jobs and had to decline. Fairley's email back suggested that we meet. The email contained a request for some general information on my problem, and I emailed back a thumbnail summary. I agreed to meet him an hour later. Fairley's email indicated that he had chosen an open patio as the meeting spot, long views in all directions but one, and that one direction was blocked by a large, windowless wall.

Twenty minutes before the appointed time, I was there. Jocko had told me that Fairley was a snappy dresser, so I was on the lookout for something other than shiny trousers and a baggy jacket. The place was sparsely populated, and it turned out that I was the only guy waiting on his own. Several well-dressed men entered but found other tables to sit at. Tired of feeling like a fifth grader waiting for his name to be called, I took some time to peruse the newspaper I had brought. Evidently the clocks all began running fast while I wasn't looking.

"Mr. Royce?"

I looked up, wondering who had hailed me.

"Daniella Fairley", she said, she being a tall brunette, shortish slightly curly hair, flat sand-coloured shoes, holding an oxblood leather case, and wearing a pale-brown suit, carrying the jacket.

"Don't feel you have to make any special effort at accommodating me, Mr. Royce", she said, offering her hand. "I apologize if you were given the impression that I was male. It's called *getting in the door*." It appeared that she had walked unerringly to my table. Unless Jocko had given her a picture of me, which was doubtful, she had simply read all the signs accurately, saw me as the only likely man waiting for someone, and just jumped right in. In any case, early indications were that she was good.

I rose, we shook hands, and then we sat.

"You have Jocko's recommendation of me. I can give you plenty of testimonials, if you wish. I've been in the business seven years, and I'd prefer not to hear any of this 'but you're a woman' stuff. Are we okay to go ahead on that basis?" she asked, flashing a smile that was half friendly and all business.

By that time I had recovered, and I found that I was both impressed and intrigued. During this time, a waiter had come to our table, we had ordered, and our drinks had been delivered.

"Yes. We're okay", I replied. "But let me say right off the top that I vet anyone before I commit to working with them. I'll explain my problem, we can talk about it, and by then I expect to be able to engage you or not."

It took me about five minutes to give a good outline of what had happened and why I thought I needed the services of someone like her. She asked about ten questions, and after I had answered the last of these, we both leaned back in our chairs, showing every indication of enjoying the afternoon. Her questions and responses indicated that she was more than adequately competent.

"It might be that I come up with a negative answer", Fairley said, looking at me squarely.

"Then I will conclude either that nobody has me under surveillance or that they're doing it so competently that you weren't able to detect it."

"I intend to make sure that the second of those possibilities will be remote. But it's always possible."

I just nodded.

"But if there is someone out there watching you", Fairley continued, "I expect to confirm that and to determine who is doing the watching."

There seemed to be nothing to say to that. Fairley took a sip of her wine.

"Let's suppose that there's someone watching and I can tell you who it is", she said, setting down her wine glass. "How do you intend to use that information?"

"Well, I'm not a street fighter", I replied. "I don't intend to go and beat out of him what he's up to. But there has been a death in my bookshop, and if there's a watcher and he is the sort of person I think he is, then two things will need to be considered. First, if the watcher is an associate of the stiff that I found in in my shop, then it's likely that he's looking for information, and he might think that he can get it directly from me. So, I'll take some measures to protect myself. Second, if he's a certain type of individual, then that will confirm that there's information out there of some value to him and that it's probably connected to the book that he, or someone, nicked from my shop. In which case I'll want to work fast to figure out just what that information is and to make use of it in a particular way."

"What way is that?" Fairley asked, still completely deadpan.

"To make it clear to the watcher that the game is over, the information has been acted upon, it's no longer of any value to him."

"Do you have some plan for this?"

"Yes. I do. But once I know what the information is and why it's important, I'll need some help to make it clear to my watcher that the game is over."

Fairley nodded. "And that help…?"

"…might be something you could line up. If you're interested."

"Let's just say that for now, yes, I am interested. This seems to be far from the usual grubby two-day job."

We both sipped our beverages.

"Who's involved in this from the police?"

"Detective Sergeant Barnett."

Fairley nodded but displayed no other reaction.

"You understand that we need to keep well clear of any police investigations."

I nodded. "Yes, I'm aware of that. But I'm not sure how I can find out what the police…"

"I'll look after that", Fairley said in a way that closed the matter decisively.

"Okay. Where do we start?"

Fairley shook her head. "We don't start anywhere. It will be just me. But I'll need to look at your shop and your home. Is there any other place where you spend a lot of time?"

"Yes. My restaurant."

At this point, Fairley just eyed me speculatively, apparently not expecting this sort of departure. After a few seconds she returned to business mode and said that we should get started.

And she meant exactly that. We finished our drinks, I paid, and then we went to the bookshop, my home, and then the restaurant. At the bookshop, I showed Fairley where the body had been found, and, by means of a long series of questions, she led me through Rice's discovery of the body, the visit by Barnett and his medical examiner, and the follow-up I had with both of them. She looked at all the windows and the two doors, asked to see the burglar alarm system, tsked a bit, and suggested a name I should contact to have the system beefed up somewhat. We spent very little time at my home, and not much more at the restaurant. But at the end of these visits, we sat in the restaurant at a table upstairs, well away from where the usual noisy crowd parks.

During these visits, Fairley had taken quite a few notes. Seated at the table in the restaurant, she went over those notes, asked more questions, jotted down a few more items, tapped the notebook with her pen a couple of times, then looked up. In an air of finality, she now closed her notebook and put notebook and pen in her case.

"Good. I'll get to work right away."

"When will I hear from you next?" I asked.

"When I contact you. So please give me the best contact information for you."

This I did.

"And please don't try to contact me", Fairley said. "If you need to get hold of me for any reason, just stick a small blue card somewhere in the window of your shop."

"How long do you think this will take?" I asked.

"If someone has you under surveillance, it will be either almost constant or occurring at regular intervals. Either way, I should be able to detect them in short order. I would guess that it will take less than a week. But if I do detect someone watching, I'll ask you to meet me someplace far from any of your frequent haunts, to discuss what the next steps should be."

Fairley held my gaze, and I just nodded agreement.

"Here's my standard contract, modified for your situation as I understood it from what Jocko told me, and our brief email exchange." She placed an envelope on the table. "Please correct anything you think isn't factually accurate."

I nodded.

"Since I don't expect the job to go on for a long time, I'll submit only one invoice when this part of the work is finished. *Finished*, by the way, means either I've detected someone and identified them, or I've concluded that you're not being watched. It's all in the contract. Please take a look at it now."

I did that.

"Any questions?" Fairley asked.

I spent a moment thinking about this, since it appeared that I wouldn't be seeing her again for a while.

"Yes. Let's assume that you identify someone. How do I go about discouraging him from anything further?"

"Well, that depends. If it's evident there's been something illegal going on, we can always hand over everything to the boys in blue and let them run with it. But it also depends on what he's looking for and why he's looking. If a big prize is involved, it could take some fairly heavy-duty discouraging."

"Such as?"

"Don't worry about that just now. The best thing you can be doing over the next few days is to try to figure out what's behind all this. Once we know that, we'll have some idea of this guy's incentive and whether it will be easy or difficult to discourage him."

At this, I just did some more nodding.

"Any more questions?"

"No. No more questions."

She inclined her head toward the contract, which I read through again and signed.

"Good!" Fairley said, smiling broadly and offering me her hand once again. "I'll be in touch again when I have something."

Fairley made to rise from her chair, then stopped.

"By the way", she said. "This book that you recovered, is it in your shop now?"

"Yes."

Fairley nodded. "I suggest you put it in a safety deposit box."

Fairley and I rose and I walked with her down the stairs and to the door. I had had precious little experience with male investigators, and none with women. But I had no doubts about this one, and it seemed that we were off to a good start.

I returned to an empty table and sat for a few minutes, pondering my first brush with Dan Fairley, favourably impressed by whatever arrangement she had made with Jocko to have a fighting chance at winning jobs, and a new respect for Jocko, the sly old vulture.

In the background, I recognized the urgency of the immediate problem I faced and began wondering seriously how I would go about resolving the riddle that seemed somehow to involve *Stylus of Death*.

Chapter Ten

Back at the bookshop, I checked that everything was running smoothly. Rice seemed to have things in hand, and for a few moments I watched the customers come and go, none of them, apparently, talking of Michelangelo. Retrieving my newly reacquired copy of *Stylus of Death*, I headed back to M&B Resto by way of my bank.

To my delight, the restaurant was much busier than when I had left just a couple of hours earlier. In the kitchen, the fume hood was running full bore, Hinge was lashing up dishes of all sorts, and my temporary server, Michelle — *soon to be made permanent,* I thought, as I watched her work — was sprinting back and forth from the kitchen hatch, laughing and joking with the customers. Her high-pitched, falling-tone, infectious laughter burst forth at regular intervals. The twin dumb waiters were pumping like pistons in an ocean liner, and even The Colonel had diverted some of his attention from the *Critique of Pure Reason* to take in the buzz.

In the kitchen, I checked the food inventories and the stock of wine, smiling at the depleted state of the latter. A generous flow of wine, I had found, was the best indicator of the health of my restaurant's trade, and I made a list, which turned out to be satisfactorily long, of the labels that needed replenishing.

"Everything okay, Hinge?"

Hinge returned to me a baleful one-eyed stare, a good sign that God was in Hinge's kitchen.

"How do, Michelle?"

"Great!" she said, stopping for a moment and exuding that hard-to-pin-down but appealing scent of busy, overheated, happy woman.

"Looks like you fit right in", I commented.

"This place and I were made for each other, Rolls", and then she sped off. Spoken as though it were a self-evident fact just being repeated. No hint of angling for tenure.

Having taken the pulse of the place, and after spending a half-hour chatting with customers, I headed off home to bend my mind once more to the big riddle.

Seated at my desk before my home computer, I found myself circling along the same old track, a path bereft of any further clues and just leading back onto itself. I had to find some way out of this closed loop and into another region of thought that would be productive.

Okay. Everything rested on assumptions, but it seemed at present that the chief underlying assumption was that Rod McGrath had uncovered something that was linked to *Stylus of Death*, something that in turn pointed toward something of value. McGrath could have come across his *something* entirely by accident, but then he would have needed to recognize that, whatever it was, it was important. His background pointed to nothing intellectual whatever, no interest or skill in puzzles, in fact nothing suggestive of accomplishment or complexity. Could he have acquired something from a colleague, or from a client? And then somehow Tim Reynolds had become involved as a partner? An odd arrangement, it seemed. Reynolds as senior partner in terms of smarts and ability to plan, but a junior partner in terms of inside information. An inherently unstable situation, one would have thought.

Just then, however, something else occurred to me. Would McGrath have sat on any important information for any length of time, important in the sense that it could be made to yield quantities of lucre? The immediate answer was *no*. So that meant he must have found out fairly recently about my copy of *Stylus of Death* and whatever information it concealed. I thumbed quickly through the package of information Jocko had sent me.

There it was. Well, there something was.

McGrath had been involved in finding a home, through a well-known fence, for some Royal Navy gear. Now, McGrath wouldn't have been involved in trading high-end naval weapons on the black market. If this hint about supposed naval gear was to be believed, it had to be something small and of high value.

That could refer to something related to a country's national security, but this also would be entirely out of McGrath's league.

Something old? Of value to a collector? If it was really *naval*, was it perhaps a ship's bell? A captain's log? Some item of value or of personal significance from a captain's cabin? Something of that nature from, say, the eighteenth century, the Old Admiral's time, could be worth a lot. So perhaps there *was* some link to the naval Barrington. But how could McGrath have come across something like that? How would he even have been able to identify such an artefact? Answer: he wouldn't. But he could have been the middleman, the visible man shielding the invisible man, the chump who would take the fall if the whole thing went south.

But there was one gaping problem here.

It couldn't be the case that McGrath had already found a home for whatever it was he had come across. In that event, none of this current fuss would have taken place. So was the prize still in play, somehow? Had McGrath double-crossed the invisible man and kept the prize for himself? Very unlikely. Did McGrath somehow have the thing in his sole possession? Possibly. That could explain a few things. But it was still just a distant possibility. The fact that the book, *Stylus of Death*, came back to me seemed to indicate that the puzzle remained unsolved. No, it looked as though McGrath was fully and finally out of the picture and he could be removed from further consideration.

And that inscription in the book, *Samuel Barrington 1979*. Was that a date? A locker number? A safety deposit box number? And how had this book come into McGrath's world, presented itself to him as a key to something of value?

None of this was leading anywhere. I scratched my head in irritation, got up to make myself a cup of coffee, and forced myself to change lanes, to think about what the next step was for M&B Resto. This wasn't the result of any sudden culinary brainwave. It was just a pragmatic way to give myself a break from all this fruitless circling around McGrath and the fog of closed-loop possibility that seemed to cloak him.

It worked.

Before I realized it, I was inventing experimental restaurant menus in my head, planning possible literary gourmet events, reinventing recipes from old York, having just brought back to mind the delightful book of desserts and drinks based on what had once come out of the Fort York officers' mess. Now wreathed in smiles, I recognized that this was just the antidote I needed. My fussing over McGrath and the big puzzle had now been pushed to one side. It was clear to me that the fevered speculation in a vacuum that I had been engaging in would need to give way to some searching that was much more systematic.

Coffee in one hand, and notebook and pencil in the other, I walked through from my office to the small sitting room, where I parked and then began marking out the basis and scope for some disciplined information searching.

This planning took about an hour. Refining and streamlining its results took another half-hour. Only then did I return to my office and symbolically restart my computer to signal a break from my recent and somewhat troubling two hours of phrenesis over things McGrathian.

And so I settled in to a spate of organized computer searching. As for any organized search, it took only a few minutes for the initial approach to throw up further possibilities, but these had to be either integrated systematically into the overall plan, or parked until a natural home was found for them. A dozen articles on Admiral Barrington appeared on my screen. Multiple succulent hints rose up before me on naval finds of significance from the eighteenth century. Several long threads of inquiry led to battles and other naval engagements. I found three extended essays on naval archaeology. I was by now a happy mule roving in fields of virginal information clover. The effort itself had become its own reward. Looking in the directory I had opened when I had started this spate of searching, I was astonished to see that I had copied and saved more than sixty items — articles, essays, news clips, heritage notes. This might have gone on indefinitely had my stomach not sent a shot across my mental bows.

I checked my watch.

Holy shit! I had been at this for more than four hours.

But my stomach was right. Time to get something to eat before I passed out. I had the wherewithal in my kitchen to whip up a nice batch of Sicilian pasta. Twenty-five minutes later, I was seated before a bowl of this spicy concoction and a nice bottle of Nero d'Avola to keep it company. As I ate, slowly and deliberately, I pondered at low revs.

First, the naval motif as a search basis had yielded a lot of material that was at least potentially relevant. There still was no really firm link to my copy of *Stylus of Death*, apart from the possibility that Samuel Barrington did indeed refer to the Old Admiral. A second but hazy connection seemed to be emerging as well, but it looked a distant second. The way forward now seemed to be first to do justice to my meal and the two glasses of wine that I had allocated as my current ration, and second to go back to my searching until it became evident that I had found everything there was to find. Years of searching had given me the means to recognize when a search had essentially exhausted its ore body. That intuition told me that I was close. I finished my pasta dish amid happy thoughts of the restaurant.

Another hour at the computer and I was convinced that I had entered that wheel-spinning stage when the same things kept appearing on the screen and nothing new was being uncovered.

Time now for some study and consolidation.

I printed out what seemed a whole ream of material, poured another glass of Nero d'Avola, and settled into my reading chair. As I worked my way through the paper, the notes I was jotting on the pad to my right accumulated. Two pages. Five pages. Eleven pages. Ultimately nineteen pages of closely packed notes.

A large and well-populated landscape had now formed in my mind, and I began working through the notes I had made, trying to extract any themes, patterns, clues. Multiple times I went back to the items I had printed, which were now numbered and marked by subject under about ten headings. Three or four times I put down my pen, rose from the chair, walked around the room, and in general tried to let things settle and digest. When I had finished digging through my nineteen pages of notes, I had three-quarters of a page of summary points. But this wasn't good enough.

Rising once more from the chair, I stretched, walked around the room again for five minutes, then settled back down to go through all the pages of detailed notes once more. At the end of that exercise, most of the summary points had been modified, and their total volume had increased from three-quarters of a page to almost a page and a half. I read through these six times.

Two figures had emerged from the great mass of detail. One was the Old Admiral, of course, and that was where it looked like I should place my money. The second was an obscure philosopher at the University of King's College in Halifax, who apparently had a flexible and wide-ranging mind, judging from the number of fairly diverse programmes he seemed to turn up in. I was a bit surprised to be coming across something new at this stage, when I had already done so much searching. Some of the papers he had posted were quite interesting. But there was something rather more interesting, something I could easily have missed, and something it seemed that I *had* missed.

His name.

My primary search turned up *S. Barrington*, buried on a high-numbered page of Google, which seemed to be why I had not noticed it earlier. But when I did spot it and dug further, I got his full name.

Samuel Barrington.

I set down my pen. It was now almost 3 am. I had been hammering away at my problem for more than ten hours. But I felt that I had made some solid headway.

Don't get too cocky now, Rolls.

All right. What *did* I have?

A brutal sceptic would reach an unedifying conclusion.

I had discarded dozens of names, private individuals mostly from current times who all had the name Samuel Barrington. And I had discarded them not by elimination but by failure to find a reason to include them, because I could see no possible connection between any of them and my book.

I had retained, by default and based on a rationale that was thin to the point of not existing, two names: an admiral who had died over two hundred years ago, and a present-day philosophy professor. Some Hobson's choice!

But I had to remain upbeat.

Taking a leaf from the book of a rediscovered hero, the same Dimitriou in *Stylus of Death*, I poured myself a large glass of limoncello, put on a disc of Verdi arias, and just let myself drift.

The limoncello lasted as long as the Verdi, and my drift had become a rapid fade.

Bed was the answer.

But even that, I reflected drily, was at that moment a default option.

Chapter Eleven

The window in my bookshop is not large but it's a good display area, and I use it. There's always about twenty books arrayed in the window; I change them regularly, and I keep track of what books have been in the window when and for how long. Despite my late night, I was up at about eight thirty, went off to the bookshop right away, spent about half an hour changing the window display, and stuck a small piece of blue card in front of the book in the bottom-right corner of the window. Rice was busy keeping things ticking over, and I left him to it.

M&B Resto was a bit quieter than usual, but it was still an active gastronomic site. The wine I had ordered to breathe new life into the restaurant's failing supplies had arrived and was sitting on a small pallet at the back of the kitchen. So I spent fifteen minutes putting it in the so-called cellar, which isn't actually underground, since that would have committed too much time to retrieving wine and filling orders. The cellar occupies, instead, a largish closed-off space right at the rear of the kitchen, where the old electrical panels had been before I rewired the place. This space is serviced by a small heat pump unit that keeps the contents at just the right temperature, and the floor-to-ceiling racks here hold about 1600 bottles. As the total stock of wine for an active restaurant, it's a bit lean, but we weren't intending to try for any sort of oenological supremacy.

Hinge will make bread if he has to, but today he was happy to defer to me. My long night of cerebral questing needed an offset, and the physical activity and the sheer olfactory delight associated with all the steps on the way to fresh bread did me good. I had noticed that it never hurt business either, and as the four different types of bread baked and their heady aroma filled the dining area, noses began twitching, palates awoke, saliva glands began pumping. Pavlov's approach wouldn't have worked if his dogs had not been fed promptly. The same applies in the Resto, and fresh bread was always made available to those watering mouths at the earliest possible moment.

If you enjoy making bread, and I do, then time does not need to be costed religiously. The activity provides its own payback, as something that meets the needs for therapy, culinary creativity, and connection to an ancient source of human welfare, and that generates a product which is at once humble, aristocratic, and physically attractive. The old phrase *the staff of life* just about says it all.

When freshly sliced bread and trays of butter began leaving the kitchen, it was clear to all that a moment of gastronomic truth had arrived. In the kitchen, I watched the loaves vanish from the cutting boards, and the flow of bread out to the dining area was a thing of beauty.

But fresh bread is also a fantastic loss leader, and the thing that it can stimulate best and most readily is the sale of accompanying appetizer items, items that are inherently profitable. That was happening now. Plates of bread, trays of thinly sliced meats and smoked salmon, dishes of olives, cornichons, artichoke hearts, and delicate cubes of old cheese galloped happily toward the alimentary black hole the public section of the restaurant had become. The upstairs area had likewise been activated, and bread and its accompaniments seemed to be going up on the dumb waiter by the hundredweight.

Good bread takes time to make. Of the four largish batches I had made, about a third would be held back for later use. The other two-thirds was current consumption. But getting the bread made, out of the ovens, cooled, and ready to be sliced and put onto plates had taken several hours, and at two thirty, my baking and clean-up completed, I stopped for a ham sandwich. I had barely finished the sandwich when my vibrating cellphone signalled the arrival of an email message.

It was from Fairley. In response to my blue card, she suggested that we meet, and had given me a location uptown. After an easy run on the subway, I made my way to the stated location, a pub called The

Isherwood, and found Fairley sitting in one corner of a large back patio separated off from the rest of the neighbourhood by high brick walls.

Fairley had ordered a half carafe of wine, and two glasses sat on the table. We exchanged greetings, she poured wine into my glass, we made a ritual toast, and we sipped.

"I got your message", she said, referring to my blue card. "Anything urgent?"

"Not urgent. But I've made some headway on just what might be involved here."

"And?"

"And it looks like some sort of naval artefact from the Seven Years War, or at least that period. Don't know exactly what. But I can think of things that would make collectors very interested."

We talked about it some more, and I answered her questions, filled in some gaps.

"Is that why you wanted to meet?"

"Yes. Well, there was no requirement to meet, but I did want to bring you up to date."

"Do you think this is a reasonable step forward?" Fairley asked, appearing somewhat sceptical.

"Yes. I do. If I can find out more specifically what is involved, then I've got a chance at determining where that something is. If I know that, then I expect to be able to start planning some countermeasures, getting some defences in place."

I sipped my wine, hoping that I was coming across as being hard and successfully at work.

"Have you identified any watchers yet?" I asked.

Fairley set down her glass.

"Yes, I have."

"Do you know who it is?"

"No, not yet."

"Does that mean you think it's not Reynolds?"

Fairley shook her head decisively.

"Oh! I know it's not Reynolds."

"Oh?" I said, hoping for more.

"Yes. It's not Reynolds, because Reynolds is dead."

This news triggered a significant mental earthquake, and it took me a few seconds to recover.

"Dead?"

Fairley waited for me to formulate a question that warranted an attempt at an answer.

"Dead?" I repeated. "How did you learn that?"

"Police contacts. The police found him late last night. Looks like an execution, apparently."

"So. Then who is watching me? And just where are they doing the watching?"

"I don't know who is doing the watching, at least not yet. And the only watching I've detected so far has been at the bookshop."

"So, have we made any real progress?" I asked, feeling that some wand of evil magic had converted my upbeat mood coming into this meeting to a cloud of confusion and an urge to retreat.

"Oh, yes, we've made progress. Although I don't know yet who the watcher is, I do have a couple of photos of him. His name should be forthcoming within the next six hours or so."

I went quiet for a moment.

"What should I be doing?" I asked after a fairly long delay.

"Normal routine, in general. But don't do anything out of the ordinary", Fairley said.

I looked at her and was aware that I was scowling.

"Normal routine? Someone else is dead, and I presume that he didn't expire because of a broken heart. This isn't a game. It isn't you who's sitting in crosshairs."

"I understand your situation, Rolls. Really. I do. But until I have a name for your watcher, I can't suggest anything else, aside from locking yourself in your home with a shotgun. There always was risk. The body in your bookshop made that amply clear, even though it appears that McGrath died of a heart attack. Now someone else is dead. I don't know why yet, but I'm not relying on it being an unrelated coincidence. If whoever is watching is trying to find out something from you, they're not just going to bump you off."

"Perhaps not, but they could try for a snatch—"

"Which is why your surveillance detail now has two people instead of just one. The second has some serious martial arts capability."

I wasn't convinced, and I didn't mind letting it show.

"Try not to worry. By this time tomorrow I expect to know who your watcher is, and what his background says about him. Once we have information like that, we'll know better what measures to take, if any."

Fairley looked down at the table briefly.

"I want you to know that my clients are special. I take their problems, and their security, very seriously. Your situation is different from the sort of thing I'm usually asked to do, but it's nothing I can't handle."

We just sat looking at each other. I was aware that my facial expression was set hard.

"I'm going to speak frankly. I hear what you say. It all sounds fine and lovely. But please reassure me that your background puts some meaning into those words."

Fairley sat there for a moment, seeming to come to a decision.

"Okay. Have you heard of JTF2?"

"The Special Operations Forces Command?"

"Yes. So you've heard of it."

"Heard of, but that's it. How does JTF2 figure in all this?"

"I was in JTF2. Two years."

"A woman?" I asked, in offensive, knee-jerk incredulity.

Fairley's expression immediately displayed impatience and anger before she wiped them both away.

"Try to join us in the current century. Yes, a woman. And yes, I was just as good as any of the men. And yes, I had their respect. And no, I left because I had spent enough time in the armed forces and not because I was pushed out."

I didn't know quite what to do, since there was no convenient hole to crawl into. But I was appalled at the sudden realization that under what I considered my cultivated and sophisticated humanist reality I was basically just another sexist pig.

Fairley smiled.

"Look, don't feel too badly about this. If you were a dyed-in-the-wool asshole, you would have turned me down as soon as you saw me. Besides, I'll tell you something. It wasn't all that long ago when my own prejudices left me hugely embarrassed. It was at a party. The man I struck up a conversation with turned out to be a househusband. A proud, happy, and competent househusband. I made all the wrong assumptions and just put both feet into it. So none of us is completely clean."

Once I had recovered my voice, and a bit of aplomb, we talked some more, about general things. My mood improved as I put the shards of my self-esteem back together. More importantly, I understood much better the capabilities of the person who sat across from me. She asked about my background. I gave her the short version of the improbable path to my present shaggy overlay of literary scholar *manqué*, bibliophile, gastronome, and general money grubber. She laughed in genuine pleasure.

"Your restaurant sounds like quite a place."

"It is, if I do say so. You need to come by sometime for a tour and a meal."

"I'd like that. Very much. Just say when."

"Well, I'm there most days. Your schedule is probably limiting. Just take your pick."

Fairley looked at her watch.

"I need to be off. But I'll be in touch just as soon as I have anything new and significant. Is any time okay? Even late?"

"Yes. Please. Any time."

We rose, smiled at each other, and shook hands once more. It was businesslike, but now there was warmth there as well.

I watched her walk away. Her movements were economical, something I hadn't noticed until just now.

There was work ahead of me. Reynolds dead. Definite confirmation of a watcher. Watcher identity expected soon. That would herald the arrival of decision time. And here I was still waving around vague feelings of what this was all about. Naval artefact from the eighteenth century! What the hell was that supposed to mean? Fairley probably thought I was just another misty-eyed artsy type, expecting the secrets of the universe to lie buried somewhere in "The Love Song of J. Alfred Prufrock".

Having had the temerity to scowl at Fairley earlier, I now scowled at myself much more ferociously. *Time to get seriously to work, you sexist prick.*

Chapter Twelve

Leaving the meet with Fairley, I returned home via the bookshop. In my den, sitting before my computer, I fumed at myself in angry disdain. Images from the meeting returned to me. There I was, faced by a capable investigator who was trying to do a serious piece of work, for *me*, while I rested happily in some floral Coleridgean glen, radiating post-orgasmic smugness, adrift on a sacred river, thinking that flashing eyes and floating hair would tell me everything I needed to know.

"Fucking idiot!" I shouted. "Moron!" Several other hard-edged, rough-hewn curses were barked into my cell.

Under the prod of my anger, impatience, and frustration, my fingers flew over the keyboard, while in the background the memory of the hazy incompetence I displayed at my meeting with Fairley struck out like a lash. But then a pragmatic voice let me know that, beyond a certain point, venting wasn't going to advance me an inch, so I called forth my sergeant major persona. Craggy-faced, lantern-jawed, impeccably uniformed, he herded his flabby charges onto the parade ground for a bit of aerobic sinew-tightening. Focussing more fiercely on my computer, I set to work again.

All right, soldier! No more dicking around! Take the obvious clue! My sergeant major bellowed his orders. *Barrington 1979. Throw away all the airy-fairy bullshit! Barrington is the admiral! What happened in 1979 that could be significant? Come on! Bend your back to it, candy-ass!*

Google and I began searching. Pretty much right away, I identified the two volumes of Barrington's papers produced by the Navy Records Society. I ordered both volumes. They would take a while to arrive. I continued searching online to try to find out just what they contained. Within a few minutes, I satisfied myself that I wasn't going to be able to see the contents of these two volumes online without paying a fee, but other items soon flashed up on the screen. I discarded most of them peremptorily. A few showed promise, and I scanned those few for gold flecks. Refined searches were fashioned. Gradually, there appeared a few leads having some potential, snippets dredged up from the aether's thin gruel. Within this material, one article indicated that not all Barrington's papers had survived, suggesting that the two volumes I had ordered would necessarily be incomplete.

Old Admiral Barrington had stood down from his active seafaring naval role, and in 1787 took up the post of general of the Royal Marines. He died on August 16, 1800, in Bath.

As good a place as any to die. *Much better than most,* I thought, recalling time spent in Bath years earlier.

Eyes front! The sergeant major roared.

Suitably chastened, I set aside the reminiscing and kept digging.

Quite soon, the same material began reappearing. It seemed that Barrington had been a private person. There was a lot about his naval exploits, especially in material that had been produced in the ten to twenty years following his death, but nothing on his private life appeared, apart from the fact that he had never married. From these items, it became clear that Barrington had not been present at the actual taking of the Fortress of Louisbourg in 1758, but had been dispatched in 1760, under Captain Byron, to help demolish it. That Byron, I was surprised to learn, was the poet's grandfather.

I discovered also that Barrington had a friend in his later years, a Colonel Barre. I turned toward the colonel and dug further. But I soon concluded that I was just sinking a shaft into an oreless depth.

Barrington also had four siblings, one of them being the Bishop of Durham at the time of Barrington's death. This Bishop-of-Durham vein looked somewhat more promising, so I began digging in that direction. Hope brightened when I learned that the bishop had written a history of one of his other siblings, William Wildman Barrington, who had been an eminent politician. I located a digitized copy of the bishop's book, expecting a more generous hoard of clues. But in his book the bish had mentioned Samuel only once, in passing.

I dug further. The articles continued to pile up, even though they delivered only thin suggestions. I saved them and ploughed on.

Time advanced. More articles suggested pay dirt, and I saved and filed them. Other articles, seeming to harbour more distant promise, were flipped into the bin marked *potential nuggets*.

After three hours, I stretched, then rose and began walking around my small den. Stiff arms and legs were soon loosened. Cobwebs and fog cleared from my mind. I began feeling somewhat better about things.

Hey! Candy-ass! What the hell do you think you're doing?

A good prod was one thing. But I had been looking for a tough-love cheerleader, not a bully.

Hey! Sergeant Major! You've done your job! Now piss off back to barracks!

That was better. I had taken charge again.

Back at my computer, and feeling a lot more assured, I began sifting through the pile of potential nuggets. Overall, it was rather disappointing. At best, only second- and third-rate detail was surfacing. Not useless, but certainly nothing leading to the game-changer I was hoping to find. I went back to Google and some basic digging, but this time aiming more deliberately at secondary sources. My fundamental assumption, if one wants to call it that, was that somebody else might have been interested in Barrington and might have done some heavy lifting that I could avoid.

It was slow and tedious. And not encouraging. The odd tangential reference appeared, but didn't point to anything new and basic. Another hour passed. Then a further hour crawled by. I stopped, rubbed my face, looked out the window, and promised myself another fifteen minutes. Ten minutes into this quarter-hour of injury time, two words leapt from one of the Google hits.

Personal recollections.

There it was. A post by an amateur English historian, Geoffrey Andrew Fielding, based in Bristol, it seemed. He was describing what he claimed were notes prepared by Admiral Barrington, late in his life, on his naval career. I would need to check the Navy Records Society volumes when they arrived to see if this material was included. My sense was that it would not be in those two volumes, since Fielding, who was apparently a keen amateur historian, would almost certainly have known this and would not have made a big deal over something already in the public domain. So I read through his post carefully.

But it was not only a teaser, containing almost no detail; it was an isolated article, apparently not one that Fielding had published anywhere. I searched through it with interest. Appearing to relate highlights of what was in the document by Barrington that Fielding had unearthed, there were references to images from Barrington's illustrious career in the Royal Navy. Louisbourg was mentioned. Reference was made to three paragraphs on Saint Lucia and the Toulon Fleet of the Comte d'Estaing (and a query on the spelling). There was a sentence or two on Grenada, some comments on the Barfleur, an indication of text on the relief of Gibraltar...

But what exactly were these notes that Barrington was said to have prepared, and where had Fielding found them?

Internet silence.

I did a search on Geoffrey Andrew Fielding and came up with an obituary.

Without a lot of hope, I pursued all fourteen references to Fielding extending to the second page in Google. I was about to throw in the towel, when I came across a brief eulogy delivered by an emeritus history professor at the University of Bristol, who recounted his friendship with Fielding and applauded Fielding's work as an amateur historian. *It's worth a shot*, I thought, *having come this far*. A bit more digging yielded an email address for this professor emeritus, and I quickly prepared and sent off an inquiry to him.

Professors whose names appear where members of the general public can find them tend to get a lot of mail. Depending on their specialty, they can receive volumes of mail from people who feel they have been uniquely blessed, have found the secret to some part of the universe, and are looking for validation and recognition. So it's hardly surprising that many emails to academics go unanswered. I fully expected mine to be one of them.

Turning to what I had collected during the day, I was a little disheartened, but not surprised, to conclude that the sum total was not very much. I had learned a little more about Admiral Barrington's career exploits, had advanced practically not at all in uncovering his private life, and was frankly somewhat astonished that this stunningly accomplished family appeared to have attracted so little interest. (But then I had been studying the relevant literature for only a matter of hours. What do you expect, Royce? Unlimited literature and practised expertise at the drop of a hat?) Most significantly, I had come across nothing that would make sense of the name and date entered in my copy of *Stylus of Death*, or why that particular book had warranted that particular inscription.

Since I had spent quite a few hours on digging, reading, and thinking, I went once more through the mass of material I had collected, made notes on the search schemes I had used, made sure that I had copied and pasted to my Word versions of the articles the links identifying where they had come from in cyberspace, and put the whole thing to bed.

I'm a believer in giving the subconscious free rein, and I do this by switching off my conscious mind for the topic of interest and going off to do something totally different. In this instance, that something was a trip to the restaurant, where I planned to move among the guests, chat, laugh, joke, argue, and prepare myself a steak in a three-mustard sauce and a huge ratatouille. And that's what I did.

The evening was relaxing. The setting, the company, the discussion, they all reminded me why I undertook this mad restaurant venture in the first place. I hung around until half past midnight helping Hinge clean up and readying everything for the following day. Then I went home, crashed, and enjoyed the sweet dreams of the just.

The next morning, there was business to do at the restaurant and the bookshop before either opened, so I bent my mind to both, being alone in each of my two establishments. I left notes for Hinge and Rice and headed for home at ten thirty. Back at my computer, I sat thinking before I turned it on. Thinking about Barrington. I asked myself what else I could do, where else I could look.

I must have sat pondering for almost half an hour before I switched on my computer and prepared to do battle again with, or maybe against, Google. Hard to tell sometimes. There were quite a few new email messages, and I scanned through them quickly. About twenty were related directly or indirectly to restaurant and bookshop. Looked like they all could wait.

Except for...

Williamson? Did I know anyone called Williamson?

It was my emeritus professor.

Thank you for your inquiry Mr. Royce. My answer is straightforward, but might not have the detail I believe you are seeking.

Geoff Fielding did indeed come up with something, but unfortunately its provenance is far from clear. It does appear to be notes produced by Admiral Barrington in late 1799, but Fielding never did tell me where he came across them or what led him to them. I do have a copy of the material, but it was transcribed by Fielding, so any non-textual hints in the original are lost to me. I attach a copy of Geoff's transcription here.

I would be interested to know, out of curiosity, what has led you to pursue this historical wisp.

I assume that you are writing from within the UK, but I have not come across your name until now.

Wow!

Opening the attachment, I scanned it quickly on the screen, noting that it was in excess of forty pages, then saved it and printed the entire document. The notes were cryptic, factual, and quite dry. It read almost as though the document had been produced against its author's better judgment. Nothing surprising in that. If they were what they seemed, then they were notes drafted by a military man. They were meant to be just a sober record of events. But for me they were indeed living history. I could feel the tingle across the centuries. Fielding had left his impressions as marginal comments, and the effect on him had been similar. In one case, *Droll remark but fantastic implications! This could upset some serious academic apple carts!!!* In another case Fielding noted, *Wonderful! This note reveals an entirely new insight!* I couldn't help regretting that I hadn't come across Fielding a year earlier.

Was this document related to the date 1979? Is that when Fielding had found Barrington's notes, if that's indeed what they were?

Checking under Properties in the Word document yielded a date, but it wasn't 1979. However, that proved nothing. But first things first.

I immediately wrote back to Williamson, thanking him for his quick response and for the document he had passed on to me. Relating the full background on how I came to be in contact with him would have certainly convinced him I was a flake and would have ended our exchange on the spot. So I simply stated that I owned a bookshop in Toronto and that this particular interest in Barrington was raised during one of my purchase transactions.

The published volumes of Barrington's letters and papers intrigued me, but I had no option but to wait for them to arrive. In the meantime, I was determined to extract what I could from the material that I did have.

The notes Fielding had transcribed (if that was what he had done) described the scene at Louisbourg in some detail. The note documented the characteristics of the fortress using what appeared to be a practised military eye. The size and strength of the fortifications were reported to be impressive, even though the damage from the earlier siege in 1745 was still evident and left the fortress vulnerable. But Barrington and others had evaluated the place in light of their instructions from London: to reduce it completely to rubble, thereby making it unappealing and unfit for any possible future occupation by the French. It took more than five months of continuous work to carry out this order. Everything of value was salvaged first and then the walls and defensive structures were blasted to ruins.

The French garrison at Louisbourg under Chevalier de Drucour had surrendered in 1758. They had been treated well, and were ultimately repatriated to France. They had probably destroyed any documents of strategic significance before surrendering, and the English victors under Amherst had almost certainly searched the place for anything of value. But I suspected that those charged with destroying Louisbourg would also have looked for anything of value, and might have looked more diligently than did the victors two years earlier, who might well have been drunk from elation.

I must have spent the best part of an hour poring over Fielding's document. There was a tantalizing hint. It looked as though a search had indeed been made of the fortress in advance of the demolition crews and that a significant amount of vaguely specified *material* had been crated and sent back to England. Would those searching have kept their own souvenirs? Almost certainly yes. Did Barrington retain anything? Unlikely, but possible. Things that might have been good keepsakes would be the logs of French ships, and the ships' bells. In 1758, there were ten French ships at Louisbourg. Five of them were sunk to try to block the entrance to the harbour. Of the remaining five, three caught fire and burned during the siege, and two were captured. Barrington wasn't present at Louisbourg in 1758, so any trophies they might have found in 1760 would have been material not scavenged two years earlier.

It's easy to forget just how significant Louisbourg was at that time. It was an enormous and significant defensive structure. Its capture by Britain in 1758 was an important event, one that opened the way for Royal Navy warships to advance to Quebec City unhindered and without fear of attack. Everyone associated with the capture and destruction of Louisbourg must have been aware of the significance of their exploits. I knew that some large items had been removed from the fortress as trophies of a sort. The two cannons sitting in the University of Toronto campus, in front of Hart House, are just two such items. It would be surprising if the men preparing to demolish the Louisbourg structures had been able to find *nothing* worth nicking.

So, let's suppose that Barrington had left Louisbourg with some sort of keepsake, either something he found or something he confiscated from his men. Papers? A logbook? A ship's bell? Perhaps a wine goblet that had belonged to Drucour? A small seal, escutcheon, coat of arms?

It was all maddeningly vague, and on its own hardly enough to be the source of a consuming mystery or a source of the conspiracy and skulduggery that led to the appearance of a body in my bookshop.

It's always darkest just before dawn. That bit of hoary folk wisdom, evidently sent from somewhere to bolster my fading enthusiasm, did precious little bolstering, but it flagged for me a possibility that might not have arisen otherwise.

Barrington died in his lodgings in Abbey Green in Bath on August 16, 1800. A quick check told me that Abbey Green is an attractive street in central Bath. On his death, all Barrington's possessions would have gone somewhere.

That *somewhere* was one of the things that now had my attention.

Chapter Thirteen

Time check. Approaching noon! Where the hell does the time go?

My searching to learn more about Admiral Barrington and his life had given me a good amount of detailed background. This was reassuring in that it put me in the picture in terms of times and places.

But I now realized that I had to back away from this detail. Fairley's team was out there watching whoever was watching me. I expected that I would soon know who that watcher was. But the watcher wasn't just spying for fun. There was something important that he (presumably a he) or his boss wanted to know. And likely they were hoping some action of mine would lead them to that something. But they might well have been monitoring the customers who came and went from my shop.

Something important. Something somewhere out in the world. That was the first thing I had to try to figure out. I didn't know what the something was. Perhaps neither did they. But the kicker was this: they probably knew things that I didn't know. And I might know things that they didn't. What I needed to do was scan this puzzle from a higher level.

Go back to the beginning, Rolls, I said to myself. I went over old ground once more. Thinking again of the *why* and *by whom* of the inscription *Samuel Barrington 1979* in my copy of *Stylus of Death* revealed nothing new. Whatever in the book was of significance for my watchers remained concealed from me. And was it, for some reason, the inscription itself that was important? I could find nothing else significant about that particular copy. So for the time being, and as a default, let's follow the idea that the inscription is important. If there was anything to all this, then it did seem that knowing the *what* and *why* of that inscription was the key to understanding whatever was the source of all the interest here.

In my mind, I walked back over how this episode had begun. Suppose that McGrath had not died of a heart attack there in my shop. My guess was that they would have got away with it. Most likely, I would have detected no break-in, and almost certainly would not have known that the book had been lifted. And that situation might have existed for months.

If all these suppositions were true, my thieves knew two things prior to the break-in: (1) they knew that I had that particular copy of *Stylus of Death* in my shop, and I had come up with one route by which they could have determined this; and (2) they had some idea of the link between that book and the something important.

But having gone to all that trouble, they had then contrived to get the book back to me. By then, they must have been aware that I knew somebody had filched the book. Otherwise they would have had some difficulty devising a way to return it to me that wouldn't look very odd. Returning to me a book that I wasn't aware was missing? One implication was that the information they had going into this elaborate book heist was either wrong or incomplete.

Too elaborate, it seemed to me.

I had already worked out a sort of rationale for why they chose this nighttime hit rather than just buying the book. To go to such extremes implied an extraordinary level of caution, and as far as I could see this had to be linked to the significance of whatever it was they were trying to find. It looked as though they didn't want anyone to know that someone even was interested in this obscure mystery novel. In that case, they certainly wouldn't want a third-party purchaser to be involved in acquiring the book.

The likely implication of all this was that although my watcher and I might know different things, neither of us had enough to crack the puzzle.

But there was one significant difference here: my watcher knew enough about the puzzle to know the value of whatever it concealed.

Okay. So where did this leave me?

Well, if this chain of reasoning was correct, the watcher probably knew who had owned the book before it became a used book. This implied either that the watcher had known that my copy of *Stylus of*

Death had reached me via Raymond Lansdell and his used book emporium, or that they had traced it some other way. How?

I thought about this. It would be a tedious but straightforward matter just to troll all the used bookshops, checking the shelves for a copy of *Stylus of Death*, or, less probably, asking in each shop if they had a copy and, if so, could they take a look at it. I wouldn't keep a record of inquiries like that, and it's very doubtful that I would remember such an inquiry, especially if they had asked about two or three books, *Stylus of Death* being one of them. I recalled from my discussion with Lansdell that he had acquired the book as part of an estate sale. If my watcher knew that I had acquired the book from Lansdell, then the last thing I wanted was to be seen going back to him to ask more about how he had obtained the book, from whom, and along with which other books. Too late to worry about that now. And this might indicate a way to gauge the level of the watchers' information. Had they actually tailed me when I went to see Raymond? I needed to ask Fairley about this.

If they had watched me, that could mean a number of things. First, it might mean that their interest in the whole matter arose after I had bought the book from Raymond. That did happen, after all, about eight or nine years ago. If they had known earlier that Raymond had the book, and they knew of its significance, wouldn't they have just pinched it from his shop? Second, it might mean that they were just trying to confirm that some of the things they suspected were really true.

And if they hadn't watched me when I went to visit Raymond? Well, that could mean any of a number of things.

As I had been thinking, I had also been jotting down notes. I looked through my notes now. It seemed that a previous owner of the book, perhaps its sole owner, had entered the inscription, and that owner knew the significance of what he or she had written. That owner of the book was now presumed dead because the book changed hands through an estate sale. This was where more suppositions had to be entertained, even though this might seem to border on the ridiculous.

Suppose Samuel Barrington was indeed the Old Admiral. And suppose that the original owner of the book was someone for whom the Old Admiral meant something. What would that imply?

I stopped here. Admiral Barrington had had an illustrious career. He had served in the Royal Navy in many parts of the world.

Would there be events, situations, whatnot, that might be of interest today, but linked to one of his many naval campaigns?

Almost certainly.

Was I going to begin digging into his complete naval history?

No.

Once again, the urge just to forget the whole thing pressed itself upon me. The possibilities were enormous. Choosing any one on a flip-the-coin basis was just a mug's game. But then I couldn't escape the shadow that stretched out from McGrath's body and threatened to darken my life. So, what to do?

It seemed that there was only one way forward, as doubtful as it seemed. I would need to make yet another supposition.

Okay. Suppose that the previous owner of the book was someone who lived here in Canada — probably a safe assumption — and who had an interest in the North American theatre of the Seven Years War. That seemed to be the only way to bring Barrington into the picture in a meaningful way.

Question: was the watcher thinking along the same lines? Had the watcher been involved in some way with the previous owner of my book, someone who presumably was now dead? This provided a possible link but seemed to indicate no way forward apart from trying to trace the path followed by the book from that owner to me. Lansdell thought he remembered a surname: Graham? Gorley? Greeley? That was of no immediate use.

I needed a reality check. I had constructed this extended chain of assumptions and suppositions that led me, possibly, to the east coast of the continent in the eighteenth century. It was better than nothing, but not much. The real help I needed here, though, was an independent set of eyes. When I related all this to Fairley, would she just laugh in disbelief at a serious case of self-deception? Or would she find something of value in it, some variation I hadn't thought of, some solid thread, something to lead forward?

So, arrange a meeting with Fairley.

In preparation for that, I spent twenty minutes writing out my point-form notes so that they would make sense to her. Doing this allowed me to pick my way through the whole rigmarole once more.

It didn't seem any more convincing on paper than it had in my head. But Fairley would be my touchstone.

This seemed to be all I could do on my own at the moment, so I headed off to the bookshop to play my blue card, consult some directories, and place another call to Jocko. From there, at ten minutes to one, I went straight to the restaurant.

M&B Resto was home to that happy, noisy fug that always brings a smile. Hinge was in his element, and the dishes coming from the kitchen looked superb. Michelle was the picture of cheerfulness, carrying a tray filled with orders for Table Six, and she waved at me as she passed, displaying complete delight in her work. There was housekeeping to do, including reviewing the menu that would be in place for the next few weeks, doing a stock inventory, and going through the mail. All those tasks took about forty-five minutes, leaving me with a list of eighteen menu items, from which I had to choose ten, a long list of things to be purchased, dealing with a request to use the restaurant for a special event, twelve bills to pay, and the weekly update of the website. Paying the bills and reviewing the menu were completed quickly. The website update I would do later from home. Later in the day I would make calls to suppliers to replenish stock. In the midst of all that, my cellphone buzzed.

Fairley.

"What's up?" she asked, before I could say "Hello".

"We need to talk", I said cryptically, hoping the background restaurant sounds would excuse any apparent bluntness.

"Good news?"

"Not sure. But we need to meet", I replied.

"Okay. Same place. Three o'clock this afternoon okay?" That was a bit more than an hour away.

"Yes."

"Until then", she said, and broke the connection.

I spent a few minutes talking to Hinge and Michelle, making sure that everything was okay, no rub points that needed immediate filing. Nods and smiles told me that I could piss off and let them get on with it. Fifteen minutes talking to the restaurant clientele was never wasted and always enjoyable. Then I made my way back home, deciding that I could plan, but not complete, an update to the website before meeting Fairley. At five minutes to three, I was seated at a table on the patio of The Isherwood, when Fairley walked in. Today she was dressed down, wearing jeans and a plain pale-blue cotton blouse. She crossed the patio and sat opposite me, every movement efficient, economical. Candidate descriptors suddenly clogged my brain: gracile, elegant, polished, agile, fluid...

Fairley pulled a folder from her leather documents case and gave me a Mona Lisa look.

"Do you greet all your private investigators this way?"

What! I said to myself. And then realized that perhaps my scrutiny of fair Fairley's form had been none too subtle. But really! I hadn't been undressing her with my eyes! Although ... I guess maybe what I had been doing was sort of ... well...

"Forget it, Rolls. I'll take it as a compliment. But you might want to work at being not quite so transparent."

Before I could formulate what would have been almost certainly a feeble response, Fairley ploughed ahead.

"I know who the watcher is now. A known quantity. Got a record. But not a particularly nasty piece of work."

She looked at me directly.

"But you wanted to see me. What's up?"

In turn, I pulled out my folder and walked through the long trail I had developed. Fairley listened without interrupting.

"I'm concerned", I concluded, "that this is just a castle in the air, and I need an independent judgment. What do you think?"

Fairley spent a good ten minutes looking through my sheets. She asked me questions, penetrating questions, and I answered them as best I could.

"So, give me your opinion", I said, almost hoping that she would pour cold water over the whole thing, tell me that I needed a holiday.

"It's entirely plausible, as far as I can see", she said at length. "And I don't see anything else that comes close to explaining the few pieces of information we have. I think we just move forward from here."

I didn't really know what to make of that. I sat there, mute.

"Suppose all this is basically true", she said. "What would you do next?"

That question was met by silence, and the silence lengthened.

"Frankly, I have no idea."

"It's okay, Rolls. I'm not trying to embarrass you. I just want to know what you're thinking."

"Well, I'm not thinking anything. That's the trouble just now."

"I'm fairly sure that's not the case. I suspect that your doubts are masking something that you do have in mind."

Fairley smiled encouragingly and took a sip of wine.

"Let me guess at what you might be thinking. You might want to provoke the watcher into doing something, showing their hand, giving us a hint."

"Might I?" By that point I felt totally incompetent. Fairley smiled again.

"Yes." At that point she leaned forward and refilled my glass. "Okay. Here's the situation as I see it. They're watching you. They probably believe that you don't know you're being watched. They almost certainly don't suspect that they're being watched. So in this game we have the advantage. For the moment. Okay?"

I nodded.

"Good. Now if we do something just on a suck-it-and-see basis, something that makes them wonder what we're up to and forces their hand in some way, there's a good chance that they'll begin to suspect something. What will that cause them to do?"

I said nothing.

"Well, one thing it might cause them to do is to embark on another course of action, one that we can't foresee at present. In that case, they might gain the upper hand. So, if we want to force their hand, it has to be in order to learn something that will perhaps confirm some of your thinking, and maybe change the game in our favour. Maybe they would reveal, unsuspectingly, some assumption they've made. Something like that would have a good chance of leaving us ahead of them no matter what they choose to do next."

"And that would mean…?" I began. "That would mean learning something that would allow us to understand what's behind all this business and end this whole standoff?"

"Precisely."

"So, I'm not sure…"

"Okay. Here's my reading. We've gone over the what-we-don't-know and what-they-don't-know stuff already. But they're probably chastened and feeling a bit vulnerable having discovered that possession of your copy of the book on its own hasn't given them what they need. They know that the body in your shop lost them their advantage, and it alerted you to the fact that there's something important, perhaps valuable, out there. Must be. I can't see what else would be driving all this. Perhaps they've got to the same point as you on a Barrington connection, and if so they're almost certainly concerned that you've got that far as well. I think we need to shake them up. But we need to do it in a way that doesn't let them know that we know they're out there, and without letting them know that they're being watched."

"So what are you suggesting?"

"Leave the bookshop for two days and go somewhere."

"Where?"

"Well, it could be anywhere. But I would suggest Halifax."

"Halifax?"

"Yes. Think about it. That's where the remainder of the estate sale items were sent by Lansdell. Our watchers might know about that, but probably they don't, so you going down east will just make them wonder and not cause them immediate concern. But Halifax is also linked to Barrington and whatever that connection implies for them. It might also be associated with whatever they're pursuing."

"But won't I just be a sitting duck out there?"

"Hah! Not a chance! This will be a test, remember? An experiment. We'll be watching it closely. And we'll be watching you like a hawk. Remember what I said about my clients."

Fairley talked further about what we might do. A plan began forming. I started to feel better about it, about the possibility of this whole business being wrapped up, the puzzle solved, the watchers shaken off like so many flies. At just after five o'clock we stood, shook hands, and left. As I walked away, I reflected on the homework I had been given: to draft a travel plan and a series of visits in and around Halifax that would look entirely ordinary to a casual observer but might raise serious flags before the eyes of my watchers.

Chapter Fourteen

By the time I was back home and seated before my computer, the Halifax idea had ripened fully in my mind. I had been to Halifax twice a long time ago, and immediately I began wondering why I hadn't gone back. Now that I had an additional purpose to go, other than just being a tourist, I would end that long span of neglect.

I called up a Google map of Halifax. I remembered the Citadel, of course, and the Old Town Clock, or Prince Edward's clock, and especially the waterfront. But looking in more detail, I was intrigued by the developments, new since my most recent visit, all along the southern shore and Lower Water Street — Bishop's Landing, the new farmers' market building, and the great amount of reconstruction and new building around and beyond the railway station. A quick search showed me that McKelvie's restaurant was still there but that MacAskills' in Dartmouth was long gone.

It was only then that it hit me: Barrington Street.

Was that *my* Barrington?

Another bit of searching revealed that it was indeed the same family, probably named after Samuel's brother William.

And then I just had to check. Surely it couldn't be that simple! Surely it would be the first thing anyone checked once they picked up on the street name!

What was at 1979 Barrington Street?

It took little time for me to determine that although there had been an address 1979 Barrington Street in old town Halifax, it was one of the buildings demolished to construct the Cogswell Interchange, and it took very little extra digging to turn up many direct, blunt comments decrying this road junction as a massive wart on the city's face: 1960s demolish-and-develop mentality let loose to do its worst.

My interest in spending time in Halifax was now fully piqued. This could be an engaging lark. Now that we knew who the principal watcher was, we could see his response to a trip I made to Halifax. Would he show any interest in, even be aware of the books Lansdell had shipped there? If not, that would tell us something. Would he think that my presence in Halifax indicated that I had uncovered a critical piece of information? How he reacted might also be telling. It seemed evident that what I would do in Halifax needed to be planned with a view to testing as many independent hypotheses as we could.

But there was one query I had to make first.

Detective Sergeant Barnett tried the who-am-I-speaking-to routine once more, but as on the previous occasion, I didn't let him get away with it. After a lot of poking on my part and whining on his, I learned that the police investigation was mired in about the same spot as before. As I ended the call, I got in a dig by thanking him for the update on his progress. *What the hell! My tax money, right?*

Then it was back to the task at hand. What would I do in Halifax?

I had by now formulated a number of tests, the results of which could be of value.

First, it would be very useful to get some idea of whether my watchers had specific information on just what they were after. Second, it would be useful to learn whether something I did while I was there prompted a strong response. Third, just who might be sent to tail me in Halifax could be revealing.

But none of what I did down there should look staged. And it would be wise if a Halifax trip had another objective that would appear to them to have no link to the Parmenides–Barrington nexus.

Regarding this last-mentioned idea, I thought immediately of Malcolm Anderson, a classmate at university, someone I had got along well with, who had gone on to get a doctorate and was now in the English department at Dalhousie University. We exchange Christmas cards every year and offer pro forma invitations: *if you ever are in Toronto/Halifax, let me know.*

Okay Malcolm. I'll take you up on it.

But back once more to the question. What would I do in Halifax?

Well, certainly I had turned up a number of leads that might be pursued there, partly because of this *Stylus of Death* connection, but partly because my interest in things historical is a light sleeper, and had awakened now with a vengeance. There were quite a few places to troll for information, and I had identified about twenty books that looked like they could contain useful background material on the Seven Years War and on Halifax as a naval base during that conflict. But I intended also to do a fair bit of plain old Halifax rubbernecking. And I had now determined that I would spend at least a few days in Louisbourg, the place that was possibly the origin of all these leads I was trying to reconcile and pursue.

It took me only about fifteen minutes to set up an itinerary: three days in Halifax, two days in Louisbourg, and two days in Wolfville. Counting the half-day travel time each way between Halifax and Louisbourg, it came to eight days altogether. I had identified eight bookshops in Halifax–Dartmouth–Bedford that I wanted to visit, plus the superb city public library and the library at Dal. From the relatively large amount of Google searching I had done, I had produced a list of nine documents relating to Louisbourg that seemed important. I had already obtained five of those, and going through them was part of my preparation for the trip. The rest of them I could obtain either at Louisbourg or in Halifax. Of course, there was no hope of picking up any threads from Barrington's time, but I did have a suspicion that just being there, seeing the historical markers from those earlier days, would hone my senses, make me more aware of hints from the past and better able to identify and interpret anything I might stumble upon.

I was about to send the itinerary to Fairley, but then I paused. Were we secure? I sent Fairley, instead, a question. *Is there a possibility that our email exchanges are being monitored?* Her reply came back almost immediately.

I've put security in place. If anybody tries to snoop, I'll know right away.

So then I sent the itinerary. Within five minutes she returned an email saying that it looked fine, and to her query about Wolfville, I said it was just for me.

She followed up with another question: how was I going to alert the watchers to the fact that I was out of town?

My response: I wasn't. The bookshop would be open, they would know soon enough that I wasn't around, they would send someone to ask Rice where I was, he would know where I had gone, and I would provide him no reason to keep that information secret.

Good! She replied.

I presume, I added in response, *that her watchers would keep tabs on anybody sent to Halifax to track me down.*

Too right! She emailed back in antipodean emphasis.

I booked a room in the Cambridge Suites for the time I would be in Halifax, a little B&B in central Wolfville called The Vineyard Arms, located a nice looking inn not far from the fortress site in Louisbourg, and rented a car for the duration. I then spent a good three hours listing topics and questions that I wanted to make sure I covered while I was in Nova Scotia. There would be a lot of camera work, and I downloaded tourist information, maps, and general historical commentary.

By then, it was after eleven in the evening — too late for a heavy meal. But I had the wherewithal for a light salad in the fridge, and, accompanied by a glass of pinot gris, it set me up for the night. I spent about an hour reading, and then I crashed.

I awoke at seven the next morning, clear of eye and mind, and decided right away that between now and my departure for Halifax four days hence I would spend fully half of every day preparing for that trip. The bookshop was gliding briskly on light winds and an even keel, and needed little or no attention from me. So the other half of my time would be spent at M&B Resto.

Those four days flew by. I made sure that everything was well-stocked at the restaurant, that both Hinge and Michelle had my cell number, and I made many pointless comings and goings from the bookshop — pointless from a book business perspective, but having a real point for my watchers, in that my sudden failure to come and go starting a few days hence would be unmistakeable.

And then the moment came. I caught an early morning express to Pearson Airport. At seven thirty I made a call to Fairley, as agreed, and at twenty minutes past eight the wheels left the runway. I was fairly steeped by then in the history of the Seven Years War, was looking forward to a week of historical sleuthing, and was vaguely curious as to how my watchers would discover and deal with my absence from the bookshop.

Fuck 'em, I thought. This could be, no, would be, my opportunity to begin drawing a line beneath the whole affair. Fairley had my complete itinerary, she had my cell number, and just to be certain, I had agreed to check in with her every second day.

At Stanfield Airport I picked up my rental car, a Ford Focus, the smallest car they had available although a little Fiat would have been nicer. I then made the longish drive into Halifax, arriving eventually at the corner of Brunswick and Sackville Streets after recovering from only one wrong turn just after leaving the Macdonald Bridge. Car parked and bags stowed in my room by one o'clock, I set out on foot to reacquaint myself with the "Warden of the North". Three bookshops and about six kilometres later, I was back at my hotel, flopped out for a late afternoon snooze. It had been a good start. At the second bookshop I visited, the owner recognized the name Raymond Lansdell, and in fact recalled a shipment of about forty books that had been sent to him.

"Good collection", he told me. "Sold well."

Under further questioning, he remembered nothing significant about them, apart from their excellent condition and the fact that they had all been about the founding of Halifax and the Seven Years War.

"Barrington?" he asked in puzzled surprise, in response to my own question. "You mean Barrington Street? Here?"

I explained a little about the Admiral, but either because he had given the books in Raymond's shipment only the most cursory examination, or because he had just shelved and forgotten them all, he knew basically nothing about Barrington.

At seven o'clock, I found a place close to the hotel, had a decent dinner, then returned to my room and called Malcolm to arrange to meet him for lunch the next day. I then settled down to read and make notes. Just after midnight, I had packed up for the night and was crawling into bed, when I became aware suddenly of a large loose end flapping in my mind. Up to now I had been considering things only from the level of an Admiral Barrington. But it took a lot of manual effort, a lot of sailors, to run even a single Royal Navy ship, and it had occurred to me that the story of those men in general could also be significant. I climbed out of bed, powered up my laptop, checked a couple of saved files, did a quick search, and then added the Maritime Museum to the list of spots to visit in the morning.

In this saga, I had long since gone from the initial great, sweeping brush strokes and was now in those areas of fine historical detail that required the equivalent of pointed round brushes. In times past, I was now certain, the sequences that determined how important a given event would be were at least as uncertain as they are today, and probably much more so. It was at this nuts-and-bolts level, therefore, that I would find the pointers on how and where I should be looking. As I climbed back into bed, I had that reassuring feeling at the back of my mind that there was something significant just around the corner.

***

At six forty-five the next morning, I slammed into well-rested but sudden and full wakefulness, feeling that the night couldn't have lasted more than twenty minutes. But there was a full day ahead and no time to waste, so after a quick shower, shave, and light breakfast, I was striding downhill along Sackville Street. It was a gorgeous, cool morning. A few ragged shreds of mist lay low over the outer harbour, and the sun brought out the raw, rugged beauty of the shores and headlands that stretched away before me. Georges Island and, further toward the sea, McNabs Island floated serenely. At the harbourside, I found a spot to sip a cup of coffee while looking out over the water and being serenaded by the shrieking and squawking of a thousand gulls. At quarter past nine, I drained my cup, walked to the Maritime Museum, and was first through the doors when they were unlocked at nine thirty. I located the woman whose name, Angela Armstrong, Google and I had found the previous night, and when the article of interest was laid out before her, her answers confirmed what I had expected.

"And that's it?" she asked in some surprise, looking at her watch to check that we had been talking only fifteen minutes.

"Yes. That's it. And thank you."

"You're most welcome. But I must say that you're the first person to ask about this particular bit of my research. And also the first person, as far as I'm aware, to ask about desertions from the Royal Navy in Halifax. Could I ask...?"

"Most certainly. I'm interested in artefacts from the Seven Years War that might have left Royal Navy ships here. I wasn't aware until quite recently how many deserters the Navy had to deal with."

I asked her what sort of information she had access to in that regard.

"Quite a bit. The Royal Navy was always interested in locating, arresting, and dealing with deserters, so their records were good. But I'm guessing you're interested in something specific."

"Yes."

I told her.

"A specific ship?" she asked.

I said "yes", gave her the name, and asked whether she would be willing to do some digging. She was clearly quite intrigued, and said that she would begin looking right away.

"It shouldn't take me too long. How can I get in touch with you?"

"I'll be in various places doing various things. Could I call you two days from now, about midmorning?"

"Sounds perfect", she replied. There was then an odd smile. "I hope you'll let me in on what's behind this."

"Yes. I will. Once I have the full picture clear myself. And I'm very grateful for your help."

She evidently was dying to know more, but seemed okay with waiting a little while longer.

We chatted for another ten minutes; she asked me how long I would be in Halifax, and I gave her a vague answer, promising to contact her in two days and to put her fully in the picture as soon as I could; then we wrapped up our meeting. Her handshake was firm, and she made sure I had a couple of her business cards. Then I left.

A brisk walk brought me to the superb Halifax Central Library on Spring Garden Road, where I checked several things, made a few notes, and asked how easy it was to do external searching. Then it was on to the library at Dal where I made copies of three items before taking a stroll around the campus prior to meeting Malcolm.

Malcolm had asked me to meet him at the entrance to the Marion McCain Building. It was easy enough to find, and as I walked toward it along University Avenue, I was paying no particular attention to my surroundings. But then, there he was, striding toward me, a big familiar grin lighting up his face, and I could hardly believe my eyes. I was greeted by the same youthful, mobile expression. The same blond forelock hung down almost to his eyes. He moved in that same loose-jointed gait that signalled complete relaxation but also steel-spring readiness.

"Henry, you old bugger! You haven't changed a bit!"

"Nor have you, Malcolm. If anything, you look even younger. This place must suit you."

"That it does. I wouldn't be anywhere else."

We stood looking at one another for a moment, then gave a laugh of recognition.

"Hungry?" he asked, but then charged ahead without waiting for an answer. "This way. There's a good spot not far from here."

As we walked, I asked Malcolm to bring me up to date; he asked me what brought me to Halifax; gradually we each filled in our stories. When Malcolm decided to try academia, Halifax had not been his first choice. He recounted his years in graduate school, a period during which we had drifted apart, mainly because I was no longer at the university.

"I really enjoyed my time in graduate school. That was what prompted me to take a run at academia. I had my sights on Victoria, for reasons that are lost to me now. But then the offer came in from Dal. When I came down here for the interview, it took only about three days for me to be snared by the place."

"What? Dal, or Halifax?"

"Both", he replied. "The winters here can be brutal, but the people are fantastic. And Halifax is full of history and interest. For a smallish city, there really is a lot to do here."

"So, no looking back?"

"Hah! None whatever! I hope to be on tenure track next year. This way, Henry."

"The Loaded Ladle?"

"That's it."

We got our food, sat, ate, and talked for almost an hour.

"When do you need to be back?" I asked.

Malcolm waved a hand dismissively. "I have a lecture at three, so plenty of time. Care to walk back to my office?"

"Sure. Let's go."

On the way, Malcolm described his main area of interest in some detail, the study of interactions among English, French, Gaelic, and First Nations cultures, both historic and contemporary, in Nova Scotia.

"There is one hell of a lot of raw material to work on here, and a few of my students have got into it in a big way. We now have some common programmes involving Acadia University and Cape Breton University. It looks like it might be just about to take off."

"Exciting times", I said, finding his enthusiasm infectious.

"Beyond anything I could have imagined", Malcolm replied.

We made our way to his office, which I found surprisingly tidy, but two large whiteboards on one wall were filled by notes, diagrams, names, dates, and a few unrecognizable scribbles. Names of authors that I recognized right away, among the dozen or so that peppered the scribbles, were Alistair MacLeod, Antonine Maillet, Ernest Buckler, and Thomas Raddall.

"But tell me a bit about your bookshop! And your restaurant! That's some combination!"

I began relating the story of the bookshop. Once I started, I couldn't stop. The telling of its acquisition and renovation soon gave way to the bookshop equivalent of *The Canterbury Tales*. There were the Keystone Cops exercises that took place whenever another bookshop owner visited, putting forward his plausible excuse for "dropping in". And then there was the memorable and deadly serious race for a prize estate.

"Have you ever seen any old Dave Allen reruns?"

Malcolm nodded, chuckling at something.

"Do you remember the skit where two families were solemnly taking their loved ones to the cemetery, but neither group wanted the other to get there first?"

"Ha! Yes!" And we both laughed at the recollection.

"It turned into a deadly serious race. They both broke into a run…"

"Well", I said, once we had caught our breath. "There was this estate sale. A once-in-ten-year opportunity for a used bookshop. And the woman selling the books, her husband's library, hated books, hated libraries, and let everyone know that it was first come, first take. I rented a van. There were almost three thousand books involved. She had said ten o'clock. And 'don't piss me off by showing up early'. I set off, hoping to get to the place by five to ten, no earlier. And there he was, the bugger. Jimmy Thornton, my arch competitor. And he really is competitive."

"We must have chosen almost the same route. We were racing neck and neck along Hoskin Avenue. Dangerous as hell. Students scattering everywhere out of our way. We could have killed somebody. But then he pulled ahead of me when I got stuck behind a street sweeper. I don't think I've ever said "Fuck!" so many times in a five-minute period. Anyway, I caught up to him again, but he was a good hundred metres ahead. It looked like I was toast."

"So what happened?" Malcolm said, genuinely tickled by something he never would have associated with a used bookshop.

"I came around a corner, grumpy and angry, and there he was."

"And? There he was what?"

"Stopped for speeding! A cop taking his time writing out a ticket."

By that time I was laughing as though I was back there, giving Jimmy a friendly wave as I sailed past.

As part of this explanation, the question of my name came up.

"Rolls?" Malcolm said, clearly amused at my explanation. "Okay. Rolls it is."

Malcolm began laughing once more at my implausible account of becoming a bookshop and restaurant owner.

"You mean that it actually happened just that way? What a story, Henry, er, Rolls! You must document it!"

I waved him off that notion, only to have him begin grilling me on my stock, my customers, what sold well, and my own interests, and I soon found that we were deep into some interesting comparative discussions of genres, authors, and the whole dynamic of established literature, new writers and trends, and the tastes of readers. His questions, and my answers, made me realize that I actually know much more about the current world of writing and reading than I was aware of.

But another hour and more had now sprinted past. Malcolm glanced at his watch.

"I'm going to have to throw you out now. I need a bit of time to prepare for my lecture. There'll be some discussion with students after the lecture. There always is. But do you have time to get together for a pint and some dinner later? Say, five thirty? Where are you staying?"

"The Cambridge Suites, Sackville and Brunswick."

"Perfect. That's quite close to where I live. Fiona is at a conference in Philadelphia for the next two days, otherwise it would be a threesome." Fiona was Malcolm's live-in girlfriend — soon, by all evidence, to be his wife. "I'll meet you at your hotel. Is five thirty okay?"

"Fine. Until then. This has been excellent. I'm really looking forward to this evening."

Our hands closed in a firm shake, which led naturally to a heartfelt bear hug.

Our reunion had been much more than I expected, and the walk back to the hotel was one of happy reflection.

I had now been away a day and a half. Time to check on my watchers.

The first call went through and Rice picked up right away.

"How are things, Rice?"

"Good. Usual rushes of customers. Sales are good, no complaints at all."

"Excellent. Has anyone asked about me, wanting to know where I am?"

"Yes. One guy, yesterday afternoon. About forty, I guess, medium height, short brown hair, wanted to talk to you about an estate sale, wouldn't leave his name. I said I could deal with estate sales, but the prick wouldn't talk to me. Said he would catch up with you when you were back."

"Did he ask when I would be back?"

"Yeah, but I told him I didn't know. Only knew that you were in Halifax, didn't know why or doing what. Said I thought you were probably taking some vacation."

"Good. Thanks Rice."

We talked briefly about a couple of interesting questions other customers had asked, then ended the call.

The second call brought Fairley onto the line at the second ring. "Someone was asking for me at the bookshop. Have you seen any action?"

"Yes", Fairley said. "We saw our man go into the bookshop yesterday at about two o'clock. Had him followed from the time he came out again. He caught an Air Canada flight to Halifax yesterday evening at six fifty-five. I had a guy waiting at Stanfield Airport, and he followed our man into town. He booked into a cheap place off Robie. We've got him covered."

"Why didn't you alert me to this?" I asked, making no effort to hide my annoyance.

"Because you need to look natural. Don't worry about him. We're all over him. He spent the day today trying to find out where you're staying."

"Oh yeah? How's he doing that?"

"The brute force way. He seems to be making the rounds of hotels. Probably asking if you've checked in yet."

"So he'll find me eventually."

"Maybe. But try not to worry. My guy in Halifax has your cell number. He'll contact you if something turns up that you need to know."

I felt a bit better about that. Plus there was the fact that the day after tomorrow I would be heading toward Louisbourg.

Chapter Fifteen

The evening with Malcolm would have been a balm for any soul. I had not counted on picking up so easily the reins from a university friendship and finding that we basically started where we had left off more than a decade earlier. Four hours flew by, then we repaired to Malcolm's condo on Dresden Row, where I was stunned by the view.

"It's a little on the pricey side", Malcolm explained, "but nothing that Fiona and I can't handle, and it was essentially love at first sight."

We sank a couple of glasses each of a nice Balvenie, and chatted desultorily about things past, present, and future. Malcolm seemed well anchored and on a clear trajectory forward, which made me wonder about my own existence, at best vaguely oriented and maintained on course by a compass of doubtful functionality. At just before midnight, I made the few minutes' walk from Malcolm's oasis to my hotel. I had already prepared a decent plan for the following day, but I was in no state to review it at that point, so I just crashed.

When I awoke the next morning, my existential doubts from the previous evening had been stowed, and after a quick breakfast I set about my day as planned: several additional bookshops, and more than half the day in the Nova Scotia Archives. Nothing much came from the bookshop visits, except the contacts that bookshop owners are always interested in making. The time at the archives was a systematic slog, but one that did turn up a few things of interest. As I was leaving the archives at just past four thirty, I placed a call to Fairley.

"No", she said. "Nothing new to report, except that our watcher hasn't located you yet. And on that front I have a suggestion."

"Okay", I said. "Shoot!"

"It looks like he's been concentrating on B&Bs and the smaller cheaper hotels. But it's only a matter of time now, I suspect. Once he starts on the larger hotels, probably this afternoon, it won't take him long."

I wasn't at all sure about the subtext here.

"But don't we want him to find out where I'm staying?"

"That's a good question. He doesn't know what you've been up to, and we certainly don't want it to look like you're just sitting waiting for him to find you."

"So, just what are you saying?"

"Well, I assume that you're making some progress, and that's part of the purpose of your visit. If he's able to lock onto you, then your freedom of action will drop to zero. He will be very careful not to lose the trail. If he picks up the trail of where you were some time back but still doesn't know where you are at the moment, the field will remain open for you. The game will still be on."

"But then what exactly are we trying to do?"

"He thinks that you're unaware of being watched. We're watching him, but he doesn't know that. We want him to know roughly, but not exactly, where you are. And we want him to have to guess at what you're doing."

"Has he tried to figure out where I've been in Halifax and what I've been doing, even if he doesn't know where I'm staying?"

"I think so. He's visited several bookshops, including three that you've been to. So he might know that you've been to those three. He's also spent quite a bit of time on Barrington Street, and two stretches of several hours each in his hotel. Likely talking to his boss and spending time online. Although just what he might be looking for I can't say."

"But part of the purpose of this trip was to try get him to tip his hand. It doesn't look like that's happened."

"No. And that makes me wonder whether the other side has now recognized somehow that they had completely the wrong end of the stick, that they in fact know a lot less than you do."

"Does that put me at any disadvantage then?" I asked.

"I don't think so", Fairley said, but her tone of voice didn't indicate enormous confidence.

There was a pause here.

"You're due to leave for Louisbourg tomorrow morning", Fairley said.

"Yes. Early. At six thirty. Why?"

"I suggest that you leave the hotel tonight. But don't check out. Head toward Louisbourg."

"Hang on! I can't make it there tonight!"

"No", Fairley said. "I know that. But how about driving to the airport and checking in at a hotel there?"

I was following the logic now.

"I see. Let him think he's found me in Halifax. The desk at the Cambridge Suites will just tell him that I haven't checked out. So he'll stooge around here for a day or two until he concludes that something's gone wrong. But won't that just lead him to suspect that we're onto him, trying to shake him?"

"Possibly. But he won't have any real evidence for that."

We walked through the whole thing once again, all the details. There seemed to be no dangling ends. And so it was that I returned to the hotel, packed, extended my reservation for another three days, called the Quality Inn at the airport to make a reservation for that night, got in my car, and headed back to Stanfield Airport. By eight o'clock that evening, I had checked in at the Quality Inn, had eaten a nice Caesar salad, and was settled in my room reviewing what I wanted to do and see in Louisbourg over the next two days. Those two days would be the last of my planned time following likely Barrington threads in Nova Scotia. There would be another two days of pure R&R in Wolfville. Time was passing quickly, and I was aware of a sense of mixed anticipation and letdown. The anticipation was Louisbourg itself, the reconstructed portion of the fortress, what had once been the largest military establishment in North America. I was aware that Parks Canada had done a massive amount of research on practically everything associated with Louisbourg, and I was interested in seeing what was available. Thinking back to my discussion with Malcolm, and being informed by my recent intense reading, it was clear to me that the events at Louisbourg between 1745 and 1760 were a major nexus in relations among the English, the French, the Acadians, and the First Nations. I could hardly wait.

But I knew also that this was just the stirrings of my own internal Clio, that the events during these years had few connections, and those connections being possibly only tenuous ones to me, to my bookshop, to the body in the Ps, and to the whole Parmenides mystery, whatever it was. I was really no closer to getting to the bottom of all that, and the realization gnawed at me.

There was one other thing to do in the morning: get back to Ms. Armstrong at the Maritime Museum and have her update me on the research she had more than willingly volunteered to undertake.

At ten o'clock, I turned in, expecting the morrow to bring a day of mild intellectual excitement.

***

Morning broke clear and sunny. I was out of the airport hotel very early and fully enjoyed the drive to Louisbourg, feeling a slight and rather inexplicable frisson as I crossed over onto Cape Breton Island. My hotel for the next two nights was just a few kilometres from the Louisbourg fortress, and to unwind from the three-hour drive from the airport, I took a quick stroll along the seashore. A light swell was washing up on the rocks, a refreshing breeze came in from the sea, and the sky was delicately draped in skeins of cirrus. The day appeared to hold promise and was free of any imminent threat, since I had killed no albatross, either literal or metaphorical.

Back at the hotel, I sent an email to Ms. Armstrong, apologizing for not contacting her directly by telephone, promising to do so the moment I had the chance, and asking her to send anything she had found to my email address. Having done that, a late breakfast of scrambled eggs and smoked fish established place and mood for me, and at ten thirty I was on my way to my first visit at the fortress.

The Fortress.

Maybe it was the day, the weather, the sky.

Maybe it was being somehow sensitized to history because of the research and reading I had done, although it takes only the slightest prod to have my historical sense operating at full charge.

Maybe it was some unsuspected, some unanticipated expectation that had been raised within me by this whole Parmenides mystery.

Whatever it was, being confronted by the physical reality of the Louisbourg Fortress overwhelmed any preparation I had made for it, my hoped-for ability to take in the fortress without breaking mental stride was blown to matchwood.

Quite simply, I found that I was in awe. The presence of the place had me in its grip from the first instant. How many kilometres I walked that day I have no real idea, but it must have been at least fifteen. I saw everything I could: the gates, of course, la Porte Frédéric and la Porte Dauphin; the full length of the quay; and as much of the walls and reconstructed fortification as possible. I saw the governor's apartments, the King's bastion, the military chapel, the engineer's residence, the *commissaire-ordonnateur*'s residence, the King's garden. I saw the lime kiln, the ice house, the iron collar, the Louisbourg Cross. I visited the powder magazine, the barracks, the bakery, the forge, and the stables.

But it was the sounds and the smells and the whole atmosphere of the place that really grabbed me. It was a clear day, so there was no mist, but the smell of the sea was everywhere. Every so often, there was a *Boom!* and a cloud of smoke drifted past, and then the smell of gunpowder was everywhere. There were aromas of freshly baked bread and roasting meat. It's common, or so it seems to me, to find reconstructed pioneer settings that are just sad, frozen in time, as though the history is dead, displayed like Lenin's corpse. It was different here. The history was alive! The individual buildings were working displays. And the sheer size of the site, the imposing nature of many of the buildings, well, for me it scooped up all those elements of the eighteenth century that I assembled in my head and breathed real life into them.

It was like being in a waking dream.

At about two thirty I had an excellent lunch at l'Épée Royale Café, and later, at the information centre, I collected a ton of information and an armful of books.

My interest in the destruction of the fortifications in 1760 caught the attention of one guide, and she spent a good half-hour with me, evidently delighted at being able to drop breathless touristic mode for a while and slide into fully appreciative historic mode. She was well informed, and she directed me to five books and documents that dealt specifically with how the English had gone about systematically reducing the fortress to ruins.

At five o'clock, I was back in my room at my hotel, sorting through the pile of material I had collected during the day, and beginning the large task of getting my head around what I had seen and learned. A first quick cut through the mound of pamphlets and documents I had assembled helped me sketch out a programme of reading I was excited to undertake, whether or not it all related to my Parmenides mystery. This was material that I had to master. I lay back on the bed, letting my mind flit across the contour map of still-glowing excitement that had been carved into me by my day at Louisbourg. I was aware of making the decision, without doing so consciously, that I would return the next day to glean whatever else I could and to take many, many more pictures.

I must have dozed off, because when I checked my watch it said almost seven thirty. The inn had a good dining room, and I was about to head down there for dinner, but then decided that dinner at one of the restaurants in the Fortress itself would have more class. I checked a few brochures I had collected during the day, picked a restaurant, and called to make a reservation.

So then I drove back to the eighteenth century, found Grandchamps Restaurant, unpacked my French, which won smiles from the staff, and had an excellent meal. Time flew, I chatted happily with my server, lingered over what was probably one glass of wine too many given that I had to drive back to the inn, and was just about the last person to leave.

Back at the inn, I coasted reluctantly once more into the twenty-first century just after eleven o'clock. Two more hours of reviewing the day's documentary takings, and stopping frequently as pictures from the Fortress rose in my mind, swept by all too quickly. At well past one o'clock I ran a hand over tired eyes, told myself that staying up all night was just not a good idea, and, with a reluctance that surprised me, filed away the documents in my luggage. Tomorrow, I would return.

As I was climbing into bed, I suddenly remembered my inquiry to Ms. Armstrong and opened my email account. As good as her word, she had sent a short email and nine attachments. It was pure gold dust.

Some of her material was general historical background, but at a level that put in sharper perspective the activities of the Royal Navy over a two-year period in Halifax and Louisbourg. So far, my time in Nova Scotia had had the hopeful objective of forcing my watchers' hands, causing them to reveal something, tell us something new. There was no guarantee here, since it was all based on a long chain of suppositions, but it was the best shot we had at trying to figure out what was going on. Unexpectedly, it was also giving me a lot of background — historical, geographical — and it was a pleasant break. There were visceral links to Admiral Barrington here, but it was clear that they were background only, and possibly not even relevant background.

But one of the items of information in Armstrong's package related to something that had never occurred to me — whether it was important remained to be seen. Armstrong's information included three accounts describing desertions from Barrington's ship, the HMS *Achilles,* in Halifax during the period 1758 to 1761. Fifteen men had deserted the *Achilles* during that time. (Another of the notes she sent reported that there were between 20 000 and 30 000 desertions from all Royal Navy ships during about that period in the entire North American theatre.) Of the fifteen men who had slunk off the *Achilles*, five had been found, captured, tried, and convicted of treason, and three of those five had been hanged from the yardarm. The kicker here was that I had all the names of the deserters, including those who had got away. My muse was leaping up and down in excitement. But against the background of all the things centred on *Stylus of Death*, it seemed just an interesting byway.

I sent Ms. Armstrong a quick email offering profuse thanks and a commitment to be in touch again as soon as possible.

Two of the attachments she had sent looked interesting, even if they were off the mark. One recounted the story of the naval yards at Halifax from the city's founding in 1749 to the end of the Seven Years War and the final abandonment of Louisbourg by the English in 1768. The second focussed on the Battle of the Restigouche, the last naval engagement of the Seven Years War. I read through it quickly, since it was all of interest, and noted the references to the *Achilles* and to Barrington.

Halfway down the second-last page, I stopped. Clio was overwhelmed and dropped away in a dead faint. I was just a happy historical sleuth, although it seemed that I needed to look more closely at the Battle of the Restigouche.

Chapter Sixteen

The next morning, I awoke facing the possibility that my plans for the last few days of my Nova Scotian interlude might need to be altered. It appeared that probably I had been chasing a chimera, something that had all the trappings of a genuine solution to my Parmenidean puzzle, but which now appeared to be taking me down the wrong path.

Okay, that might be a bit melodramatic. I hadn't found proof that what I was looking for, what I had thought *Samuel Barrington 1979* was a clue to, was wrong. The document provided by Ms. Armstrong at the Maritime Museum indicated that there was another, and much more likely, possibility. I was convinced that the answer still was connected somehow to the Seven Years War. It was just that a link to Louisbourg now appeared much less likely. I ran my hand through my hair, feeling at once both frustrated and intrigued, while I considered how to spend my remaining several days in Nova Scotia. What I needed was a firm footing. What I was getting was a series of conditional pointers: maybe it's this; maybe it's that; maybe it's something else.

Okay, Rolls. What's the status now? What are the next moves?
Status.

I had finished at Louisbourg, and the information I had got there was certainly interesting and might yet prove useful. But nothing indicated that I should spend any more time there. The basic hard reality was that all my searching had led to nothing that allowed me to confirm that *Samuel Barrington 1979* pointed to anything in Louisbourg 1760. And I could see nowhere else to look that might provide any further new information pointing toward such a connection.

Instead, the best piece of evidence now seemed to indicate that 1760 was indeed a date of interest, but that it was tied to a different geographic location. That was what was emerging from the Maritime Museum documents. And when I stood back from it all, it was clear enough that the decisive event at Louisbourg occurred not in 1760, but in 1758. It was in 1758 that the Louisbourg fortress fell and passed from French to English hands. By comparison, the destruction of the fortifications in 1760 was a mop-up operation at best.

So what was the something else?

There were two somethings else that took place in 1760, but for me these now seemed only of general historical interest. One was the event that finally marked a fundamental change to the future of the northeastern part of North America: the capitulation of Montreal, when Governor General Vaudreuil-Cavagnial and General Lévis surrendered all of New France to the English armies led by Murray, Havilland, and Amherst. Could this have anything to do with the Barrington nexus? Hard to say for certain, but it was looking doubtful.

The other something else, at least the something else that was making more sense to me, was the Battle of the Restigouche. It had been the last naval engagement of the Seven Years War. But the Battle of the Restigouche resulted in no dramatic tipping of the scales, nothing that one could term *decisive* on a larger canvas. The really decisive change had been authored by Wolfe and Amherst at Quebec City.

The problem here was that Admiral Barrington was present at the Battle of the Restigouche, but not at the surrender of Montreal. Hence, if the name *Samuel Barrington* really was central to this puzzle, it seemed that the focus should be on la baie des Chaleurs.

And it was just this that the article from the Maritime Museum seemed to be nudging me toward. The article was a copy of something that Professor Samuel Barrington at University of King's College had submitted to *History Today*, something that was not yet published or perhaps not even accepted and entitled "Twilight Thoughts from the Seven Years War". The article provided interesting commentary on the reflections and activities of French forces on realizing that they had lost New France, and the same for English forces on their acquisition of what would turn out to be half a continent. Eight references were listed, one of them being the book *Frigates and Foremasts* by Julian Gwyn, and a second to another book *La vergue et les fers* by Alain Cabantous. But it was one of the other references that caught my eye, a paper entitled "One Year in Logged Activity of HMS *Achilles*". That paper was by Professor Barrington, dated 1979, and described as an "unpublished note". Recalling that I had come down this long path on the back of string of poorly supported presumptions, I had to make great efforts to resist jumping to conclusions. But the incentive certainly was there. *Samuel Barrington 1979*. It seemed to meet all my criteria. It might well be what lay behind the inscription in *Stylus of Death*. In fact, it just might be my grail.

Or not. And hence the need for academic caution.

But I had to get a copy of that reference.

One other point, and out of curiosity more than anything — it was almost certain that this paper would link directly to Admiral Barrington. Had Prof. Barrington become interested in this at least in part because he had the same name as the admiral?

When I had first glanced through the *History Today* article the previous evening, the reference to this elusive "One Year in Logged Activity" paper hit me like a shock wave. I read the article again, closely, but it had nothing particularly interesting to say to me, nothing that would shed more light on my puzzle. There was a good deal of information in the Gwyn and Cabantous books on desertions from the Royal Navy and the Marine nationale française, respectively. None of that came through in Barrington's article, however. Was there something more in the paper he had referenced concerning the HMS *Achilles*?

I had then found Barrington's web page at University of King's College, but the paper didn't appear among his works. Fair enough, I suppose, since the relevant website heading was *Published Works*. I had located an email address for Barrington and sent him a request, but an automatic reply said that he was out of the country and not responding to email. A call to the university brought me eventually to an admin assistant who said that Barrington was combining research and vacation, that he would be away for another three weeks, and that, no, she could not give me his cellphone number. She was unfamiliar with the unpublished paper and said that even if she could find it she wouldn't be able to send me a copy without consulting

Barrington. I left my name and contact information with her, said that I was very interested in speaking to Prof. Barrington. She said she would see what she could do, but no promises whatever, although she thanked me for my interest and for the call.

All this just told me that something to do with the Seven Years War remained at the centre of my puzzle. It also encouraged the assumption that whatever this something was, it might well be linked to the behaviour of individual sailors from one of those two opposing naval forces, but more likely from the Royal Navy. The two countries had been locked in combat at several locations in New France, the taking of Louisbourg was a *big deal*, and some physical reminder of that victory might well provide important bragging rights for some individual combatants. It was Barrington's article and especially his unpublished paper, which, through the number 1979 provided a tantalizing possible link to the inscription in my copy of *Stylus of Death*. It was all this that was turning my gaze toward la baie des Chaleurs.

It was now almost eight o'clock, and I was still in my room at the inn near Louisbourg. Notepad before me and pen in hand, I walked through the material once more, carefully, noting the significant points, trying to see whether my string of suppositions showed any sign of giving way to something that could be called, with a straight face, a logic train.

No such sign leapt out at me.

No alternative, it seemed, but to go back to Google.

Turning to my laptop, I undertook a series of searches involving la baie des Chaleurs, the Battle of the Restigouche, Admiral Barrington, and the HMS *Achilles*. Details of the battle began appearing immediately. References to the supply ships sent to New France from Bordeaux under Giraudais also began appearing. Then there were articles on the *Machault*, the lead ship in this expedition. Papers by a number of academics began clamouring for my attention, modern-day hairsplitting debates on fine points of history marched upward across my screen, and there was an odd article concerning a death of someone called Roberts in 2013, suspected to be a homicide but unproven and involving receding layers of speculation. Almost all these I discarded, focussing on the ship, the *Machault*, now the central exhibit at a national historic site.

And the *Machault* was the French warship that had been the primary victim in the Battle of the Restigouche.

It would be, most likely, just a wild goose chase, but...

Next moves.

I packed up my laptop, closed my suitcase, and prepared to check out of the inn. But not right away.

A few phone calls later, I had cancelled my reservations in Wolfville, located a place to stay in Campbellton, and managed to find passage on a small plane from Halifax to the local airport at Charlo in New Brunswick, not far from Campbellton.

Then I started heading back to Stanfield Airport in Halifax.

Three hours later, I pulled into the rental car lot, handed over the car, subjected my charge card to something of a battering, and headed toward the terminal. As I walked, I called up the number for the local airline that I would be using.

"Air Chaleurs! Ici Deschamps!"

I introduced myself.

"Ah! Monsieur Royce! Where are you now?"

"I'm just walking from the rental car lot to the terminal. Where should I be heading to meet you?"

Deschamps gave me cheerful and enthusiastic directions, and soon I entered an area identified as General Aviation. A smiling, wiry gentleman, looking for all the world like Ace McCool, was striding confidently toward me. He waved, ran a hand through his unruly black hair, and directed the most infectious smile my way. I couldn't help but smile back.

"Vous êtes Monsieur Deschamps?"[1]

The wattage in his smile tripled.

"Mais c'est fou raide! Vous parlez le français!"[2]

I confirmed that that was the case, including conditions requesting that the rate of speaking and use of argot be limited, but he brushed all that aside and extended his hand. *"Yvon Deschamps. Par ici, s'il vous plait"*[3,4], he said, pointing toward a red single-engine plane sitting a couple of hundred metres away. There were

---

1 "Are you Monsieur Deschamps?"

2 "But this is brilliant! You speak French!"

3 "Yvon Deschamps. This way please."

4 Note that this is not *the* Yvon Deschamps. This Deschamps is too young.

yellow flames painted down the side of the fuselage. Maybe he really was Ace McCool.

As we walked toward the plane, my French received the most vigorous exercise it had had in months, but having to switch from elements of history and an intractable puzzle on the one hand and applying serious effort at here-and-now communicating on the other was a surprisingly welcome change. A lot of that had to do with Yvon, I came to realize, since he evidently had much more to say than he had time to say it. The speech that tumbled out of him, combined with his irrepressible good humour, left me with the entertaining but difficult task of extracting the correct meaning from a flood of words.

I found that I was consistently about half a sentence behind, so it took me a moment, even given a sudden break in this verbal flow and an expectant look, to realize that he had asked me what my given name was.

"On m'appelle Rolls en anglais."[5]

"Rolls! Comme la voiture?"[6]

"Oui."[7]

He decided that *Roule* fitted more easily into a flow of French, so that would be my name for the duration.

We reached the plane, and by then I was beginning to master Yvon's monologue in French, understanding it more easily, and in fact quite enjoying it. Yvon placed my small suitcase in the baggage hold, which was not much larger than a generous glovebox, we climbed into the plane, he made sure I was belted in and that I had pulled on my headset, then he started the engine. There was a short, clipped, and efficient exchange between Yvon and ground control, and we moved out onto one of the taxiways.

Things looked quiet. There was another short exchange with the traffic controller, and we were given the okay to take off. The little engine roared, we accelerated down the runway, and when there were still several miles of tarmac ahead of us, Yvon hauled us skyward. We climbed as steeply as the plane allowed, moved into a

---

5 "They call me 'Rolls' in English."
6 "Rolls! Like the car?"
7 "Yes."

long turn, eventually levelled off at about 5000 feet, and headed off to the northwest. I looked across at Yvon and saw one ecstatic fly boy.

My headset crackled.

"*Pourquoi est-ce que tu vas à Charlo, hein? Une femme?*"[8] And he broke into a laugh.

I explained to him that he wasn't too far wrong. That she was indeed waiting for me.

Yvon cast me an openly speculative look, and I smiled and chuckled at him. I really had his attention now.

"*Ce n'est pas une femme, mais le plus vite que nous sommes ensemble...*"[9], and I let the sentence trail off.

And then, of course, he had to know.

I told him it wasn't a woman. It was a warship. Several expressions flitted across his face, but the one that finally claimed it was immediate curiosity.

"*C'est un navire de guerre, Yvon. C'est le* Machault."[10]

"*Ahh! Le* Machault!*" And he was off on the next quest. Now that he knew *what*, he was burning to find out *why*.

I'm afraid I gave him a long-winded, not very clear, and not very accurate answer. But the essence of it was that I was trying to unravel a mystery.

Well, he wanted all the details, said he could solve mysteries, that he was my man. I replied that I hardly knew where to start, so it would be impossible to explain it to him. He didn't believe me, but he switched straight away to asking me about myself, what I did. I gave him the thumbnail version.

"*Une librairie! Et un restaurant!*" His broad enthusiastic smile told me that I was his kind of guy. He asked many questions. I answered them all. Then I asked him if he ever got to Toronto.

He shook his head.

"*Trop loin pour Sophie.*"[11]

"*Mon avion*"[12], he clarified when I didn't get it right away.

---

8 "Why are you going to Charlo, hey? A woman?"
9 "It's not a woman, but the sooner we're together..."
10 "It's a warship, Yvon. It's the Machault."
11 "Too far for Sophie."
12 "My airplane."

I told him that if he ever did make it to the fleshpots of Central Canada, he should look me up. Any time. Supplies of reading matter and food would be on me. This was greeted by a great laugh of approval.

We talked about other things. Time passed. I almost forgot about the need for a taxi at the other end. When I raised this, he said there was no problem, pulled out his cellphone, and made a call to someone called Robert. There was a lot of rapid-fire kibitzing in French, but I understood enough to know that Robert would be waiting with his taxi at Charlo.

As we glided over the landscape, Yvon pointed out to me what was drifting by below: first Wolfville, then Fundy, then Moncton and a haze off to the right that was Prince Edward Island, then the Miramichi, all separated by what seemed endless miles of forest. Then we were coming up on Bathurst, and Yvon pointed off to the right and embarked on a long explanation of Caraquet and its significance. From Bathurst, we followed the south coast of la baie des Chaleurs, then began a slow descent toward Charlo. There was a quick exchange with the tower, and Yvon guided Sophie in to a perfect landing. We taxied to the tiny terminal, Yvon allowed the engine to idle for a few minutes, then switched it off.

"Bienvenue à Charlo et au Nouveau-Brunswick!"[13]

Yvon asked me some practical questions about my stay, and most importantly where I was going next. Back to Halifax, after I finish here, I said. Yvon said he would be very pleased to fly me back, and I said I would contact him. We climbed out of the plane, Yvon recovered by bag, and then we stood facing each other.

Yvon was already planning my next visit. *When you return, Roule, give me some advance warning*, he said. *We'll do a little tour.* His handshake was firm and friendly. As we walked the short distance to the terminal, I pulled out my wallet, and proffered a fifty-dollar note, even though this short flight had not been cheap.

"Quoi? Comment?"[14] he stumbled.

I insisted.

---

13 "Welcome to Charlo, and to New Brunswick!"
14 "What? What for?"

"Non, Roule! Câlisse! Ne sois pas stupide!"[15]

We argued a bit, but eventually he took the fifty, offered his thanks through a massive infectious smile, and clapped me on the shoulder.

We found Robert and his taxi, and Yvon surprised me by asking me in English where I wanted to go, after first offering a *Salut!* to Robert.

"Campbellton", I said.

Yvon had a rapid, idiomatic exchange with Robert, none of which I caught, then he pushed me toward the cab, we shook hands strongly once again, exchanging *"Maudit Anglais"* and *"Maudit Français"* mock insults through roaring laughter, I climbed in, and the cab sped off.

Campbellton is only a few kilometres from Charlo, and I asked Robert to take me to the Quality Hotel, which he confirmed was the best, if the most expensive. In a few minutes we had stopped under the hotel's portico. I pulled out my wallet. Robert waved his hand in denial.

"Non. C'est déjà payé. Yvon, he has paid it."[16]

There seemed no point in arguing, and the incomprehensible exchange between Yvon and Robert likely had sealed this little arrangement. I said goodbye to Robert, went into the hotel, and checked in. In my room, I looked for local car rental agencies, and found that Enterprise was practically around the corner. I phoned, booked a car, then headed back down to the lobby.

The rack of brochures on what to do locally contained many items of interest, and I grabbed a few that made reference to the *Machault*, although I already had downloaded and studied the Parks Canada information.

In my rental car, I consulted a map and set off toward Pointe-à-la-Croix, across the river, where the national historic site is located.

I have to say that it was impressive. I spent over four hours there, more than half of it talking to interpretation centre staff and picking their brains for the more obscure technical books and papers not on display in the museum. The rest of the time I spent

---

15 "No, Rolls! For God's sake! Don't be stupid!"
16 "No. It's already paid."

examining the sections of the *Machault* that had been recovered and put on display, the reconstructed captain's quarters, and the excellent model of the ship. But the impression that I had feared was already settling over me.

What am I doing here? I said to myself.

Okay, fine. This gives me a much clearer picture of Giraudais' French expedition. I had identified four more substantial documents on the history of the battle and the events leading up to it. And I could now imagine the scenes in the estuary as impending defeat closed in on the *Machault* and her crew. But I wasn't going to come up with any hot new piece of evidence, never before suspected or unearthed, something that would shine the ultimate beam of illumination onto my Parmenidean riddle.

Come on, Rolls. You knew better than to expect a silver bullet. The best you could have hoped for was background. The most you could expect, when you're swimming in a sea of suppositions. Get a grip!

That was the best advice on offer. If there was anything further that was important to solving the Barrington puzzle, chances are it already lurked, waiting to be found, among the now significant pile of documents I had amassed. I thanked the staff who had been unstinting with their time, left the museum, and drove back to Campbellton and my hotel.

By now it was after four o'clock. I decided to make another sweep through the documents that seemed most relevant since my focus had shifted away from Louisbourg, have some dinner in the hotel restaurant, work through the rest of the evening, get a decent sleep, then head back to Halifax. The specifics of doing that were undefined at that point, but most likely would involve Yvon. He said just to contact him, that he would fit it in.

I worked for two and a half hours, circling back several times to the elusive material, whatever it was, that Prof. Barrington claimed to have found, and in general retuned my approach. None of it produced an *aha!* moment, but it needed to be done. Just before seven, I called Yvon and arranged to have him fly me back to Halifax. He would need to let me know the exact time, he said, because he had to juggle another small job, but he said he would send me an email. I told him that there was no schedule I needed to keep to, apart from getting back to Halifax sometime the following afternoon. I then ate, worked for another three hours, and called it a day.

It was a cloud of melancholia that accompanied me to bed, my sense being now that this whole side trip had been an interesting but unproductive diversion. I had succumbed to the lure of metaphorical fool's gold, a misinterpretation of plain ordinary static generated by a crossed-wires view of my puzzle.

Despite all that, I had a sound sleep, and awoke riding the crest of a mood that was inexplicably upbeat. Checking my email, I found that Yvon requested me to be at Charlo at two thirty that afternoon. I replied confirming that I would be there. That gave me another few hours to slog away at the great amorphous mass of material I had collected. Passing on breakfast, I settled down to work at the point I had left off the previous evening.

At eleven thirty, I decided that I would have some lunch in half an hour, check out, return the hire car, and organize a taxi back to Charlo airport. I was wrapping up the morning's work and made a last check on my email, not expecting there to be anything important.

A few messages, for information only, had been forwarded to me concerning the bookshop and the restaurant. Interesting but not requiring any action. As I was looking through these items, another email arrived.

It was from Prof. Barrington.

Checking with my admin assistant, and she told me of your query. Flattered that you were interested in this little thread of my work. Copy of my 1979 paper attached. Let's meet sometime. S.B.

I couldn't open his attachment quickly enough. Reading at breakneck speed, I digested the essential contents in fifteen minutes.

Lunch was cancelled. This I needed to study. Although I had only a picture in outline, the tingle of imminent discovery rippled through my body.

I was gutting Barrington's paper when another email arrived. From Fairley.

Where are you? Let me know soonest. Something odd is going on. Am investigating. Will keep you informed. Be careful, Rolls.

Chapter Seventeen

I wasn't at all sure what Fairley meant. But I sent off a quick email reply saying where I was and what I was doing next. Having done that, I decided to wait for a few minutes to see whether she would reply with anything further. Four minutes later, she did.

Your watcher has been waiting at Cambridge Suites for two days. I have an odd feeling. Can you stay anywhere else when you return to Halifax? If so, please do that. Let me know where. Phillips, the second of my team watching your bookshop, called out to another urgent job, so a bit short-handed. Will be in touch again soon.

It sounded as though Fairley was trying to deal with her own set of irritations and annoyances, and that her shortage of direct information on what was happening in Nova Scotia was making her move up a notch or two on the careful index. A call to Malcolm Anderson provided me an alternative place to stay in Halifax for one night. Fiona was back home, Malcolm said, but that was no problem since she was keen to meet me. Then I just concentrated on what was coming up: return to Halifax, one more night there, then fly back to Toronto the following day.

In working through the mechanics of the next twenty-four hours or so, I found that I was now ready to get back to Toronto, despite my reacquired affection for Halifax, and indeed for the Maritimes, or at least those parts I had had time to visit this trip. Yvon would take me to Stanfield Airport, then I would probably take a taxi to Halifax, despite the cost, turn up at Malcolm's place, and look forward to another few hours of his and Fiona's company. Then back to Stanfield Airport the next morning, catch my midday flight to Toronto, and return to bookshop, restaurant, and established routine of life. That was when the doubt began to surface.

I began wondering vaguely why my Halifax watchers had been pursuing their task in what seemed to be a fairly laid-back fashion. What had they been hoping to find just by watching? What were they looking for? To see whether I went anywhere unexpected? If that was the case, then their watching must have been limited to just Halifax, since as far as I knew they had no idea where else I had been. Did that bother them? If I gone somewhere or done something unexpected, what then? And would they just throw in the towel once I returned to Toronto? I had to speak to Fairley about this. It occurred to me, and it wasn't a welcome thought, that whatever the interest was that someone had in me, likely it would not just go away. In fact, any such interest, seen specifically from a Toronto perspective, might have been heightened by my Atlantic caper. I mulled this over for some time, not getting anywhere, and still dogged by the same feelings of unease.

And then I stopped. What if…?

I dropped everything, went down to reception, was told that the nearest Walmart was not far, in Atholville, located it on a map, jumped in my car, and drove there straightaway. I bought what I needed, drove back to the hotel, and let myself into my room. I was about to call Fairley when my phone buzzed.

"Hello. Rolls?"

"Yes."

"It's Dan Fairley. Are you still in Campbellton?" There was a lot of background noise.

"Yes."

"Tell me exactly what your movements will be between now and when you return to Toronto."

I didn't much like the sound of that, but I walked through everything I had organized.

There was a long pause.

"Okay", Fairley said, her voice conveying nothing that sounded like confirmation, relief, conviction, or any of the things I found that I was wanting to hear. We talked a bit more.

"All right", Fairley said, sounding as though she was wrapping up the call. "Phone me when you land in Toronto."

I promised that I would, and we ended the conversation.

I wasn't in the right mood for returning immediately to work on my puzzle, so I called Robert and organized a taxi back to Charlo, packed my suitcase, checked out of the hotel, returned the rental car, and then walked back to the hotel to wait for Robert. He turned up fifteen minutes later, drove me to the airport at Charlo. I paid him and we said a pleasant farewell.

The Charlo airport is little more than an airfield. In the terminal, there are a few seats, a tiny place to buy refreshments, and that's about it. To me, the place had the feel I thought would be associated with flying lessons, bush pilots, dentists going fishing, and bookshop owners pursuing mad schemes. I settled in one of the plastic seats that wasn't cracked and called Yvon to tell him that I had arrived about forty-five minutes early.

That's okay, he told me, since his other job was now finished and he would land at Charlo in about ten minutes. He had to refuel, and then he would come and look for me in the terminal. I sat there, prepared just to wait, but then the feeling of uncertainty that rumbled inside me induced me to get up from my seat and amble around the small terminal. I made six slow circuits of the terminal space and had pretty much memorized everything it contained, for want of anything else to distract me, and then saw Yvon waving from across the floor, his big smile turned up to full power.

From there, it was straightforward. Almost.

That was when I asked Yvon if he could do me a favour.

"Your cellphone?"

"Yes, my cellphone." And I explained what I wanted him to do.

"Okay", he said, clearly puzzled. "Okay. I don't understand why", he said, but he agreed to do it. Before handing it over to him, I sent two text messages, one to Rice and one to Michelle, saying I was having trouble with my phone, and if they needed to contact me to do it by email. Then on the way to his plane we stopped at his locker in the Charlo terminal and he deposited my cellphone.

We walked out again to his plane, he stowed my bag, we climbed in, and after a short exchange the tower cleared him to leave. We followed roughly the reverse path we had taken earlier when Yvon brought me from Halifax, and he maintained his good-natured travelogue during most of the trip, complete with the occasional bursts of belly laughter that I felt could have cheered up the terminally depressed.

The glorious sweep of the Bay of Fundy soon came into sight ahead of us. The day was exceptionally clear, and we could see the entire Parrsboro Shore, up the Minas Basin almost as far as Truro, and down the bay toward Annapolis Royal. At that point, Yvon had a short exchange with traffic control at Stanfield Airport.

I kept examining what was below us. I knew that Blomidon was down there somewhere, the apple orchards in the Annapolis and Gaspereau Valleys were clearly visible, as was the campus of Acadia University as we approached Wolfville. The tide was out, and I looked down on extensive mud flats, could make out the lines of dikes, imagined the aboiteaux they once contained, and I could feel all the rich, eventful, varied, and tragic history of the place drawing me back, willing me to return. The lovely town of Windsor drifted by on our left, and then it was lakes, forests, and rugged terrain until we began encountering the outlying built-up area of Halifax near Sackville.

Yvon must have sensed my mood, since it was clear that he was going to do a large circle around Halifax, overfly McNabs Island and Cole Harbour, and approach Stanfield Airport from the east.

"*C'est bon ça, hein?*"[17] Yvon's voice, softer now, more mellow, came through my headset.

"*C'est merveilleux, Yvon! C'est un pays magnifique!*"[18]

"*Quand tu reviens, mon gars, je vais te montrer quelques tranches de paradis.*"

"*Il me tarde de revenir!*"

"*Oui! Mais quand?*"

"*Et si on disait la semaine prochaine?*"[19]

Yvon shook his head in mock despair.

---

17 "Beautiful, isn't it."
18 "It's gorgeous, Yvon! This country is magnificent!"
19 "On your next visit here, my friend, I'll show you some views of paradise."
"I can't wait to come back."
"Fine! But when?"
"And if I said next week?"

"*C'est tout les torontois! Trop à l'aise!*"[20]

I smiled at Yvon. He smiled back. Here was a guy I really could get along with!

The lakes, forests, and rugged country flowed past beneath us, but soon air traffic control was giving Yvon his instructions, and we swung around toward Stanfield Airport which was now below us on the left. I knew I should have been thinking *port* and *starboard*, but there had been too much else going on. Yvon brought us down to a graceful landing, and we peeled off to a taxiway and headed for the general aviation area.

This time, Yvon tied the plane down since he was finished for the day, and he indicated that a tipple *à la prochaine!* was called for.

"*Mais pas à l'aeroport!*" he said. "*Je vais maintenant en ville. Toi?*"[21]

I indicated that I was also going into Halifax, and soon we were in Yvon's car, speeding along Highway 102. Yvon's conversation continued, irrepressibly but not vacuously. He had things to say, interesting stories to tell. We entered Halifax, and I was surprised yet again at how quickly one can reach the centre of this compact city. Yvon found a place to park not far from Malcolm's condo building in Dresden Row and led me unerringly to a watering hole I never would have located on my own. We shared a drink. We shared expectations for a reprise of my visit, and then, after a heartfelt farewell, Yvon headed for the door, turned, and gave a final wave and a smile that lit up the whole room.

I checked my watch, saw that it was now past five thirty, left the bar, and made my way toward Malcolm's condo building. It had clouded over, threatening rain, and the afternoon had become dim and grey. I passed several large buildings and approached the main entrance to Malcolm's place.

Suddenly, I was gripped powerfully, my right arm pulled up behind my back.

"Don't say anything. Don't look at me. Just keep walking."

---

20 "Just like a Torontonian, all too easy!"
21 "But not at the airport"
"I'm going into town now. You?"

Chapter Eighteen

"What the hell—"

"Don't say anything! Just keep walking."

I disobeyed. Immediately. I stopped, even though the pressure on my arm ratcheted up sharply, turned my head, and scowled.

"What the hell's going on Fairley?"

My arm was moved into a zone of real pain.

"Keep walking, Rolls. Go into the lobby of your friend's condo building over there. We can talk in the lobby, at least for a minute."

Fairley frogmarched me along the sidewalk at a brisk pace, we entered the main door of Malcolm's building and sat on the small sofa just inside the door.

"We have less than a minute here. Then we need to go somewhere else."

"You're damn right we do", I said, "you need to explain to me just what the fuck's going on here!"

There were now quite a few people walking along Dresden Row, and it was only a matter of time before someone turned to come into Malcolm's building.

"There's a hole-in-the-wall pub less than a block from here", I said, referring to the bar Yvon and I had just left. "Let's go." And I rose, took Fairley by the arm the way a gentleman would in days of old, and we covered the short distance to the bar in less than two minutes. Neither of us said anything until we were inside and seated. A young server placed a drinks menu on our table, I asked him to give us a few minutes, and when he was out of hearing range, I turned to Fairley.

"Why are you in Halifax?" I asked abruptly.

"Why are *you* in Halifax?" Fairley countered. "You're supposed to be in Campbellton."

There was something wrong here. But then I suddenly worked it out.

"No. My cellphone is supposed to be in Campbellton, and you're assuming that I'm with my phone. So that means you've been tracking my phone."

My suspicions were now inflating fast.

"You weren't answering, I had to know what was happening. I—"

"Oh yeah? Well now *I* need to know what's happening. Why is it suddenly so important for you to know exactly where I am?"

"Because I didn't want you to walk into what might have been a trap at the Cambridge Suites. Because the watcher has basically been camped there, instead of being out looking, as though he knows something we don't, as though he had a very good reason just to wait there for you. And because my own guy, that bastard Phillips, is now here in Halifax, for what reason I have no idea, but certainly not because I asked him to come here. So, now, please fill me in."

I shook my head.

"Not so fast. There are things going on here that I don't know about. You need to explain them to me. At the very least, so that I can regain my confidence in you."

"In me!"

"Yes, Dan. In you. This caper started off dark when a body appeared in my bookshop, and it has got continuously darker. I was being watched in Toronto. Then I find that what was supposed to be me flushing some turkey out of the undergrowth actually involves somebody shadowing me seriously here in Halifax. Now I discover that you're here, the last place I expected you to be, and you tell me that one of your own people is also here, doing God knows what on some rogue operation. I'm the only guy who seems to be out of the loop in all this, but I'm the guy who has most to lose. So, you need to convince me, and convince me fast, that you're still on my side."

I gave her about three seconds to say something, then jumped in again.

"Okay. I'll ask some questions then. When you called me, I'm assuming that all that background noise meant you were already at Pearson Airport. Why didn't you tell me then what was going on?"

"I didn't want to alarm you."

"Didn't want to alarm me? And practically snatching me off the street just now? I wasn't supposed to be alarmed? You hardly cut the figure of a Girl Guide selling cookies. What was that all about?"

"I needed to talk to you, and I needed to get you off the street fast before the other side caught up."

"And how did you know that somebody was tailing me when I arrived? How did you know all that stuff about my tail looking at B&Bs and moving up to chain hotels?"

"When you left Toronto", Fairley began, "I contacted a guy here in Halifax I've worked with, and—"

"One of your JTF2 crowd?"

"Don't knock it", she said, her voice suddenly harder. "I got to know a lot of very capable people during the time I worked there. Those contacts are one of the strengths I have in my work today. So, yes, it was one of my JTF2 crowd."

"So, what happened? Somebody identified me at Stanfield, followed me into Halifax, and your guy followed the follower?"

"That's exactly the way it was, except your follower lost you at the exit from the Macdonald Bridge. My guy followed him toward the North End, then watched him start checking B&Bs. The odd thing about all that was he didn't seem to be very concerned."

"And what did you read from that?" I demanded.

"That they had another source of information."

Another source of information, I thought. That could explain quite a few things. It also made it hard to avoid the conclusion that the other side had been ahead of us all along, and explained this relaxed and laid-back manner to watching me. Almost a case of non-surveillance.

"Did you know about Phillips then, what he was doing?"

"No", Fairley said, obviously cross with herself at being caught out like that. "It took a few hours for my suspicions about Phillips to be raised."

"And when did Phillips come to Halifax?"

"Not long before I spoke to you, although at that point I thought he was just working locally on what he said, another 'urgent job'. I didn't know about Halifax until about six hours later. Several hours after he went off to his 'urgent job', I tried to contact him. He didn't answer, so then I tracked his phone. The bastard!"

Fairley thumped a closed fist lightly on the table, then appeared to suppress her anger. She sat quietly for a few moments, cooling down.

"That was a neat trick, giving your follower the slip at the bridge. How did you get the sense you were being followed?"

"I didn't. I had no idea. And it wasn't a trick. I just got lost, did a lot of twisting and turning trying to pick up my planned route again."

Fairley looked at me for a few moments. It was quite clear that she was unhappy at the ragged, poorly scripted, and potentially dangerous way things had unfolded.

"I underestimated you", Fairley said finally, "coming up with that cellphone manoeuvre." I guess she thought she was complimenting me, and didn't expect my mood and my face to darken in response.

"Come off it, Dan! You're not the only one who can work things out. You think I'm just some flake who's been lucky at playing bookshop and restaurant owner. To make either of those things just squeak by takes work and imagination. To make them even modestly successful takes a lot more of both. I've had to handle a lot of problems, anticipate a lot of situations, construct a lot of plans A, B, and C. It's called survival. So, please! Give me some credit!"

"Sorry. I didn't … I mean … Oh shit!"

I glanced across at her. It was easy enough to see that she was working hard to right her own ship of self-assured competence, to mask the signs of what was likely a scathing round of self-recrimination. I was suddenly ashamed of my overreaction.

"Have you eaten?" I asked.

Fairley looked up, evidently surprised at my suddenly mellowed tone, and shook her head.

"Do you have a place for tonight?"

"Yes. I booked a room at the Prince George before I left Toronto."

I reached across the table and picked up a menu.

"They've probably got something edible here", and I began scanning what was on offer.

"Aren't you meeting your friend?"

"Yes, but he said he wouldn't be home until about seven. And I haven't eaten all day."

Our server had drifted past several times, saw each time that some heavy discussion was in play, and faded into the background again. He was hovering close to our table once more.

I caught his eye.

"Could you bring us two double scotches?" I asked. "Do you have Dalwhinnie, or Balvenie, or Singleton, or something decent?"

He had Dalwhinnie, so I had him scuttle off and pour us a couple.

"What if I don't like scotch?"

"Well, then mine will be a quadruple. Not going to pour it into the potted plants, am I?"

Thirst must have been written in the air above us, because the glasses of scotch were set on our table without delay. The golden liquid found our cockles quickly enough, it knew what to do when it got there, and the evening began looking up almost immediately.

We both ordered steaks, but mine was very modest and accompanied by just a small salad since I expected to be eating later with Fiona and Malcolm. Fairley decided on a much heartier meal — a good-sized steak, jacket potato with sour cream and chives, and a large Caesar salad. Our food arrived promptly, and for a hole-in-the-wall pub, someone in the kitchen knew what they were doing.

As we ate, we talked about what this venture to Halifax had revealed. I walked through the essentials of what I had discovered, noted that there were a few lines of research I needed to do urgently when I was back home, and said that I wanted us to start thinking about how to bring this whole business to a conclusion.

My flight back to Toronto was about midday the next day. Fairley knew this.

"When are you going back?" I asked.

"Tomorrow evening."

I gave her a questioning look.

"I have something to attend to. Won't take more than a few hours."

The *something* likely involved Phillips.

I was glad I wasn't him just then.

"Have you checked out of the Cambridge Suites yet?"

"No", I said. "I was planning to do that within the next half-hour."

"You going to do that electronically?"

"Electronically? Why? The place is just five minutes away."

"Do me a favour", Fairley said. "Check out electronically, but don't do it until about four o'clock Halifax time. I know you'll be back in Toronto by then, and I know it will cost you an extra day, but … I'll deduct that day's charge from your account."

"Why do you want—"

"You're probably getting concerned about the cost of all this", Fairley said, interrupting and striking out on a different tack. "And by the way, have the police back in Toronto made any progress?"

By that time I had worked out that my checkout time had something to do with plans she had here. There were now three questions in the air. I tackled them in reverse order.

"No. The last time I spoke to Detective Sergeant Barnett, about, what, a week ago, he danced around a bit, and it sounded like his investigation had become stalled permanently. The cost of this venture is what it is. Barnett is interested in just who and how, not why. I need to know what's going on. I don't want to be the victim of another who and how. And I'm assuming that the delay in checking out is to give you time to do something."

Fairley's expression was blank so I just nodded, indicating that I understood but also hoping that my frustration concerning this game of spooks would show.

We edged away from that awkward supposed end of discussion and talked about non-project things as we ate. Fairley asked about how I came to own a bookshop, and I gave her an abbreviated version of how it had all come about. I asked what led her to join the armed forces, and she gave a vague answer that seemed to centre on family and relationship problems. On my questions about her present PI work, she was more forthcoming. It sounded as though she really enjoyed the work, and I was surprised at the variety of jobs she had been involved in.

Meals consumed, we sat sipping our coffee and talking about what came next, agreeing to get together the morning after we were both back in Toronto. Although I was looking forward to the understandable chaos of both restaurant and bookshop, the previous few hours hadn't been reassuring. My life had been engulfed by a cloud ever since McGrath's body had turned up, and my apparent inability to rid myself of that cloud was disquieting.

Chapter Nineteen

Fairley and I left the pub at just before seven — she headed to her hotel, while I walked back to Malcolm's condo building. When I dialled the code for his unit from the lobby, a reply came back immediately and he buzzed me in. My evening with Fiona and Malcolm was another relaxed four hours of takeout Thai food, discussion, laughter, music, and some excellent local wine.

At about eleven o'clock, Malcolm and I carried the dinner things into the kitchen, I helped load the dishwasher, and then we began tying ribbons on the evening.

"How will you get to the airport tomorrow?" Fiona asked.

"Oh, I'll just take a taxi."

"Nonsense!" Malcolm exclaimed.

"Nonsense indeed", Fiona said. "A taxi to the airport will cost a fortune. If Malcolm drives you, you'll have another hour together. I would tag along if I could, but..."

Malcolm was nodding, basically challenging me to object. "If you don't mind arriving an hour or so early at the airport, I would enjoy driving you. I don't have a lecture until two o'clock."

I tried to talk him out of it, but it soon became clear that any such attempt would fail, so I accepted.

"I'm sorry you have to sleep here on the sofa, Rolls", Fiona said, still not quite used to calling anybody *Rolls*.

There then followed some one-upmanship back and forth on "places I've had to sleep", and I won that contest by my description of an overbooked youth hostel in Narvik, and my night spent stretched out across the tops of three washing machines in the hostel's laundry room.

"So your sofa is luxury", I pronounced in conclusion.

Fiona brought sheets, a blanket, a pillow, fussed about making the bed, and asked me several times if everything was okay.

"You use the bathroom first, Rolls", Malcolm said, and then they both bid me good night. Obviously, I didn't know how tired I was. I must have been half-asleep already when I began to undress, since the next morning I had no recollection of anything after brushing my teeth.

I awoke early, early enough to see just how extravagant the sunrise is in Halifax. Great wispy bolts of red, orange, and yellow cloud were thrown into loops and folds across the sky, as though awaiting the attentions of some cosmic tailor. When Fiona emerged, already dressed and asking about coffee, I had folded my sofa bedclothes and gone back to watch as the morning continued to break.

Malcolm appeared a few minutes later, shaved and sporting that bright look of someone who enjoys his work and can't wait to get started.

We settled in to a nice working-day breakfast. Malcolm and Fiona noted to each other, in what sounded already like marital code, what the day held for each of them, and when they would both be back at Dresden Row. Fiona asked me what was coming up for me once I returned to Toronto, and they both seemed intrigued at my list of routine tasks for bookshop and restaurant. In response to a question from me, Fiona talked a bit about her IT work, which she said was enjoyable and going well, but there were hints in the background that she would be moving on to something different in not too many months. Just after eight o'clock, she took her breakfast dishes to the kitchen, set her briefcase and handbag on the end table near the door, and took my hands in hers.

"It's been so good to get to know you, Rolls. Malcolm has a lot to say about you. I hope the next time you're in Halifax we can spend more than a day together."

She gave me an unselfconscious hug, and we said a few more versions of *farewell*.

"Have a good flight back, Rolls."

And then she headed off into her day.

"Another cup of coffee?" Malcolm asked.

I nodded, he poured, and we sat and chatted for another forty minutes.

"If we leave here at about nine forty-five, will that be okay for you?"

"Absolutely fine", I said, then we carried the remaining breakfast things to the kitchen and spent ten minutes washing them by hand.

It didn't occur to me until we started down in the elevator that we would be emerging from the underground garage, making my departure from Halifax almost unknowable, even if someone had been watching Malcolm's building. We chatted more as Malcolm threaded his way effortlessly through the Halifax traffic, over the Macdonald Bridge, and onto Highway 102 to the airport.

Our goodbyes at the airport were brief but backlit by the glow of a rekindled relationship. I watched Malcolm walk off toward the car park and reflected briefly on our common student past and the different courses we had followed since then. There was the usual rigmarole of check-in and security, a short time spent reading in the departure lounge, and then we were shuffling toward the waiting airplane. During the flight back, I paid little attention to the clouds, water, and land passing below. Once we landed at Pearson Airport, I knew that I would be in a different space wrestling in a different way with different faces of the same general problem. But set against that, I was returning to the comfortable rituals of running a bookshop and a restaurant and to contact with the people who inhabited those two distinct spaces. My short time in Nova Scotia had put all that in a new perspective: the significance of these two Toronto ventures and how deeply they had become embedded in my existence, but also the importance of breaking step from time to time, gaining more knowledge of another of the indefinitely large number of dimensions that make up our social world.

Heading straight home, I began reconnecting with my Toronto reality by checking email. Dozens of the messages that rose up the screen to meet me could be dealt with some other time. There were about fifty messages having to do with some aspect of restaurant or bookshop, and I skimmed them all, determining that eight had to be tackled immediately. It was still just after three o'clock, and recalling the hour time difference between Halifax and Toronto dispatched my vague sense on why that didn't seem right. I used that surplus hour to call the bookshop and the restaurant, and found, not to my surprise, that they were both humming along nicely, but that a social call by me to each would be welcomed. That seemed a good way to switch realities.

Rice was all smiles. Sales had been better than usual, almost a dozen requests had been made for obscure books that Rice had promised to try to find, and although the P body was now just a rapidly fading image in day-to-day operations, it still seemed to be preoccupying our competitors. Rice was pleased when I offered to take on half the items on his list of requests for obscure books.

My welcome at M&B Resto was tumultuous, causing me to think that a customer appreciation day was not just a good idea, but one whose time was past due. In the kitchen, Hinge offered a wan smile, the equivalent in anyone else of delirious happiness. Michelle gave me a ritual hug en passant, and at the next pass set before me a welcome mug of coffee, which I discovered soon enough had been fortified by at least two ounces of brandy. Evidently, the world was as it should be, and I slipped into the routine of checking the indicators of restaurant health. The values of those indicators, at one end of their scales, would flag the need for the gastronomic analogues of oil top-up and tire inflation. This check revealed values for which the only interpretation could be *buoyant*.

Big smile.

But even the best-designed machines need continual attention, and inevitably a list of tasks emerged from this check. A half-hour spent with the clientele was good for everyone. I then spent an hour placing orders for the restaurant's larder and freezer, paying bills, and deciding that tomorrow morning should bring a surprise offering of breads of various sorts.

Back home, I dealt with a few things on the websites for bookshop and restaurant, asked Fairley by email to contact me when she was back in town, and then decided to treat myself to a dinner of kedgeree.

But I didn't get the chance.

My new cellphone buzzed. Only one person knew the number of my new phone.

Fairley.

Her call lasted barely a minute. And that's how I came to be on the next flight back to Halifax.

Chapter Twenty

At the reception desk of the Hilton Garden Hotel at Stanfield Airport, I registered and picked up the key to the fourth-floor room that Fairley had reserved for me. The clock behind the reception desk said nine forty.

Fairley had the room right next door to mine. When she opened the door to my knock, the large angry bruise on the right side of her face shocked me. She waved me into the room before I could ask.

"Phillips", she said simply.

"How—"

"Never mind", Fairley replied dismissively.

"Where is he now?"

"Probably having his arm set."

I had to drag it out of her a couple of words at a time. It was perfectly clear that she was angry and frustrated that the case was turning out to be so ragged.

"I checked out of the Cambridge Suites at about five o'clock Toronto time", I said. "The very last thing I expected was to be back here just a few hours later. What's going on, Dan?"

Without answering, she moved to the mini-bar and pulled out a bottle of white wine and six or eight miniatures.

"I need a drink", she said. "Just had a three-hour nap. I had a blinding headache when I checked in."

"Hardly surprising", I said, looking more closely at her war wound. "Have you had that looked at?"

"What! Don't tell me you're a paramedic on top of everything else!"

I just shrugged, and offered, "I'll have a glass of wine and a glass of Kahlùa ", as a reply.

Fairley poured my order, and served herself a glass of wine to follow a gin and tonic, in which the gin was by far the senior partner. Gin and Kahlùa met in a clink and we took hearty slugs.

Having got herself outside half her large G and T, Fairley began looking more relaxed and more businesslike. I got the feeling she was also gathering a good deal of determination.

"I had the advantage over Phillips", she said. "I knew where he was but he probably believed I didn't know that. And I suspected, and I think this was confirmed when I accosted him, that he didn't in the least expect to see me here."

Another swig of G and T reduced it to dregs level. She rose, it looked like to fix herself a second one, but then she sank back into her seat and reached for the wine glass.

"I saw him slouched in a car outside the Cambridge Suites. Looked like he was waiting for you, either to enter or to leave."

"Surely he must know about electronic checkout!" I said.

"Of course. But if you did that, there would have been nothing he could do anyway. He was counting on the off chance. That you had left something in the room, for example. That you'd come back to retrieve it. Or that you would spend another night in Halifax. He would probably wait there until it became likely that you weren't going to show, ask at the desk if you'd checked out, and then call it a day."

"And if I had come back? Then what?"

"Well, then most probably he would have followed you to your room. Come up behind you as you were letting yourself in. Forced his way in with you. Encouraged you to talk."

"Talk? About what?"

"That is where we leave the trail of knowns. They are in the dark about something important. It might have to do with the book that was lifted from your shop. It might be something else."

"They? Who exactly are they?"

"That I don't know. But Phillips isn't really an entrepreneur. He likes working for other people."

"You mean … somebody else is calling the shots and Phillips was working for him? Or her?"

"Prudent call, Rolls. Not all bosses need to be men. I don't know who it is, but I'm pretty sure that Phillips is working for somebody."

"Shit, Dan! This just gets worse and worse."

I just sat there getting angry for a moment. Then something occurred to me.

"Was Phillips already in the pay of his controller when you hired him? I assume he's an occasional hire just for this job."

Fairley was nodding.

"Yes, I took him on just for this job. He's one of a number of people I know of, and his particular skills fit. But no, I doubt that he was already part of the Dark Side when I engaged him. Nobody knew that I would hire him and not someone else."

"So he must have been turned while he was working for you. How would the controller know that he was on your payroll?"

"That's pretty easy. Phillips, and a lot of others of his type, work in a grey area. They're stooges, mercenaries. One relies on some sort of honour system, but nobody is sworn to silence. In fact, it's never that difficult finding out whether a given person is working or between jobs, and, if they're working, who they're working for." I thought back to Jocko's information that led me to selecting Dan. "This case is out of the ordinary. It's not often that somebody will seek out someone like Phillips and hire him to work against his own current employer. That means against you. And me. It doesn't happen often because it can be dangerous."

"Dangerous? How so?"

"Well, that person then becomes a sort of double agent. Meaning that they can betray either employer. And either side, finding that they have someone like that in their employ, has to be aware of the risk. In our case, the other side hired away Phillips. They would need to give him a strong incentive for allowing himself to be bought out like that. And his new employer would want to operate on a strict need-to-know basis, telling the new hire, Phillips in this case, as little as possible."

"So that there's as little as possible to betray", I said.

"Exactly."

"So you would be trying to get as much out of Phillips as you could."

Fairley just nodded. I thought about all this for a while, becoming increasingly uneasy.

"Tell me about your encounter with Phillips."

Fairley rose with the bottle and refilled our wine glasses. She now had some colour and was moving once more with purpose and economy. I took care not to assess her too obviously, although who really knows how much sharp-eyed women see…

"I watched him for a while from a little further south along Brunswick. When there was nobody in any of the other cars, or hanging around outside the hotel, I approached his car from the rear passenger side. He was focussed on the front of the hotel. Slouched down in the seat. Leaning against his door. He almost fell out when I pulled it open. A couple of jabs left him not fully in control, and I walked him along Brunswick and then turned right down Sackville. There's a recessed entranceway, there at the first intersection, at Market Street. Not the best place to conduct an interrogation, but I had thirty seconds or so. I asked my first question, gave him five seconds to answer, then broke his right arm."

"Shit, Fairley!"

She took no notice of my interjection and didn't stop.

"He knows essentially nothing. He was in Halifax to find out. From you. Or wherever he could."

"Find out what?"

"Okay. Here it is. I think he wanted to find out what you know."

"What I know? What do you mean 'what I know'? And why didn't he just pick me up and grind it out of me?"

"He wouldn't do that, because he knew that I was involved, but he didn't know exactly what you and I were up to. He worked for me on a need-to-know basis, thank God. So, apart from our surveillance of the bookshop, he knew nothing."

"Then how did he know to come to Halifax?"

"Bingo! He didn't know it from me."

"Then how…?"

"Yes, how. There's only one way I can think of: whoever found out that you were off to Halifax, maybe by watching you, then following you to the airport in Toronto. Then they arranged for someone out there to pick up your trail, and that someone was keeping his boss informed."

"You mean, somebody, whoever's in charge, has been pulling the strings, and they alerted Phillips?"

"I can't think of any other explanation."

"How much did you get from Phillips?"

"Almost nothing. There wasn't any time. But I did lift his cellphone. Don't worry", she said, seeing my expression of alarm. "I took out the SIM card immediately."

"Where's the phone now?"

"With a friend."

"Another—?"

"Yes. Another one of *them*."

"So then how did you—?"

"He was resting peacefully when I left him." She broke into a wry smile. "There are quick and sophisticated ways of putting someone out. The John Wayne approach works only in the movies."

"So then—"

"So then I took a taxi back to my hotel, checked out, drove to Admiral Cove Park on the Bedford Basin, parked in an out-of-the-way spot, called the hotel and booked our rooms, and waited. And did some serious thinking."

"I guess all this means that my pissing around down here was just a waste of time." I must have looked dejected. That's certainly how I felt. The whole business seemed to be just careening out of control.

"Not at all", Fairley said, touching my arm gently. "You got the buggers to reveal at least part of their hand."

"I did? Tell me what and how."

And Fairley walked me through what she had deduced, in quite a lot of detail.

It was hard to believe.

Chapter Twenty-One

"So you don't think this is someone trying to find or to steal some valuable object?" I asked, at the end of Fairley's long but admirably concise summary.

"I think it could involve that. But it seems to me that it must be more than just that." Fairley looked as though she was going to say more, but she just sat there looking at the wall for a moment.

"More than that? What, for example?"

Fairley fiddled with the top button of her shirt, and I was aware suddenly that she did this quite often.

"Here's the thing. Collectors are a secretive bunch. Their competition is other collectors. If they hire someone to get something for them, they want that someone to do it quietly and invisibly. What's been happening here is very far from that. It's left behind a wide trail of noise and ruckus. I suspect that nobody would go to the extremes we see here just to snap up something valuable. There's something else in play."

"What?"

"I don't know. But I think it must be something of considerable personal importance. Maybe someone is trying to keep something from being uncovered. Or maybe all this fuss is deliberate. Maybe somebody wants anyone watching this game to conclude that some particular individual is behind it all."

"A smokescreen?" I asked.

"Maybe. Maybe a smokescreen behind a smokescreen. But of one thing I'm fairly certain. Whoever's calling the shots here has police or military experience."

I had no response to that. I was too busy dealing with all the other details. But my face must have signalled a question.

"I can see you're wondering why. Why police or military?"

"Yes. I am", I replied.

"It looks as though there's been a mastermind behind everything we've seen here. A planner who looks after everything, in great detail. Somebody who leaves no possibility unassessed."

I wasn't sure whether she had consciously concluded something, or she just had a strong feeling. That must have showed in my face, which evidently had been read again.

"Feelings are important", Fairley said with some emphasis. "You get to know which ones to pay attention to and which to discard. This one can't be brushed off. Don't ask me why."

I was now making every attempt at a blank, uninformative facial expression.

Fairley laughed. "Don't like having your mind read, do you?"

"Yeah ... Well I ... No, actually..."

"Forget it", she said, waving a hand dismissively. "We have work to do now. How long can you stay here?"

"As long as I need to. Several days, if necessary." I looked at Fairley who seemed to be thinking hard. "Why?" I asked.

She took a sip of wine, ran a hand through her hair, and then despite an attempt to hide it, broke into a huge yawn.

"You need to go to bed, Dan", I said, draining my glass and rising. "Early breakfast?"

"Hmmm", she said, nodding and gazing at nothing in particular. There were large smudges under her eyes. She really was beat.

"Seven thirty downstairs", I said, then I opened the door and left.

Back in my own room, sleep was the last thing I had in mind.

I was pleased that I'd had the sense to bring my laptop with me. There was now a large amount of material I had amassed, and being able to see it on the larger screen of a laptop would be kinder to my eyes.

I fired up the laptop. Then I began a series of online searches, broad in scope initially, but in much finer detail eventually. My search routines I saved deliberately. I wasn't sure what I would find, but if any result turned out to be golden, I definitely wanted to be able to duplicate the search that found it. I started out on the topic of the Seven Years War but linked that to various current-day individuals. At the beginning, I had in my head a sort of outline for my search strategy, but as I worked, it became more complex. I took fifteen minutes off to jot the outline down in a notebook. I gazed at what I got, no flash of inspiration leapt off the page at me, so I just carried on searching. The searching, however, now was moving along some fairly well-defined lines.

Vast amounts of material came up, something that seemed to happen for even the simplest, most innocuous search. I sifted through truckloads of material. It looked like it was all gangue, hardly any ore, and even the ore I found was low grade.

Midnight came and went. Two o'clock rolled past. At quarter to three, I saw some gold flecks in my pan. I had discovered that there are lots of books out there on the Seven Years War, and almost as much text talking about those books as the books themselves contain. What I had come across was a short article in an obscure journal about modern-day interest in the minutiae of that war, but it was a few paragraphs in the article on individuals who stood out in all this. There were a dozen or so academics noted, but there was also a list of fourteen amateur historians of the period. It was these amateurs who had captured the interest of the author of the article, judging from how the text appeared suddenly to become more engaged.

Of the fourteen names, nine of them were Americans, mostly living in New England. Three lived in England, one of those being the now-deceased Geoffrey Fielding. One lived in Wolfville. And one lived in Toronto. The two Canadians were of immediate interest.

It was easy to determine that the woman from Wolfville could be discounted, since I quickly came across a human-interest story of her work that had appeared in a local newspaper. She had been, apparently, a lovable local eccentric, but had suffered a sudden descent into dementia that had resulted in her transfer to a care home. It was this that had triggered the article. The man from Toronto was named Greer. And I was disappointed to read that he was now dead. But my disappointment soon turned to intense curiosity.

One newspaper account gave thin details. He had died in his own home, violently, and under circumstances that had not been clarified. "Possibly an accident; possibly homicide", the account had read, the police being unable to determine which. Google and I did some more digging.

Robert M. Greer had become independently wealthy in some aspect of stocks and bonds. He was a bibliophile, and from the age of sixty-three he had indulged his passion for history. "He was intensely interested in history", the article quoted his brother. "He became obsessed by the Seven Years War. At the time of his death he was deep into some particular aspect, but he never did explain to me what it was. I'm sorry now that I didn't ask him."

Me too, I thought.

But then came a reminder. *It's late. You're tired. And now you're getting sidetracked. This is just a distant possibility. Forget it.*

Good advice.

I saved what I had found, made a long note on the route by which I had arrived at this information, switched off, and crashed for the night.

There had been some sort of dust storm during the night, because when I dragged myself out of Lake Molasses at six fifty the next morning, I tried to rub the grit from my eyes. It didn't work. After a quick shave and getting dressed while cursing myself for leaving only four hours for sleep, I was in the hotel restaurant by seven thirty. Fairley was already there tucking into a plate of pancakes. She looked fresh and rejuvenated.

"Morning, Rolls. You look like you've just had your last night on death row."

I muttered something about a sadistic hangwoman and went off to get some grub.

"So", Fairley began as I sat down, my tray containing a mound of scrambled egg, a piece of toast, and two cups of coffee. "Looks like you sat up most of the night. Working, I'm guessing."

I stuffed my mouth full of egg, not keen to do any talking for a few minutes. The egg, toast, and first cup of coffee soon did their thing, and the day's prospect mellowed from one of shattered glass to something more like a room lined in cotton wool.

We ate in silence for a while. Fairley looked at me regularly, probably trying to judge my fitness for just about anything. I glanced at her briefly, noting that the bruise on her cheek had ripened, despite her attempt to hide it under a layer of makeup. Apart from that, she seemed to be loaded for T. Rex, if not something even more ferocious.

"Did quite a bit of searching last night", I said, setting down knife and fork.

"Find anything?"

"Yes."

I related what I had learned about Greer.

"Is this relevant?"

"I can't be sure."

"Well, what makes you think it might be relevant?"

I hesitated, knowing that my mind was dangling yet another supposition before me, but that this one, if it turned out to be true, might be a ringer.

"You remember me telling you about my visit to Raymond Lansdell, when I was tracing the path of my copy of *Stylus of Death*?"

There was a delay, and then a doubtful "Yes."

"You remember Lansdell's recollections of the name, the owner of the library, the estate sale where my book came from? You remember he said Graham, or maybe Gorley, or maybe Greeley?"

An even more doubtful "Yes."

"What if it was *Greer*?"

I knew she didn't buy it. I knew I couldn't really buy it. But I knew also that I wasn't just going to discard it.

We simply peered into that pit for a few minutes, then carried on with breakfast.

I waited for Fairley to finish her pancakes, noting the same economy of movement I had noticed recently, but hoping that my mode of observation was more subtle now and wouldn't drop me into disfavour again.

What the hell, I thought. *The descriptor* good-looking *is used for a reason.* But I shifted my gaze to an unattractive painting on the wall just in time.

"You said we have things to do. What things specifically?"

"Right in there, eh", she said, smiling. "To hell with the conversational foreplay."

"That's not what's on the agenda, is it? I didn't fly all the way out here just for a bit of foreplay, did I?"

"No. Not in your case. But some other men I've known…"

I wasn't sure whether to take that as a slight on my manhood, or a compliment on my gentlemanhood.

It looked as though Fairley had reflected on her previous sentence.

"You're a good guy, Rolls. Please forgive my coarse edge. Two years spent in JTF2 with a bunch of guys who were definitely not shrinking violets, and a rough day yesterday hasn't done anything for my own social graces. My apologies."

I looked up and was somewhat taken aback to see from her expression that she really meant it.

A couple of smiles and a few seconds of silence took us onto another plane.

"I'd like to do a few more hours searching and reading. Sometime today", I said. "It doesn't matter when. From what you say, it seems that there's something needing four eyes."

"I want to find out what my guy got from Phillips' cellphone. We should look at that together. There could be stuff that you know about but I don't. I'll give him a call at eight thirty, so", glancing at her watch, "in about another half-hour. Let's meet in my room at eight forty-five."

I nodded, rose from the table, and began carrying my tray to the dirty dishes hatch. Fairley remained seated, evidently feeling the need to commune with her coffee.

Back at my computer, I retrieved the material I had saved the night before and went through it again. Despite the fact that Greer was likely connected only remotely to the case, if at all, I decided that he was worth a bit more time. It was not yet eight o'clock in Toronto, but I put a call through anyway to Jocko, a man who, it seemed, never slept.

"Do you know what time it is Rolls? If you want me to do something for you, you're on premium rate. If you don't, then—"

"No price is too high, Jocko. How hard is it to get information on a closed police investigation that never resulted in any charges?"

"Shit! Not only is it difficult, it's dangerous! Finding someone in the police who will break all the rules? Payments under the table that will draw serious attention if they're spotted? Easy for you. All you need to do is ask me and then pay. I'm the one carrying all the risk."

"Well, could you suggest someone who might do it for me?"

"Whoa! Hang on! I didn't say it was fucking impossible! What do you need?"

I explained it to him.

"When do you need it?"

"Yesterday would be good", I said.

"Yeah! You and every other fucker!" There was muttering and the sound of paper being shuffled in the background. "I can do it by tomorrow midmorning. Not earlier."

"Excellent, Jocko! I'm not in Toronto, so when you have something just email it to me."

"Okay. With my invoice." And the connection was cut abruptly.

Looking back over my notes, I realized that there were far too many possible threads that seemed to be, or at least had the potential to be, linked to this mystery. There was only one way forward here. Just drop all the ones that looked least likely, without any evaluation. Then look into the ones that remained until it became clearer whether or not there was something there.

Time check. Eight twenty-five. I had ten minutes.

Looking now for specific connections to Greer, I started on McGrath and Reynolds. Quick searches brought out nothing but short accounts of their demises. Nothing unexpected there. But it proved nothing either way.

But then I rethought the matter. *Rather than thrash around like this, let's wait to see what Jocko comes up with.* Besides, very soon it would be time to go next door and see what Phillips' cellphone would yield. Just then, my own cellphone rang. It was Fairley.

"I just had an email exchange with my cellphone guy. He got something from the phone and he's going to email it to me. Might take half an hour. Come over at nine thirty. No point in sitting around here."

"Okay", I said. "Nine thirty."

I decided to use that time to go through the material I had downloaded over the past few days and try to organize it along a timeline, and generally see whether any pattern emerged. I had forty-five minutes.

In half an hour, I had produced a set of notes in time order. Sitting back and squinting at it, I was not surprised when nothing earth-shattering leapt from the page. I was pondering all this when a ping announced the arrival of an email.

It was from Jocko. A result coming back this soon most likely meant that he had hit a snag and was looking for advice. I almost ignored his message, but then I decided to take a quick look.

He hadn't hit a snag.

In fact, he had found something.

Chapter Twenty-Two

For a long moment I had just looked at Jocko's short and cryptic message.

Rod McGrath worked for Robert Greer for five weeks as a security consultant in May and June of 2015.

Security consultant. Did that mean advising Greer on security measures? Did it mean supervising the installation of upgraded security systems? Did it mean something as simple as *bodyguard*? Physical presence to act as a deterrent?

Here was another link to McGrath, something entirely new.

Coincidence? Possibly, but that would be a last-ditch assumption.

An indication that Greer was a player in all this? Possibly.

Other? *Don't know. Need more information.*

But it was now nine thirty. Time to go to Fairley's room.

At my knock, Fairley just shouted "Come in!" She was seated at the desk, going over what was on the screen of her laptop.

She looked up as I walked toward her.

"Any luck on your end?" she asked.

I explained what I had asked Jocko to do, and what he had delivered just half an hour earlier.

"That's good", Fairley said. "Irons in the fire is good."

"What did your guy find?" I asked.

"It looks as though Phillips was fairly diligent about erasing things from his phone log. There's not much there. But we have four numbers in Toronto and two in Halifax. We traced the Halifax numbers. One is Bedford Books."

Fairley looked at me and I nodded. "That's one of the bookshops I visited here. I wonder why the numbers for Granite Books and Grafton Street Books aren't there."

"Probably deleted them already. The call to Bedford Books was just yesterday."

"What's the other Halifax number?" I asked.

"It's the number for someone called James Angus. And it's linked to an address on Lower Water Street. In fact, it's a condo in Bishop's Landing."

"You seem pretty sure about that."

"I am. My guy here checked it out."

"So who is this James Angus?"

"Nobody."

I shook my head impatiently.

"It seems to be a false name. Most likely, it's a number registered to that name but being used by somebody who's really called Angus Conway. He's well-to-do. Owns a very large condo there."

"How did you find out all this?"

"Eddie went the extra mile for me. Actually went down to the condo building. Poked around a bit."

"Eddie?"

She ignored my question.

"So then", Fairley continued, "we did a bit of checking on Conway. Seems to be a wheeler-dealer. Probably started off with family money or some sort of windfall. Put in a small fortune as an early investor when Bishop's Landing was being proposed. Came out with a large fortune. He seems to be a sort of venture capitalist now."

"James Angus and Angus Conway. And both associated with the same Halifax address. Sounds a bit sloppy."

"You're right", Fairley said. "And I'd say that it's an indication we're dealing with a novice investigator. A warning not to jump too quickly to elaborate conclusions. We're probably dealing with someone who's had some success finding oddities for collectors."

"Even so. This Angus and Conway stuff doesn't tell us much", I said somewhat plaintively.

"How about if you add in the fact that Conway is a serious history buff?"

"How did your guy find out that? At least, I'm assuming that's where this crumb came from."

"I told you. He snooped around. He's a good snooper. He could have a stranger in the next seat on an airplane talking about her miscarriage even before he knew her name."

"So this guy Conway is a history buff. There's no shortage of them."

"No. You're right. But what if I also told you that somebody called James Angus has been scooping up historical books and documents from the eighteenth century, and that he's been doing this through Bedford Books?"

"Well! Eddie again? How?"

"Yes. Eddie again. He said he just took a flyer and tried asking around."

"Not bad work at all! But this all must be costing me a fortune."

"No. Eddie and I work on a back-scratching basis. The amounts owing between us tend to ebb and flow. He happened to owe me. Now he owes me less."

"But…You must be paid somehow!"

"Yes. You pay me for my time. Eddie has his own clients. My arrangement with him just makes the time each of us invests that much more effective. Very good for repeat business."

I scratched my head.

"Where do we go from here?"

"Let's finish with these numbers. One of the Toronto numbers on Phillips' phone is your bookshop. No real surprise there. One is my cellphone. One is to somebody called Stephen Robertson. There are plenty of Stephen Robertsons in Toronto, but none of them seems to fit. At least not yet. I'm still digging on that."

"Any speculation on who Robertson *might* be?" I asked.

"Yes. I suspect he's a colleague."

"Then there's the fourth number", Fairley said, after a short interval to separate the two topics. "Looks like it might be a prepaid disposable phone. No name attached. But whoever owns it, they must have some significance for Phillips. He made six calls to it yesterday."

"Six? None before that?"

Fairley was shaking her head. "Probably quite a few, in which case Phillips just deleted them from the call log."

I leaned back to think about all this.

"So", I began, trying to work out a rationale, "this might indicate that Phillips is working for Disposable Phone and is a middle man between him and Angus Conway. Maybe Disposable Phone wants to locate the prize, whatever it is, off-load it to Conway for a nice fee, then just fade away."

Fairley was nodding. "It could be that. Or it could be that we're seeing two separate arrangements playing out. Maybe Phillips is working for Disposable Phone, but he has a deal going with Conway independently on something else. Or it might be altogether another matter."

"Like what?" I asked.

"I don't know. But just look at the variables involved here. Any number of stories could fit the evidence we have. We need more information."

I shook my head in genuine perplexity.

"I'm in your hands, Dan. What should we do next?"

"I want to talk to Eddie face to face. And then I want to have him find out as much as he can about Conway. We need to know what Conway really is up to. You seem to be making good headway on what you're doing. Why don't you just keep plugging away at it? But it won't be convenient if I'm in Halifax and you're out here at the airport. There's every likelihood that I'll need to talk to you as more information comes in, and we can't do that effectively just by cellphones. So I suggest we check out, take the shuttle into town, and find rooms in a hotel there."

We agreed on what to do, and I called and booked us two rooms in the Lord Nelson, the possibility of a much needed escape into the Public Gardens being in my mind.

It was a clear, warm day. There were few people on the shuttle, and for a short while we both just enjoyed the ride. The scenery along the stretch between Stanfield Airport and Halifax is rugged, but it's surprisingly varied even over that relatively modest stretch, and it has its own appeal.

"Tell me a bit about yourself, Dan."

It was clear that I had caught her in a completely different thought domain.

"Not that much to tell."

"Not true. Everybody has a story. But if you'd rather not..."

"No. That's fine. I don't have things to hide. Well, not *too* many."
She hesitated.

"Okay", I said. "I'll get the ball rolling. You know quite a bit about me already, just because of this PI and client business. But I can tell you a few things you probably don't know. When I entered university to study English, I was really a mass of doubt, although I didn't know it then. I had visions of an effortless climb into the intellectual stratosphere. Well. Major narcissistic shock. Despite that, I continued in my English course. I realize, in retrospect, that I enjoyed it. A lot. But on the side I toyed with the idea for quite a few months of becoming an actor. Played a number of minor amateur roles. Loved it. But I got a glimpse of a possible future from watching forty-something rep actors enjoying full-time poverty. Then I had a short period when I thought a career in science might be good. I was put off that by one of Auden's poems called 'The Average'."

"I don't know that one. But then I know very little poetry."

I recited it for Fairley.

"Pretty strong stuff!" she said.

"Fairly typical Auden, I would say. Superb poet. In my case, not a bad iconoclast either."

"Interesting", she said. "It's usually women who worry about being imposters."

"Yes", I said, trying not to be dismissive. "But Elizabeth Renzetti has interesting things to say about that."

I could tell from Fairley's expression that this might be an area to steer clear of.

"So you finished your English course and got a bachelor's degree."

"Yep. Then came the bookshop, and then the restaurant. Probably the best things that happened to me."

"You never can tell what will happen", Fairley said. "I was born in Abbotsford, struggled through a first year at UBC, dropped out, married young — disastrously — we divorced, then I joined the armed forces. And here I am."

"Those of us who are lucky probably find an appropriate slot, even if it is by chance", I said, hoping that it was an appropriate, neutral comment. "I think I did."

"A good match for your feminine side?"

I looked at Fairley in surprise. "What makes you say that?"

"Don't be offended. I just—"

"Oh no. I'm not offended. It's just that not many people say things like that. You didn't study psychology by any chance, did you?"

"No. Philosophy. Don't know why I chose that. Don't know what I was thinking. Actually, I do know. I wasn't thinking."

The landscape drifted past outside.

"When I joined the armed forces, I was completely adrift, and the routine and discipline were just what I needed. I responded well to it. It was the early days of equality for women in the forces. If you were interested and knew what to look for, the opportunities were there. But it wasn't easy. The armed forces can be a rough life. I had a lot of encouragement. And the physical skills I gained soon rid me of any feeling of helplessness or inferiority. What surprised me most was becoming aware of my own masculine side. Hard to avoid when you're surrounded mostly by men all the time. That's what made me ask that question about you."

"Have you read much about that sort of psychology?"

"You're probably light years ahead of me in reading. And I'm not sure what you mean by 'that sort of psychology'. I don't read all that much. When I do, it's usually fiction."

"Well, if you're interested at all, you might try *The Manticore*, one of Robertson Davies' best books in my view. Or the three little books by Robert Johnson, *He*, *She*, and *We*. I can send the references by email if you're interested. Here! What am I talking about? I have them all in my shop. I'll send you the books themselves."

A most intriguing smile formed on Fairley's face. "Yes. Thanks. I think I'd like that."

"You've never been married?" she asked after a short delay.

"No. Almost. Once. I think. Gwen was her name. She broke off whatever it was that we had. I took it hard. Wasn't looking at things clearly. Didn't realize the problems she had. I heard later that she was under treatment for serious mental health problems."

"Nothing since...? No. Forget that. Not something I should be asking."

"No. I don't mind at all." Then I told her about Marielle.

We were now barrelling through Dartmouth, and the Macdonald Bridge was visible ahead.

"Will two more nights in Halifax be enough?" I asked.

"I certainly hope so", Fairley said with some feeling.

"You eager to get back? Are things piling up in Toronto?"

"Oh no. I didn't mean to give that impression." She paused here, looked out the window, then turned to me wearing what looked like a scheming smile. "No. I'm becoming really curious to see what's driving all this. This is the most interesting project I've had in quite a while."

Halifax is a compact city, and before we knew it the bus had pulled up outside the Lord Nelson. Fifteen minutes later I was seated at the desk in my room and Fairley had headed off to meet Eddie.

It seems that we were both stirring the pot over the next couple of hours. It didn't take long for something to rise to the surface.

Chapter Twenty-Three

Time check. Quarter past eleven.

Ten minutes spent leafing through the many pages in my notebook that I had filled with statements, questions, and speculations gave me something to chew on. The time I had spent quickly scanning the notes that Geoffrey Fielding had attributed to Admiral Barrington left me less than convinced that this would be a good thing to pursue just at that moment. It would probably take at least two hours to read and digest, and I was concerned that it might turn out to be not relevant, even though it certainly would be interesting in its own right.

I turned instead to the file dated 1979 and sent to me by Prof. Barrington. It documented what appeared to be the results of Barrington digging around in a lot of anecdotal material. He had found some Royal Navy records concerning the movements and activities of the HMS *Achilles*. Seemed like innocuous stuff, but there was more detail than was available from other sources that I had found up to that time. He had unearthed what he clearly felt "seemed to be letters or perhaps notes" from a senior petty officer on the HMS *Achilles*. He had also generated a list of the names of men who had deserted from the Royal Navy. I began reading more closely when I realized that he had separated them out by ship. One of those ships was the HMS *Achilles*.

Did I have this information already? Maybe. The Maritime Museum. I located the notes Armstrong had dug out for me. There it was: fifteen men had deserted from the HMS *Achilles* during the time period of interest to me. But my Maritime Museum woman had found only the number of deserters. No names. It looked as though Prof. Barrington had managed to find, somehow, the names of those men. I had to talk to him, but not just now.

I looked through the names. Some of the information was incomplete. For example, Barrington had found only thirteen names. Not bad, though. Thirteen out of fifteen at a distance of more than two centuries! I reminded myself that this information likely had attached to it a lot of uncertainty. Not really having any clear idea where all this was leading, I worked my way through the list of names: B. Foresstall, Richard Galton, E. Thomas, Robert Dunn, Bailey, N. Christopher, W. Finlay, James Maitland, G. Browne, D. Wesley, Ronald Yeo, P. Norman, Wilde.

These names told me nothing. Just a bunch of people — unknowns, unfortunates, deracinated Englishmen — who had had enough of the harsh Royal Navy discipline and had decided that any alternative had to be better. There was a high probability that they all just vanished into history. How many would have been induced, ultimately, to make their way back to England? How many would have changed their names? How many found that the alternative they had chosen was not better?

I read on through Barrington's interesting screed. It was densely packed material, and I found that I had to loop back frequently to link together various pieces of the information scattered through his text. It was on one of these returns to an earlier part of his note that I confirmed one of my early suspicions: Prof. Barrington had undertaken this work initially because he was tickled by the fact that his namesake had commanded the HMS *Achilles*, that there was a Samuel Barrington line going back into history, and that this line had happened to intersect the general physical and temporal space that Prof. Barrington now inhabited. I could see the appeal.

Barrington had also unearthed material relating to the early settlements along both shores of la baie des Chaleurs. There were lists of communities, lists of family names, and he had lined up a lot of the real people with known and recognized Acadian family names. It looked as though he had spent some time on this, poking, prodding, exploring, maybe searching for links that he wanted to use in other research. But one of the names he had singled out was Jean Malaimé, and he had added an annotation: *Not a common Francophone name, as far as I can tell, and it seems to be a singleton — no other instances of that family name, or even a similar name, in any place I have looked.* And it looked as though

Barrington had been diligent. He had searched through lists of Acadian names, had tried to follow the paths of families after *Le Grand Dérangement*, and was convinced that he had actually found a few families who had trekked back from their exile in the Thirteen Colonies to re-establish themselves along la baie des Chaleurs. One family of Gaudets. One family of Trahans. One family of Boudreaus.

I moved on. Barrington had apparently tried to trace the names of deserters to Anglophone names in the area, without success. *Not too surprising*, I thought. It seems to me that the first thing a deserter would do, if he wasn't going to move far away from the point of his desertion, would be to change his name. And at that time, there was probably good reason not to travel a lot. The Royal Navy and several English armies were active in what are now Nova Scotia, New Brunswick, Prince Edward Island, and Quebec. There would be an active search for deserters. Being on the move, being visible, would have been a bad move. Finding some isolated spot and hunkering down there would have been a better course.

Barrington had also located a number of local histories. He found eleven altogether. Nine of them seemed to me to be well-intended but were really not history, just reminiscences of doubtful quality and unverifiable provenance. One, entitled *l'Histoire des Chaleurs*, looked intriguing even though it was only twenty-three pages long, but I was not able to locate a copy anywhere. The eleventh was something different: *The History of Caraquet and Pokemouche*, by William Francis Ganong.

Then I circled back to the name Barrington had singled out: Malaimé. I began some digging of my own. It took time. I located something called *The Drouhin Collection* and was astonished at its millions of individual records. I shovelled and sifted and squinted, and eventually came up with something. It was the record of a death at the age of sixty-three, in 1798, the death of someone called Jean Malaimé. Taking these two figures at face value, this information meant that whoever Jean Malaimé was, he had been born in 1735. I went into further excavations, determined to find whatever was there. There was no record of a birth that I could locate. No record of a marriage. But there was the record of a christening, of a girl, Christine Malaimé, in 1765.

No matter how diligently I searched, nothing more than that came to light.

Well. Interesting. But it proved absolutely nothing.

Suppose, however, that Jean Malaimé was a reinvented James Maitland.

The sceptic in my head went berserk: *Objection! What do you think you're doing? This is pure invention!*

Well, no, I prefer to call it a working hypothesis.

Oh! Indeed! And just how are you going to prove it?

Well ... one step at a...

Just what I thought! You're pathetic!

I thanked the sceptic for his contribution, rather sarcastically, and moved on. Although I had to admit, honestly, that the apparently arbitrary appearance of the names Maitland and Malaimé at the same time and place, while intriguing, was really just coincidence without any necessary cause or consequence.

My watch reminded me that time waits for no one, and it certainly hadn't been waiting for me over the past five hours. It was now just after four o'clock. I wondered what Fairley was doing. I wondered how Jocko was doing. I wondered what the hell I had been doing. Just then my phone buzzed.

It was Dan.

"How are you doing?" she asked.

"Thrashing around in the information wilderness. You?"

"Slow and steady. Nothing earth-shaking."

"I guess that's the life story of PIs and gold prospectors."

A snort came from the other end.

"I'm going to bash away here for another hour", I said, "then call it a day. You interested in dinner tonight?"

"Yes, sure. Where and when?"

"There are some good places not far from the Lord Nelson. I'll just keep going until you turn up."

"Suits me. I'll be back at the hotel by about five thirty. Time for a shower and a bit of happy hour?"

We signed off.

I hacked away for another hour, sat back pondering, had an interesting idea, then started closing up shop. A bit of happy hour, something to eat, and chatting with Fairley about non-work items sounded good to my battered, addled brain. There was something in the background, however, and eventually I identified it. I was impatient to see what Jocko would come up with. If his promises held as good as usual, he would likely get back to me in the morning.

There was time to duck outside and get something worthy of happy-hour expectations.

Chapter Twenty-Four

I sniffed an armpit — the left — and decided that a shower was definitely in order. Showered and changed, I had been sitting for fifteen minutes making desultory notes when my phone buzzed.

Fairley.

"The bus is just pulling up at the hotel. Give me twenty minutes. See you in your room." A grunt of acknowledgement was good enough, and when I heard the door to Fairley's neighbouring room being unlocked, I went down the hallway and filled the small ice bucket that sat next to the mini-bar.

At Fairley's knock, I rose and opened the door. She wore a colourful top I hadn't seen before, and her hair was still a little damp.

"Scotch?" I asked.

Her raised eyebrow expressed a combined note of pleasant surprise and the rhetorical question about the Pope being Catholic, and bears and forests. I poured us generous measures.

"Ice?" I asked.

"Depends on the scotch." There was somewhat more vigorous eyebrow work when she saw the name Macallan. The ice remained in its bucket.

"Not trying to lead a young thing astray, are you?"

"I doubt it would work with a woman of the world like you. But if I were, I certainly wouldn't spoil the fun by saying so. Cheers."

The clink of our glasses expressed a note of Caledonian approval, and the sound made Dan look at her glass.

"How come your room gets glasses like this?"

"It doesn't. These were obtained for the occasion. There's no way I'm sipping single malt from a shitty plastic beaker."

We sipped in silent appreciation.

"What kind of food would you like for dinner?"

Fairley looked at her scotch for a long moment, then turned to me.

"I don't know. Make a suggestion. Surprise me."

"There's a good French place not far from here."

"Not a second of hesitation, eh? Right in there like Flint."

"I aim to please myself", I said, lowering my eyes in modesty.

Fairley smiled. "You've got all the moves, haven't you? I guess that bottle of wine", and she waved at my other purchase that was crouched and waiting beside the mini-bar, "is for later? For now?"

"Well, I was thinking of drinking it on my own, but, since you insist…"

Fairley laughed.

"As I said", I resumed, swirling my scotch with practised skill, "clear-eyed woman of the world, yet here you are, in *my* room, drinking *my* scotch, casting longing glances at *my* bed. How do you know you're not a sitting duck?"

Fairley laughed again in genuine pleasure. "Great imagination, Rolls."

I drained the last of my scotch.

"*Alors. Mangeons? Sans doute tu as appris un peu de français dans les forces armées?*"[22]

"Yes. I did learn some French in the Forces. But it's gone dormant." Fairley set down her empty glass and rose. "Excellent scotch. Thanks. I'll just get a jacket."

The ten-minute walk to the restaurant was companionable. It was clear we had both decided that there would be no talk of the project over dinner. And that's what happened. I asked Fairley what it was like in the Forces. She wanted to know more about the book and restaurant business. It turned out that we both had quite a few odd and hilarious stories to tell, and I noticed several nearby diners looking our way and smiling as we both chortled our way past yet another in a series of accounts, many of them good candidates for shaggy-dog story of the year. At just after ten o'clock, I paid and we drifted back to the Lord Nelson. It was a fresh evening, and the smell of the Atlantic was in the air.

---

22 Okay. Shall we eat? You probably learned a bit of French in the Forces.

"Did you spend any time here Dan, in Halifax?"

"A bit. Not much. Maybe two weeks total."

"And where were you based?"

"Trenton."

"You enjoyed it, evidently, the whole Forces gig?"

"I loved it. It taught me who I am, who I could be."

"Strong endorsement. Does that mean you were a bit messed up going in?"

"No. Not a bit messed up. Totally fucked up. I had a good family. Really. But there were some expectations. My father doted on me. I was his princess. I never really understood how much damage that characterization did to me until I was in my midtwenties."

"Your marriage...?"

Fairley walked on in silence for a moment.

"Yes. My marriage. That was the first big casualty. I must have thought I was in Wonderland, was trying to live a fairy tale. Of course, it crashed and burned. But it could have been a lot more complicated. There might have been a child."

We walked on in silence.

"I've concluded that I'm a late developer", she said.

We began climbing the steps toward the Lord Nelson entrance.

"Glass of wine?" I asked.

"Sure, but I hope you..."

I turned to face her.

"We had some good risqué sparring earlier. We've just enjoyed an excellent meal and a discussion to match. And you've been frank with a lot of personal stuff. So, no. I won't be trying anything. We're just a PI and her client relaxing professionally and sharing a nice bottle of wine."

Fairley gave me a peculiar lopsided smile.

"Thanks."

The wine was a screw-top, one of Pete Luckett's excellent local offerings, Phone Box White. I rinsed out and dried our scotch glasses, poured, and raised my glass.

"I'm getting a feeling about this job", I said. "I hope we'll soon be in a position to work out who's behind all this shit and smoke the bugger out."

"Well! Really? Tell me all."

"It's really just that. A feeling." But I walked her through it.

"So, you think that whatever Jocko sends you tomorrow might have something important in it?"

"I certainly hope so. Otherwise this whole business is likely just to lumber on. And I want to see the end of it. Do you think anything more will come out of the Angus–Conway connection?"

Fairley sipped her wine and nodded.

"Yes, I do. But it's just a feeling, like yours."

I refilled our glasses, then sat there tapping mine, expressing a combination of pensiveness and irritation.

"What?" Fairley said.

"We'll be catching a flight back to Toronto in not much more than thirty-six hours. Is there anything more we should be doing here that we're not doing?"

"Well", Fairley began, "the only route open to me is the Angus–Conway connection, and I'll be pursuing that with Eddie's help. What about you?"

"I'm going to contact my source at the Maritime Museum. Maybe I can get more out of her, but I'm not hopeful. I'm going to try to speak to Prof. Barrington tomorrow. There might be stuff that he didn't put into his 1979 paper. Plus, that was a long time ago and he might have come across more in the meantime."

"Apart from that?"

"Apart from that, nothing. Although there's a chance that Jocko's information might change that picture."

I refilled our glasses using the last of the wine in the bottle.

"What about the unknown Toronto number that your guy Eddie got from Phillips' phone? Couldn't we just call it?"

Fairley shook her head.

"No. If he doesn't recognize the voice, he might just ditch the phone. Then any lead we might get from it would be lost."

"He might have ditched the phone already."

"Yes", Fairley said. "He might have. But we don't want to give him a reason to do that if he hasn't."

"Isn't it odd that there was no call to Phillips from that number, I mean no record on the log on Phillips' phone?"

"No. Not really. I suspect that if Disposable Phone wanted to contact Phillips, we would have used a different number. That disposable number was likely just a means for Phillips to contact him."

"So then Phillips probably wouldn't know Disposable Phone's real name?"

"That's almost certainly the case", Fairley said, nodding.

"Well, it all sounds implausibly elaborate", I said.

"Yes", Fairley said. "It does sound elaborate. And it would need to be elaborate if whatever is in play is really big. The guy in charge of all this, whether it's Disposable Phone or someone else, is being very careful."

We both sat there, looking at the ceiling and taking a sip of wine every thirty seconds or so.

Fairley finished her wine, sighed, set the glass down by the mini-bar, and smiled.

"This was a lovely evening. Thank you. I feel entirely relaxed now and I look forward to a good long sleep."

"Breakfast downstairs? Seven thirty?"

"I'll be there", Fairley said, and she slipped quietly into the hallway.

I sat there, empty glass in hand, thinking. We had just one more day here in Halifax to extract whatever might be available. I could no longer envision a clean endgame, simply because the problem now seemed to be more diffuse than I had thought just a couple of days ago.

Just two people to talk to. Angela Armstrong and Prof. Barrington. For some reason, my earlier more hopeful outlook on the future had collapsed, and in its place were two telephone calls that likely would deliver little or nothing.

Kahlùa. That was the answer. Couldn't turn in with these morose thoughts in my head. So I poured the contents of a miniature into my glass and sat there sipping and ruminating for another half-hour.

Chapter Twenty-Five

At twenty past six, my cellphone rang. I saw that it was Jocko calling me, and it took a couple of seconds for the penny to drop.

Where Jocko was in Toronto, it was only twenty past five. Something was up.

"Jocko. What's the word?"

He wasn't grumpy. He didn't even sound particularly tired.

"I've sent you a package. Check your email. I think it's important."

There was then a short delay before the really important message came through.

"I've sent my invoice as well." And that was it.

Quick shower and shave, get dressed, then half an hour to read what Jocko had sent. He had gone to a good deal of trouble for me.

I never ask Jocko how he finds out things. It's a bit like not knowing what's in the sausages you eat. You're better off. Somehow Jocko had managed to pull stuff from a police case record. But, of course, he didn't do that, and of course I didn't have the results. Within a set of unwritten rules, Jocko plays his information game. And if you don't stick to Jocko's rules, he will never work for you again.

The facts of the case looked straightforward enough.

It was a surprisingly old case, going back more than two years.

Robert Greer had been found on the floor of his study, dead. His body had been discovered by Rod McGrath, and McGrath's fingerprints were everywhere within the study and elsewhere within Greer's house, consistent with McGrath being employed by Greer. He had died from a blow to the head. There was no way to decide whether it was an accident or homicide. His head wound was quite shallow and looked not at all fatal, but it matched the corner of his desk and the corner of a table that sat elsewhere in his study. The wound also matched the corners on several solid objects within the room. It was entirely possible that Greer had suffered some sort of dizzy spell, and had fallen against one of the furniture corners. The location of the body was consistent with his head having struck any of those corners, rendering him immediately unconscious. The medical examiner believed that Greer had died quickly. There was little blood.

The police considered it equally likely, however, that someone had struck Greer using one of several objects in the room. If that had been the case, the perpetrator had wiped the offending object clean. Normally, this might have been suspicious, but if that was the way the death had occurred, whoever had wiped the object clean had been careful. Only the corners could have been wiped, since there were fingerprints elsewhere on all the candidate objects. No blood, hair, or other organic matter was found on any of these objects, indicating, but not proving, that none of those objects was involved. Somewhat unexpectedly, neither were any such traces found on any of the furniture corners against which Greer might have struck his head. So it was also possible that someone had struck Greer then carried away the weapon with him.

McGrath had been grilled intensely, but his story had never varied, and it had about the right number of loose ends that a real experience would have included. McGrath's story also had none of those features that appear too often in rehearsed accounts: every detail consistent, no small contradictions, no instances of incompleteness, no uncertainties. There were quite a few fingerprints in the study, but they had all been accounted for and none was suspiciously out of place.

The police account had also followed McGrath to his own life's end in my bookshop, but that line of inquiry terminated in the medical examiner's conclusion that McGrath had died of a sudden and almost immediately fatal heart attack. There was no evidence that any doors or windows in Greer's house had been forced, tending to rule out a smash-and-grab burglary gone wrong. According to Greer's sister, nothing appeared to be missing from his study, but she admitted to not knowing much about her brother's affairs or any valuables he might have kept there.

Also in the police files was a set of inquiries concerning the man Reynolds, whose name arose much later as the possible accomplice to McGrath at the break-in to my bookshop. This line dead-ended in the discovery of Reynolds' body, sometime after my bookshop break-in, where Reynolds had been apparently the victim of some sort of gangland execution.

Greer's sister, who had inherited the house and contents from her brother, had wasted no time. The day the police investigation concluded, she had begun liquidating practically the entire contents of the house, an operation carried out in unseemly haste. She was evidently after money. An auctioneer had sorted everything, and all but a few rare books had been shipped off to a second-hand bookshop. This estate collection of books was then broken up. A consignment had made its way to Raymond Lansdell's emporium, and it was from Raymond, some time later, that I had bought my copy of *Stylus of Death*. Some of this consignment that Raymond received, a few dozen naval-themed books, was sent on to a dealer in Halifax. It was just luck that allowed me to piece together enough material to conclude reliably that my copy of *Stylus of Death* had gone from Greer's study to Lansdell's shop to me.

The police had also examined Greer's telephone records. All but one of the numbers had been identified, and several of the people who had called Greer, or whom he had called, had been interviewed by the police. These interviews had done nothing more than fill in unimportant details.

It was the one unidentified number that had my attention. That number was the number for a disposable phone. There had been just one call from that number to Greer. That call had been made two days before Greer's body was discovered.

The police had impounded all Greer's files and had spent some time examining them. They concluded after about twenty hours of police time had been expended that these were just the innocuous records of a collector of historical artefacts. They had kept a copy of Greer's contacts, which were extensive, and a copy of the list of books and reports in Greer's library. Greer's safety deposit box had revealed nothing unexpected, and nothing that had any bearing on the case.

I closed the electronic file Jocko had sent and saved it. Then I paid Jocko's invoice, adding a hundred dollars for going above and beyond.

It was now twenty to eight, and Dan would be waiting in the restaurant.

"Sleep in?" she asked, as I eased into the seat across from her in the hotel restaurant.

"No. Important information from Jocko." And I spent ten minutes outlining what he had sent.

"Interesting", she said. "What does it mean?"

"Well, it means that I'm going to have some breakfast first, but then we have a few things to do before we leave Halifax." And I got up and walked to the buffet before she could ask or say anything further.

We ate without saying much, since I wanted to go back to my room to plan the day. Dan had pancakes again.

"They'll give you gas", I offered, pointing to her massive plate of cooked bubbly dough, but she just cast a sceptical glance at me.

Back in my room, I brought Jocko's file up on the screen of my laptop and let Dan run through it. She finished a quick read, then sat looking into space and tapping her cheek with her left index finger.

"What do you think?" Dan asked.

"I think that Greer now moves to front and centre. Let me just speculate for a moment. Greer got wind of some item of historic interest, here in Atlantic Canada, from the eighteenth century. Either he wanted it for himself, or he had a buyer. At about the same time, somebody else who knew that Greer was good at chasing things down began to suspect that Greer was onto something."

I paused there and thought for a moment.

"So I guess there are two questions that occur", I continued. "First, how did Greer get wind of whatever the find was? I think for that we might need to have a longish chat with Angus Conway. It seems that he's as well tuned-in to the local scene as anyone. Second, how did someone detect that Greer was onto something, and what happened next?"

"I guess you're assuming that this *someone* and our current Disposable Phone are one person, and that he's the kingpin here."

"Yes. And I think that's the case. There appears to be just one linked set of events stretching across the whole span of time, and in the present intrigue we've come across no links to anybody who seems to be higher in the food chain than DP."

"Okay", Dan said, looking as though she was pulling hopefully on a thread. "There are things here that don't make sense on the face of it, but might be logical given the right set of assumptions."

I said nothing, but nodded, encouraging her to continue.

"So we assume that Greer came across something that was convincing to him. How did Disposable Phone find out about it?" Here she stopped, thinking.

"Well", I said, "if Disposable Phone was in the game, then he would know people. All he would need was a whisper from the right individual—"

"For example, the collector that Greer had identified", Dan said.

"Or, another whisper from the same person, or from the same area, where Greer had got his lead. Greer would have been careful not to tell anybody just what he knew or how he came to know it. But where something valuable is involved, the one rule everyone seems to follow is *look to your own advantage*. If that means *making discrete inquiries*, then so be it."

"So what would Disposable Phone have done then?" Dan asked herself. "Answer: he would have tried to get a more direct line into Greer's nest."

"McGrath."

"Yes", I said. "McGrath. The perfect plod. Good bona fides in the area of security, clearly no genius, probably a hard worker, and because of all that, likely able to engage a reasonable level of trust."

"So McGrath finds employ with Greer, or rather employ is found for him, and he quickly makes himself useful. Probably he passes back a running account of what he sees and hears to Disposable Phone, or to a middleman."

We stopped to think about where this was going.

"And then something happens", I said.

"Something? Such as?"

"Maybe Greer comes across information that gives him a much better picture of what's out there, confirms his initial lead, maybe indicates a path by which he can snatch the prize. Greer is visibly excited by this. McGrath picks up on that. And somehow McGrath senses that *Stylus of Death* is important."

"You know that this is all just pure invention, don't you Rolls?"

"I know nothing of the sort. A comment like that implies that no option exists between waiting indefinitely in ignorance and having the full solution drop from the sky. Sure, we're inventing stuff here. But a more useful way of looking at it is to say that we're postulating, and any of these postulates can be tested. The value of a postulate is that it points toward the information that could be used to make that test. So, let's continue."

Dan nodded, looking somewhat more enthusiastic.

"Back to *Stylus of Death*. Maybe McGrath saw Greer writing the inscription in the book. Maybe McGrath noticed Greer trying to conceal the book from him. But however it happened, let's just suppose that somehow McGrath got it into his head that there was something important in that book. This would get back to Disposable Phone. DP suspects right away that McGrath had detected something, and maybe *Stylus of Death* figured in that something, or maybe it didn't. But somewhere along the line, DP decided that it was time to go to the source, try to get some information directly from Greer."

"Wouldn't that have been a bit obvious?"

"Not necessarily. I doubt that DP would have gone to Greer himself. He would have sent someone else. The approach almost certainly wouldn't have been ham-fisted, a demand that Greer tell all. They would have had some sort of oblique approach. But something went wrong. Maybe they underestimated Greer. Maybe the man DP sent let something slip that he shouldn't have. Maybe Greer tried an outflanking operation, tried to throw them off the scent, tried to convince them that the thing of interest was purely academic, of no real-world value. Things got out of hand. Suddenly, Greer was on the floor. DP's man might have panicked, but probably didn't. He likely looked for the copy of *Stylus of Death*, but by then Greer had put it somewhere safe."

"And after that", Dan continued, "it was too late. The police were all over the place. Then the sister liquidated everything. The books were disposed of. That copy of *Stylus of Death* was then in some unknown location, beyond DP's reach."

"So then the whole thing went quiet", I said.

"And it just sat there for two years?"

"Well, DP was probably probing away behind the scenes, trying to pick up the trail again."

"Ah!" Dan said. "And then somehow they managed to trace Greer's copy of *Stylus of Death* to you via Lansdell. So they planned the break-in at your bookshop. And then McGrath had his infarct, and the wheels came off the thing once more."

Dan was obviously mulling something over.

"What is it?" I asked.

"Two things. Why did Greer write that inscription in his copy of *Stylus of Death*? And what was it that was so important? What outranked the value of whatever artefact they were after?"

"Both good questions", I said. "And I've thought about them until my head hurts. I think I know the answer to the first one. And I think I might also know the answer to the second."

Dan's eagerness to know was written all over her face.

"Take the first question. I suspect that Greer came across something he thought was very important, and that something was a hint that appeared somewhere in Prof. Barrington's 1979 paper. From the police file, we know that Greer had hundreds of notebooks, he was interested in dozens of things at the same time. But this prize was something different, and however it was that Greer came across this information, he felt the need to record it. Not necessarily in an obviously titled notebook. Maybe he wrote it in the first place that came to hand. More likely, he wrote it in a book that could have no conceivable link to the prize or anything connected to it, but a place that would have meaning only for him."

Dan was nodding.

"Now the second question. Suppose it is DP who's implicated in Greer's death. If that became known generally, it would be a big deal for him. One would expect him to do almost anything to keep it secret. At the same time, he doesn't want to let go of the prize. And, if one thinks about it, given Greer's mysterious death, the risk that something could come to light showing it was homicide was always present. So the risk of DP's involvement becoming known is also there and won't ever go away. So, why not go for the prize, maybe as some sort of consolation?"

"It all sounds plausible", Fairley said, her face reflecting serious mental activity. "But how do we go about confirming any of it?"

"Well, look at it from DP's point of view. McGrath is out of the picture. Whatever he knew about DP and Greer is safe now. What DP won't know is just what it was that McGrath actually did know."

"But that doesn't matter, does it?" Dan asked. "McGrath's dead."

"Yes, he's dead. But while he was alive, what did he tell and to whom?"

"You mean Reynolds?"

"Yes. I mean Reynolds. If it was DP who had Reynolds killed, why would he do that?"

"Ah! Yes! I see. DP wouldn't know how much Reynolds might have learned from McGrath. And he wouldn't know whether Reynolds might choose to act on something he learned from McGrath. Maybe he would go into business for himself. Maybe he would blow the whistle on DP. Maybe he would try to do both."

"Exactly", I said. "Reynolds represented an unknown risk. So DP had to have him silenced."

"But does that get us anywhere?" Dan asked.

"It might. Here's the thing. DP knows that I'm involved. Initially it was just because I had that copy of *Stylus of Death*. Then it turned out that just having the book wasn't enough. So the book came back to me. The hope seemed to be that I would reveal some piece of information that would allow DP to crack the puzzle. But then one Dan Fairley comes onto the scene, and hires Phillips. Either DP knew Phillips independently, or he somehow got wind of the fact that his watchers were being watched, asked around, learned about Phillips' role, and bought Phillips off. Then Phillips goes on the rocks in Halifax, and now DP must be fairly sure that things definitely are not trending his way. In addition, DP must be aware now that you and I know more about him than would make him comfortable. He probably would love to know just how much we do know, but there would be too great a risk for him in trying to learn that."

"And...?" Dan prompted, when I seemed to run dry.

"I think we need to give DP a jolt."

"But we don't know who he is, or where he is."

"No. Not with certainty. But we can suspect that he must be keeping pretty close tabs on us. Or at least on me."

"But how does that help us?"

"It doesn't give us any direct and definitive answers. That's true. But we can rattle the cage of someone who has a very good idea where I am most of the time."

"But we don't know anybody like that."

I smiled at Dan.

"I do."

Chapter Twenty-Six

We decided that we should tag team for our last day of interviewing people in Halifax. By six o'clock — about nine hours from now — we would be finished here. I could foresee a couple of hours consolidating notes, impressions, and observations and formulating any remaining questions. We would be able to deal with small items by email, but today was the last day for those all-important face-to-face conversations.

The Maritime Museum and Bishop's Landing are reasonably close to each other, and calls to Armstrong and Conway allowed us to book an hour with each of them. I sent an email to Prof. Barrington asking if he had time available in the afternoon.

As it had appeared to me on my previous visit, Angela Armstrong's office gave the impression of someone who was industrious, interested in her work, and busy. I introduced Dan, Armstrong found seats for us, and we went through the usual pleasantries.

"I want to thank you once again, Ms. Armstrong, for your help earlier. Very useful and greatly appreciated. I hope not to take up much of your time today, but there are a few items that I wanted to make sure I have clear."

"Please", Armstrong began, "it's a pleasure to have someone from outside our usual circle take an interest in these things. And I'm still looking forward to learning more details, when you're ready to share them. But what can I do for you now?"

"We're wrapping up our stay here in Nova Scotia, all too soon I might add. Later today we'll be visiting a few other people, and I wanted to find out if you know Angus Conway?"

Armstrong's facial expression relaxed in a way that was entirely natural.

"Yes. I know Angus. I suspect everyone here in Halifax who has a serious interest in history knows him. Why do you ask?"

"Well, I won't need to bother him on the matter of desertions from the Royal Navy. The information you provided me on that is more than adequate. But I do want to ask him about aspects of the Battle of the Restigouche. Do you happen to know whether that's in his area of interest?"

"I've heard him speak of it from time to time", Armstrong said, "but really only in a general sense. I'm not aware that he's into the details of it."

I nodded.

"I wanted to ask you a few questions about that as well." Armstrong nodded, indicating that I should go ahead.

"The Acadians began moving back into l'Acadie not long after that battle. I presume that area of resettlement included the shores of la baie des Chaleurs. But I'm aware that many Acadians never left the area. Camp d'Espérance. So, I have two questions. Of those who remained in hiding in New Brunswick and PEI, how many made their way eventually to la baie des Chaleurs? I'm aware in a general sense of the work of Ronnie-Gilles LeBlanc, but is there much in the way of definitive history for la baie des Chaleurs area for, say, the ten years following 1760? That's the first question.

"The second question is more speculative. To what extent is the novel by Antonine Maillet based on solid history? I'm aware of the story of Captain Broussard, but are there other accounts that could be properly called history that relate to the resettlement of Acadians who made their way back from the Thirteen Colonies?"

Armstrong didn't answer right away but looked at me wearing an expression that I can describe only as *assessing*.

"I assume that you're referring to her book *Pélagie-la-Charrette*."

"Yes. Of course. I've tended to start thinking in shorthand."

"No. That's fine. I do have to say, however, that I find you uncommonly well informed for someone who doesn't come from this area." Armstrong stopped there, evidently expecting me to come out with some sort of explanation.

"Well, I have no personal links to l'Acadie. It's just an area of interest. And it continues to grow apparently of its own accord."

"I can answer your questions, but I'm reluctant to do so just off the top of my head. I think they deserve answers that have some depth and completeness. So, if you agree, what I would like to do is to prepare a written answer. I want to take the time to check that everything I'm saying is correct and referenced. It will take me a week or so. Is that okay?"

"It's much more that I expected. Thank you."

Armstrong was nodding again. A silence grew while she made a few notes. She then put down her pencil and focussed on me.

"At the risk of seeming persistent, I do want to express my interest in the larger story behind what you've been exploring here in Nova Scotia. I know you've said that you will let me know. I just want to register my interest."

"Noted", I said. "Letting you know that bigger picture is the least I can do. But I'm afraid it will need to wait a little longer. I hope that's all right."

It was clear that the meeting was drawing to a close, and we drifted into the more general remarks that signal preparing to leave. Armstrong shook our hands, and we left.

"So. What do you think?" I asked Dan once we were outside.

"She's straight-up. It sounds as though the Dark Side hasn't got to her. But why did you ask all those questions about the Acadians?"

"Partly just plain ordinary interest. But also to see whether she would pick up on anything. You know, perhaps the Dark Side has been trolling, and maybe one of Armstrong's responses might have revealed that. I didn't see anything though. Did you?"

"No. There was nothing like that."

In the lobby of the Maritime Museum I stopped and jotted half a page of notes from the interview with Armstrong.

"Okay", I said. "Onward to Conway."

The concierge at Bishop's Landing confirmed with Conway that we were expected, buzzed us in, and gave us directions to Conway's unit. When Conway opened the door, everything about him spoke of the comfort of generous financial independence, a life full of interesting projects, and a man happy with his situation. On entering his condo, I realized that *unit* was a demeaning descriptor. The main room seemed to extend forever, an impression made even more dramatic by the view through large windows out over Halifax Harbour.

Dan and I introduced ourselves and said we were grateful that Conway had the time to see us. Conway smiled, and it was a genuine rather than a self-satisfied smile.

"Please. Come through", he said, leading the way.

We were led into an "office" that would have shamed the main living space of most condos and were offered seats at a large oval table. Conway's desk sat in one corner, and it was covered in high but neat piles of books, reports, and folders.

"How can I help you?" Conway asked as he took a seat across the table from us. He was completely relaxed.

"We'll try to keep this short, Mr. Conway. It's evident that you're busy", waving my hand in the general direction of his desk as I said this.

Conway laughed engagingly.

"I'm an amateur historian, as you probably know. My big problem is that I'm interested in almost everything, and apart from a love of walking around Halifax I have no other commitments to temper those interests. I'm assuming that it is also some historical interest that brings you here."

"Yes. I'm interested in the Battle of the Restigouche, and particularly the history associated with the ships the *Machault* and the HMS *Achilles*. But I'm also interested in details of the movements of the Acadians in the area of la baie des Chaleurs during the time 1755 to 1765. Roughly."

Conway smiled and looked from one to the other of us.

"And, just out of curiosity, is this an interest you're pursuing together?"

"Not really", Dan said. "I'm helping Mr. Royce with some of the logistical arrangements."

"Most interesting. Does either of you have connections to Atlantic Canada? At least, judging by your accent, you're not from the East Coast."

"No", I said, looking at Dan. "We're both from Toronto."

Conway nodded, probably having already guessed as much.

"It isn't all that common for people from Central Canada to have any knowledge of, or interest in, the Acadians."

"So I've gathered. My interest in the Acadians is just something I acquired at some point, but it's a long-standing interest. A fascination, you might say. I really can't explain it beyond that."

"Ahh! The best driver for an interest in history, in my view. But how can I help you specifically?"

"Well, I want to ask you whether you became involved in locating artefacts of historical interest from that period."

"Only from the historical perspective. I'm not an archaeologist. Not a digger or a procurer. I have done historical research for people, but I don't like the thought of our patrimony being plundered."

As he said this, Conway's expression darkened. It very much looked as though his interest was almost exclusively intellectual.

After a short delay, I decided to take the chance.

"Have you ever done work on aspects of the Seven Years War for anyone in Toronto, and I mean specifically for the times and places we've just been considering."

Conway raised an eyebrow, and I was aware of a change in expression on Dan's part.

"That's a very direct question, Mr. Royce. I will say in general that, yes, I have done some work for people in Toronto, but I won't be telling you who they are. And before we go any further, I will ask that you give some explanation for asking that question."

There was no hint of aggression in Conway's manner. But it was clear that we were on ground that left him feeling uncomfortable, and that unless my explanation was satisfactory he would extend a gentlemanly invitation for us to leave.

I smiled in a way that I hoped looked confident and comfortable. Dan looked at me in a way that appeared to show her support, but really was intended to reassure Conway.

"By all means. I operate a used bookshop in Toronto. Some weeks ago, I found a body in my shop, and something had been stolen. This has led to a series of revelations, all of which point to, but don't prove, a private interest in some aspect of the Seven Years War. It seems to be an interest that involves me somehow. I don't know how or why. That's what has brought me to Atlantic Canada. I'm not a treasure hunter. And I'm not on any vengeance mission. But I do want to find out what it was that brought my bookshop and me into whatever this intrigue is, if indeed there is an intrigue."

Conway had relaxed, He looked as though I had given him more information than he was expecting.

"I can tell you with confidence, Mr. Royce, that I have no interests or involvement in anything that resembles what you describe."

Conway paused here for a moment.

"Do you have any other questions of me, Mr. Royce?"

"No. But I do thank you for your time. And I would hope that we might come into contact again on purely historical ground."

"I have a question, if I may", Dan interjected.

"Please!" Conway said, making an encouraging gesture.

"How large is the community of serious historical researchers in Atlantic Canada, including the academics?"

"Very interesting", Conway said, eyeing Dan closely. "This is only the second time I've been asked that question." And then he listed about a dozen names. "So, not a large group, as you can see."

Conway looked from one to the other of us, to see if more questions would arise, then he rose, smiling.

"I would welcome further contacts with you, Mr. Royce, and with you, Ms. Fairley. Please take copies of my business card. And give me some advance warning the next time you plan to come to Halifax."

Business cards were exchanged, Conway accompanied us to the door of his waterfront mansion, we shook hands again, then Dan and I left.

Outside, we walked south along the waterfront, toward the sales and tasting rooms of the Garrison Seaport brewery.

"Thoughts?" I asked Dan.

"I got only good feelings. He's a man fully in control of his world, beholden to nobody for anything. I got the impression he was trying to hide nothing."

"My sense exactly", I said. "But I fully expect that even now he's checking us out thoroughly."

"Fine with me", Dan said.

It was a pleasant day, and we found seats outside at the Garrison tasting room and ordered a glass of Nut Brown Ale for me, and Irish Red (somewhat surprisingly) for Dan.

"What did you expect?" she asked, a sardonic expression on her face. "Think I'd go out with the guys and order a chardonnay, or a spritzer with a twist?"

There was no answer to that, and once again I was annoyed at my readable face, so I just looked toward the statue of Samuel Cunard.

"Do you think we're any further ahead?" Dan asked at length.

"Well, we seem to have ruled some things out. But I'm still not entirely sure what our next step is. I just know where it has to be."

"Oh?"

"Yes. Whatever our next step is, it will be in Toronto."

We sipped our beer, enjoyed the sun, tried to counteract the downer feeling that came with the realization that tomorrow we'd catch a plane home.

Dan set her beer down quickly and pulled her cellphone from her jeans.

"Fairley."

Her face relaxed into a smile of recognition.

"Hi, Eddie. What's up?" As she said this she switched to speaker.

"—just cracked it about fifteen minutes ago. Can you come over?"

"Is it important?" Dan asked.

"Hard for me to say. I think so."

"We'll be right there, Eddie. Give us twenty minutes."

Chapter Twenty-Seven

The cab ride to Eddie's place took surprisingly little time. I was still used to the distances and the congestion of Toronto. In just over ten minutes, the cab stopped in front of an attractive small detached house just off Jubilee Road. I paid, we climbed out, and the cabbie drove off.

I looked at Dan. She read my thinking in uncanny accuracy.

"I've known Eddie only when we were in the Forces. Don't know his background, apart from the fact that he comes from Halifax. He was always meticulous, and I can only suppose that he carried that over into civilian life. I agree. It's a nice neighbourhood."

Dan's knock was answered by a man who had a dark complexion and black hair, was about half a head taller that Dan, but a guy who looked looked alert, tough, sinewy. He smiled.

"Hello, Dan. Good to see you again."

Dan dispensed with the formalities by putting her arms around his neck and they exchanged an embrace. Dan introduced me, and Eddie nodded and smiled faintly, but it was clear that Dan had already filled him in on my background. He led us into his house, and I noticed that he displayed the same grace and economy of movement that had impressed me about Dan.

Eddie's house was sparsely furnished, but what was there was exquisite, all heritage-style furniture. Solid maple dining table and matching chairs. A gorgeous pine buffet. Two small end tables that looked to be ash. Despite the colourful curtains on the windows and the attractive watercolour paintings of various views around Halifax, it was clear to me that there was no woman of the house.

"What did you find, Eddie?" Dan asked, as we approached a beautiful large butternut desk on which lay an assortment of electronic equipment and a partly disassembled cellphone.

"Gather round. I'll show you."

"Did you have much trouble breaking the password?" Dan asked.

"Some. It was a lot more secure than average."

"Serious security?"

"No. I'd say just extra care."

"There are three messages", Eddie said. "The first two seem to be just arrangements for meeting times or something similar. The third one seems to be the important one. I'll play that one first. But you should listen to them all. I've downloaded them onto solid-state storage. Here's the third message."

Eddie pressed a button on one of the pieces of equipment arranged neatly on the desk. There was background noise. Someone, a man, began speaking as though trying to keep his voice down but at the same time making it clear that he was annoyed.

"This is my third attempt to reach you. Where are you? Get back to me as soon as you pick this up. No excuses."

"That's it", Eddie said.

"Not much to go on", Dan commented, and I thought there was doubt and some disappointment in her voice.

"Could you play it once more?" I asked.

Eddie nodded and played it again.

I said nothing for a moment. They were both looking at me.

"Once more please, Eddie."

I closed my eyes. Eddie played it again. In the background someone had laughed briefly. There was a general rumble of conversation. No music. But also, just briefly, there was a squeaking sound, like a shopping cart wheel that needed oil.

"What is it, Rolls?" Dan asked.

"I'm not sure. Is it possible to put that recording onto a flash drive that I could take away with me?"

Eddie hesitated. "Sure. I can do that."

"I'll pay you."

"No. That's fine."

"Well, you've taken a lot of trouble here, Eddie. I know about the arrangement you and Dan have. But I'd feel better if you accepted something." I pulled out my wallet and handed Eddie two fifties.

"This is way too much."

"Not at all", I said. "You've spent hours on this. And the man's voice recorded here is a solid clue. Please. If only for me to show my gratitude."

"Okay. Thanks."

He took the two fifties and offered his hand. Some of the man's steel was in evidence.

"Can I offer you a cup of coffee? I've just made some."

Dan and I both nodded, and we all moved into Eddie's kitchen. The maple cabinets were stunning, and they gave the entire room a restful golden glow. Eddie poured coffee into three mugs that bore a JTF2 emblem, and the motto *Facta Non Verba*.

Dan was taken by the mugs straightaway.

"Great mugs Eddie. Where did you get them?"

"Had them made."

"Do you have any spares? I'd love a set of these."

"Yes. I had to order forty-eight of them. I've got about thirty left. In the basement."

"Can I buy four of them from you?"

"I'll give you four, Dan."

"No you won't. I'll pay for them. How much."

"Okay. For you the price will—"

"No, Eddie. I'll pay what they cost you. How much?"

"Twelve per mug."

"I'll get them", and Eddie headed down to his basement, returning a few minutes later with four mugs, a handful of bubble wrap, and a plastic bag.

We sat at Eddie's breakfast table and sipped our coffee. Dan and Eddie exchanged glances that spoke of a past full of things to remember.

"Do you use Dan often, Rolls?"

The question caught me off guard.

"Sorry. I was daydreaming. No. This is the first job Dan has done for me. I've never had to use a PI before. The used bookshop business is generally as dull as ditchwater."

We sipped our coffee, and I looked around Eddie's kitchen once more.

"Your place here is very nice", I said.

"Thanks. It belonged to my parents. Dad died a couple of years ago, and Mom is in a care home. She doesn't recognize anybody now."

I mumbled something that I hoped was appropriate.

"Are you still teaching?" Dan asked.

"Yes." He recognized my puzzled look.

"I studied chemistry in university. Here at Dal. Joined the Forces after I graduated. Looking for excitement. Certainly got some of that. But then I left JTF2 four years ago. Same reason as Dan, I expect. I'd been in uniform long enough."

"So, you do PI work in your spare time?"

"Not really. I'm a supply teacher. I actually get quite a bit of teaching work. But when I'm not teaching, I'm investigating."

We talked some more. Dan and I accepted the offer of a second cup of coffee. Eventually, we made getting-ready-to-leave noises. Eddie handed me a flash drive, called us a cab, and walked us to his front door where he and Dan chatted until the cab drove up.

"Look after yourself, Eddie", Dan said, giving him another big-sister hug. "Talk to you again soon."

On the way back to the Lord Nelson, I looked at Dan.

"Yes. He's recovering. He was by far the most competent and most reliable guy in our unit. But something happened to him in the Forces. I don't know what. He came out completely screwed-up. I keep in close contact with him. Believe me, he looks a lot better than he did a year ago."

I thought back to Dan's description of the business arrangement they had, work ebbing and flowing between them. It didn't make sense. Toronto is more than ten times the size of Greater Halifax, and a lot richer. It seemed pretty obvious to me that Dan had found some acceptable way to help keep Eddie in work.

"What did you hear on the recording from Phillips' cellphone?"

"I'm not sure", I said. "I want to find someone who can pull up some of the background noise."

"Do you think there's something you recognize?"

"I don't know. I'm just not sure."

But I had a suspicion. I just needed either to confirm or discount it.

Chapter Twenty-Eight

Back at the hotel, I let us into my room, and Dan and I planned the rest of the day. I said I wanted to try to get in touch with Prof. Barrington.

"What do you want to do?" I asked.

"I want to think a bit."

I was fairly sure where that was coming from.

"How about a walk later on?"

"Yes", Dan said, with enthusiasm. "That would be good."

"And dinner tonight? Do you like fish?"

"Yes."

"Have you ever eaten at McKelvie's?"

"No."

"Let's do that then. Seven o'clock?"

A nod.

"Good. I'll make the booking right now."

The directory that was in its naff burgundy mock leather folder in the room had McKelvie's number in it, and I called.

"Okay", I said. "Done."

Dan looked somewhat deflated.

"Are you okay?"

"Yes", she said, without conviction. "You can probably guess that I worry about Eddie."

"Did you two have a … *thing* … back then…?"

"What?" Dan replied, evidently distracted. "Oh, no. Nothing like that."

She stared into space for a moment, fiddling with the top button on her shirt.

"When you're as tightly knit a unit as we were, by training, by continuous proximity, by an incredible level of readiness that we had to maintain all the time, by the need to rely on each other without fail, and by the knowledge that a mission and its dangers could always be just around the corner, well, you grow very close to each other, in a way that's unknown to most civilians."

She continued fiddling with the button.

"Do you miss it?"

"I miss the camaraderie. That was something I had never known before, could not have imagined. But without all the rest of it that kind of camaraderie just wouldn't be there. Leaving JTF2 was one of those things I just made a judgment about. At some point, enough was enough. It's not that I was sick of it, or anything like that. It was a little corner of my emotional universe that was complete."

"But Eddie stayed on."

"Yes", Dan said. I guess she could see a question in my face. "We didn't talk about why I decided to leave. And Eddie didn't say…Well. Eddie never did say much."

"And when did Eddie leave?"

"I don't know exactly. I think about eighteen months after I did. Obviously we've been in contact. But we don't talk about our JTF2 time at all now."

Dan paused here, looking at some point in space.

"I think he might have left getting out just that little bit too late."

I looked at Dan, seeing this side of her more clearly now.

"And now? Isn't life rather flat for you, by comparison?"

"For a few months I thought so. Wondered if I had made a dreadful mistake. But then I realized that my supercharged life in JTF2 wasn't the real thing, it was a sort of hyperreality. I adjusted slowly."

Dan shook her head, as though shedding the remnants of a bad dream.

"I'll be in my room", she said.

"When I've finished talking to Barrington, I can tap on your door, if you like. Go for a walk."

"Yes. Just come around whenever you've finished."

And she went off to her own room.

Barrington wasn't in. He had been called away to deal with some sort of academic crisis. From the secretary's description, I didn't quite understand what that involved. Sounded about as implausible as a dermatological emergency. She said that Barrington wouldn't be back until midmorning two days hence. I explained about my flight back to Toronto, and suggested that I would set up an appointment with Barrington for a telephone conversation.

"Prof. Barrington did send something on to you in Toronto. I'm not sure what it was. He said you would likely be interested but that it wasn't anything urgent or immediately important."

I thanked her and hung up.

So, the elusive Barrington evades me again.

Somehow, I felt the immediate future weighing heavily. Maybe it was the imminence of the flight home the next day. Maybe it was just the realization of leaving Atlantic Canada and the things that had become so fascinating for me down here. Or maybe it was just the thought of going back and being yoked once again to the same old problem. Whatever it was, I was hit by the sudden realization that I needed to extricate myself from all this shit.

Dragging out my notebook, I went through the jottings I had made over the past week. It wasn't a pointless exercise, either, since it became obvious, in an in-your-face conscious way not fully recognized until then, that quite a few new things had impacted my view of my situation during my time here Down East. Had I integrated all that into a current picture?

The answer was straightforward and blunt.

No.

Turning to a fresh page in my notebook, I was about to start making a list, when the image of an amused Marielle came to mind.

"Your lists would drive me crazy", she had said more than once. "Throw away that pen and just be intuitive for a change."

Easy for her to say. And I was envious at how she could just close her eyes, turn her mental world upside down and inside out, and come up with a new approach. Just like that.

"It's not that easy", I had said to her on several occasions.

"That's because you haven't practised."

"Practise? At being intuitive? That makes no sense."

"Really? So when you read a new literary text, and come up with some interpretation, is that something that was already there, on the shelf? Or did you construct it somehow, deep down inside?"

At some level, I had always pooh-poohed talk of intuition, tossing it onto the same rubbish heap as reflexology, crystal healing, aromatherapy, Ouija boards, auras, tea leaves, chicken entrails, crystal balls, and tarot cards. But I had to admit there were aspects of the world that weren't rectilinear, weren't accessible by calculation alone. My own continuing attraction to the indirect appeal presented by literature was something that I had managed, over the years, just to take for granted somehow. It looked a bit different now, my own present circumstance, the roundabout path from *Stylus of Death* and the P body to the subtleties of Atlantic Canadian history; it was certainly requiring a flexible approach at every turn.

"Just let yourself go", I remembered Marielle saying.

I looked again at my notes, read them all through once.

Can't hurt, I said to myself, even though I remained unconvinced.

I rose from the desk, lay down on the bed, and *let myself go*. Right away, images came and went. Making serious efforts to maintain a mental hands-off position, I just let the images come and go. I do have to say that I was surprised. I was a sort of observer, not really a participant, and I observed the whole thing initially with interest, but increasingly in a detached way.

I glanced at my watch.

Two thirty.

Shit! I'd been asleep for almost an hour and a half.

Dan answered the door a few seconds after my knock.

"I was beginning to think that you might have gone out without me. Did you have a sleep?"

I mumbled something.

"Ready to go?" she asked.

More mumbling.

We set off.

The Halifax Public Gardens is a true national gem, but is surprisingly unknown to most people who haven't spent any time in Halifax. The oldest Victorian garden in North America, it retains its original character, and is one of the centres of life in Halifax. At sixteen acres, it doesn't sound large, but when Dan and I entered through the elaborate gates, it took less than two minutes to be convinced we were in another world.

"This is gorgeous", Dan said in something just a bit more than a whisper.

I said nothing. Just nodded. But it reminded me suddenly, vividly, of an essay I had written at university, something that brought me high praise in private from my lecturer. Seems it had hit a personal chord with her. It hadn't been the usual sort of essay, in that it was written in the first person, from the perspective of someone, gender undefined, who was visiting or recalling literary gardens. Even as I remembered it all these years later, the intimacy I had felt in writing it came back to me.

"What are you thinking about?" She asked.

I realized that this was the second time Dan had posed her question.

I smiled and told her about the essay.

"What was in it? I mean, what bits of literature did you use?"

"Well, there was Andrew Marvell's poem "The Garden", there was Tennyson's poem "Maud", I made a reference to Ovid, *The Secret Garden* was there, *The Wind in the Willows* was there. I made a reference to the garden in *The Importance of Being Earnest*. And there were a half dozen others."

"Do you still have it?"

"Have what?"

"The essay."

"Oh! I doubt it."

"Too bad."

"Why?"

"I'd like to read it. My ignorance of literature is almost total."

"Well, stick with me kid."

We walked on.

"Has anyone ever written a novel involving these gardens?" Dan asked.

"That's a good question. I'm not aware of one."

We looked at the small metal plaques identifying trees and shrubs. We stopped at several of the items of statuary. Dan spent some time contemplating the Boer War Memorial Fountain. Most of the time we just strolled slowly in silence. There were many people around, something I recalled from a previous visit several years earlier.

A surreptitious glance at my watch told me it was approaching four o'clock.

"How about a quick glass of beer, then back to the hotel for a nap before we strike out for dinner?"

"Sounds like a plan", Dan said, with some enthusiasm. "Is there a pub nearby?"

"As it happens…"

"Yes", she said, through a wry smile. "I might have known."

We strolled back to the gardens' entrance, then moved more briskly to the Rockbottom Brewpub, where we did justice to some lovely beer.

"Ready to go?" I asked. "I'm just about set now for a nap, a shower, and then a good meal."

And that's what happened. Refreshed after a sleep and a shower, I was well prepared for McKelvie's. It didn't disappoint.

Over dinner, we talked about Dan's early years in British Columbia, about my early years in Peterborough, about our families, about teenage loves, about early hopes and later realities. The wine flowed; our conversation bubbled; the evening flew. We laughed a lot, and before we knew it, we were outside again, watching traffic flow past on Lower Water Street, looking up Prince Street, and captivated by the ragged sheets of mist drifting in from the harbour. It was a reasonable walk back to the Lord Nelson, and Halifax was at its atmospheric best. Crinolines of light flared from the streetlamps down through the mist. The hard edges of buildings were fuzzy and mellowed, and somewhere above us the Citadel lay shrouded as it and its previous incarnations had done on many similar evenings for more than two centuries. Foghorns and warning lights spoke to each other around the harbour, and Halifax was a place of mystery.

It took us about twenty-five minutes to reach the Lord Nelson.

"A drink to cap the evening?" I asked.

"Sure. But just a small one. I don't want to make it a late night."

In the hotel bar we ordered two Spanish coffees and sipped them contentedly.

"So, back home tomorrow", Dan said.

"Looking forward to it?"

"A bit yes, a bit no."

The atmosphere of the bar was subdued and clubby. Quiet. Unhurried. Refined. Dark wood and leather. Just what I wanted.

"You looking forward to getting back?", Dan asked.

"Yes. I think so. The bookshop and restaurant are important parts of my life. I miss them. But then…" I let the sentence drift into some indeterminate place.

"Things will probably look different when we're back there. Could we get together and have some sort of debriefing, see what's changed, see where we go next with this problem?"

"Yes. We should do that", Dan said.

We drained our coffees. It was time now to hit the sack. Tomorrow morning the flight home would redirect our lives.

Once again, our rooms were next to each other.

"I've really enjoyed today. Good night, Dan. Sleep well. Breakfast at eight downstairs?"

"Yes."

Our doors closed.

Chapter Twenty-Nine

It was two thirty.

I had been asleep for a bit less than five hours. But now I was wide awake and sitting on the edge of my bed. *Why*, I wondered.

The first thought that surfaced surprised me. From the moment I discovered the body in my bookshop, this lark had cost me more than forty-eight hundred dollars and counting, not including Dan's fees. How did I know that? The answer came back almost immediately. A list of expenses scrolled through my mind, and I could see every entry. Flights, hotels, car rental, rides in Yvon's plane, books, meals, incidental expenses — somehow, while I wasn't looking, my subconscious had constructed this list.

Who's going to refund all this to you, Rolls?

This wasn't a question I had asked consciously. It had come from somewhere *way down there*. And it wasn't an idle question. Wherever the question had come from, that *somewhere* was expecting an answer.

Then there was the message Eddie had pulled from Phillips' cellphone. It was likely that the message had been sent by the man in charge. And probably the last thing that person would expect was for his message to fall into my hands, or indeed into any hands other than Phillips'. Phillips should have erased it. As a priority.

But he hadn't. Why?

You need to get this guy off your back, Rolls. Permanently.

Another message from *way down there*?

I was no longer sure just how many people were talking here, but it was time I took charge of the conversation.

So.

Fact. There were two deaths I knew of that likely were murders: the execution of Reynolds and the probable bludgeoning of Greer.

Reynolds' death was one of those rough-justice affairs that took place on the dark side. The police had made efforts to determine what had happened, but those efforts hadn't been enough.

Fact. Greer's death, on the other hand, was a case where the dark side had spilled over into the nominally civilized world. This had remained an open case, and there was always the risk for the perpetrator that some crucial piece of evidence would come to light, and he would then be on the run.

Fact. There was a financially valuable prize out there for the finding. Circumstances had brought a particular copy of *Stylus of Death* into the picture, and that had led to the break-in to my bookshop and the pilfering of that copy. But...

Fact. A heart attack at just the wrong time had thrown a serious wrench into the works. What should have remained a secret for weeks, months, or even forever became common knowledge immediately. It was this that had put Reynolds in the crosshairs of suspicion. And then Reynolds, and the risk he posed, ceased to exist.

Where did this leave me?

This question was mine, my own conscious query. And I was surprised, stunned in fact, to discover that *way down there* had an answer. Or at least a possible answer and a path forward.

Marielle's approach appeared to have worked, but only when I was asleep. From here on in, it would be a clear and unapologetic Apollonian approach. Rising from the bed, I found my notebook, sat at the desk, and began jotting. After three pages of jottings that required forty-five minutes of alternating jotting and thinking, I had an approach. I read it all over three times, made a few annotations and clarifications, and then added the major next step: talk to Dan.

It was now quarter past four. There was no hope of getting back to sleep. I flicked through the television channels, found nothing of interest, then realized that the room had access to satellite radio. I found a good classical music channel, pulled on pants and shirt, and lay back on the bed. Some great selections from Mozart, Beethoven, Schubert, and Mendelssohn saw off the next two hours in style. At six thirty I hit the shower, then had a slow and luxurious shave. By seven thirty, I was in clean clothes, had packed, had confirmed that the most recent jottings in my notebook weren't pointless nocturnal ravings, and was making my way down to breakfast.

I was surprised to see Dan already there. It appeared she hadn't been there long, since all she had managed to get was a glass of orange juice.

"Couldn't sleep", she said, by way of rationale.

"Me neither. But I made some real headway. I mean, I think I now know how to get out of this mess."

"Which mess?" Dan asked. Her tone was flat. It sounded as though she had also spent some time thinking but had come up against just a solid wall.

"Come on. Let's get something to eat."

I've noticed that when I'm away from home, and in a good mood, I can always enjoy a generous breakfast. And under those circumstances, my breakfast of choice almost always is great clouds of scrambled eggs and four or five sausages. Not all scrambled eggs — and certainly not all sausages — are made equal. But to my great delight, I found that morning in the Lord Nelson restaurant that the scrambled eggs and sausages were first among equals. I carried my tower of cholesterol back to our table and tucked in. Dan was nibbling at a meagre portion of toast and peach jam.

"I don't know how you can do that", she said, glancing at my plate then looking away quickly.

"When it comes to breakfast, I do know myself. This", and I waved my fork over the partially excavated meal, "is a sign."

"Yeah. Probably a sign that you'll infarct on the plane."

"Not at all", I assured her. "When we finish here and catch the express bus to the airport, I want to walk you through what I've been thinking. I know you'll be critical, and that's exactly what I want. I think I have a way forward."

Dan smiled. First smile of the morning.

"The scrambled eggs actually look pretty good", she said.

"Go ahead. Try some."

She did, and a look of appreciation crossed her face. Without saying anything, she rose from the table, and a couple of minutes later put a small plate of scrambled egg down, sat, and began eating. Her forksful became increasingly less modest.

We finished. Dan's colour was now equal unto the day. Staff at the restaurant took away our empty plates unobtrusively.

I looked at Dan. Her pale-green shirt and cream jeans made her look terrific.

She smiled.

"Still the same old transparent Rolls, eh? Well, you know what? I've got used to it. And I like it."

I stumbled over that one and tacked what was probably the twentieth note to my mental corkboard. The note reminded me, as had all the others before it, that it was bad business to be so readable. *And what are you going to do about it, you bumbling oaf?*

Dan looked at me, and I realized that she was still probably reading me like a book.

"Will you be able to locate Phillips?" I asked.

This sudden change to my facial tea leaves caught her on the hop.

"Phillips? Why?"

"Will you be able to find him? Do you think he'll be back in Toronto?"

"Well, yes. I expect he'll be back in Toronto. But he'll be keeping his head low. He really didn't distinguish himself in Halifax. His boss won't be impressed."

"Will you be able to find him?"

"Yes ... but ... why?"

"He's now a central part of my plan."

"Your plan?" Dan was pretty much completely in the dark, but it was evident from her face that clear and sharp and decisive mental processes were in high gear.

"Here's where my thinking got me last night. And this is what I have in mind."

And I spent the next twenty minutes walking through the puzzle as I now saw it, and how I hoped to unravel it.

Dan's first-rate mind was very quickly on top of everything.

I looked at my watch.

"We need to catch the airport express in about half an hour, so we should collect our things and check out."

Fifteen minutes later, we had checked out, paid, and the driver was loading our cases onto the bus in front of the hotel. Dan looked as though she was about to board the bus, but then stopped, walked back toward the hotel, and looked across to the Public Gardens. I came up beside her.

"We'll be back", I said.

She looked at me and nodded, and we climbed aboard.

Our trip to the airport was quiet. The day was beautiful. As we passed stretches of water, sunlight winked from them. Cloud shadows chased each other over the landscape. It felt almost as though the ancient terrain, drenched in light, was smiling and asking me to stay. The coniferous forest along Highway 102 rolled past. And then we arrived at Stanfield Airport.

"Do you know who Stanfield was?" Dan asked, apparently out of idle curiosity.

"Yes, I do. Came from Nova Scotia, and was premier there at one point. He was also head of the Progressive Conservative Party. One of the original good guys."

"Where do you learn all this stuff?"

"I own a bookshop. Remember?"

We checked in, went through security, and soon we were accelerating down the runway. I had an unaccountable pang of sadness when the wheels left the ground.

I'll be back, I promised myself silently.

Dan and I had seats next to one another, but we spoke little on the way back to Toronto. I asked if we could get together after she had a chance to take her stuff home and do whatever needed doing immediately.

"You mean today?"

"Yes. We need a planning session."

Dan nodded.

"One thing more", I said. I pulled out of my pocket the flash drive Eddie had given me. "Do you know anyone who can enhance this, separate some of this things I'm hearing on it? And is it at all possible that we might get all that sometime this afternoon?"

"I'll try", Dan said.

At Pearson Airport, we separated, agreeing to get together two hours later at my place.

It took a bit more than two hours, but at one thirty I opened the door to my place and let Dan in. She looked around with interest, and I realized that this was her first time here.

"Come through", I said, and led the way.

"Anything to drink?" I asked. "Coffee?"

She shook her head.

When we were seated, I began.

"We need to have a chat with Phillips. What do you think is the best way to arrange that?"

"Well", Dan said. "He'll need to be convinced. He and I are not exactly fast friends at the moment."

"A meeting on neutral ground? I'm hoping we can convince him that it's very much in his own interest. He must know that the guy who hired him doesn't like loose ends. So he must know that he might just vanish without trace at any point."

We talked about how we could set up something. We needed someplace very public, but where we could speak privately.

"A large hotel lobby would do. What about the InterContinental, on Bloor?"

"Yes", Dan said, nodding slowly. "It would need to be some place he could leave at any time."

"Would he be afraid of being followed, I mean, that someone else might follow him once he left us?" I asked.

"He must have some concern about that right now. The guy who hired him could already be tailing him, waiting for just the right opportunity. He must be aware of that."

"Can you set something up with him?"

"Yes. I'll need to locate him first, but that shouldn't be too difficult. When do you think we should organize a meet?"

"Today, if possible."

"Okay", Dan said, and pulled out her cellphone. After six calls, she got a number where her correspondent *thought* she would be able to contact Phillips.

"All right", Dan said. "Let's see what we can do."

She dialled the number she had been given. It was answered on the ninth ring.

"Hello?"

"Hello, Roger. Please don't hang up. This is Dan Fairley. I'd like to talk to you."

"We have nothing to talk about."

"I think we do, Roger. I think I know what your situation is. I'm pretty sure that someone is not at all happy at what happened in Halifax. I think I have a lifeline for you."

"I don't know what you're talking about."

"Oh, I think you do, Roger, but instead of this sparring, can we just get together and have you hear what I've got to say?"

No response.

"I'm going to suggest an open public place, the lobby of the InterContinental on Bloor."

"Why should I agree to that?"

"We both know that you're probably in a bind, Roger. But there is a way out. All we need to do is get together. For half an hour."

There was a long delay here.

"When?"

"Late this afternoon. Say, six o'clock."

"Will you be alone?"

"Yes."

Another long pause.

"I'll be there at six o'clock, Roger."

Another long pause. I was beginning to fear he wasn't going to take the bait.

"Okay. Make sure you're there at six. Alone."

Then the line went dead.

"Will he show?" I asked.

"Yes. I think so."

We agreed on how we would work it. Dan would be there well before six, waiting on her own in a conspicuous place. I could picture the large lobby of the InterContinental, and I knew where I could park unseen. We worked through a script. We had several hours to think of possible outcomes, possible snags, and to work out what we would do in each case.

I can get to the InterContinental in about fifteen minutes from my place, but we agreed that I should be at the hotel at least an hour before Dan, and that she should arrive via St. George subway station. To anybody watching, she might have approached on the subway from any of four directions.

"Did you get the flash drive to your contact?"

"Yes. She took a quick look at it and said she could clean it up fairly quickly. I asked her if we could do that early afternoon today. The answer was *yes*."

We caught a cab right away. In ten minutes, we were in a tiny basement lab jammed with equipment. Dan introduced me to Tina.

"I assumed that you were interested in hearing background noise more clearly, so I cleaned up five bits of background and enhanced them. Here they are."

She pressed some buttons, and immediately there were swishing sounds, and a muffled voice in the background.

"I think that's outside traffic noise. Probably not what you're looking for."

"No", I said, shaking my head.

More buttons. This time there was a regular squeaking sound that lasted for about ten seconds then stopped.

"Okay. Good", I said.

"Next", Tina said, and we heard a clear peal of laughter.

"Good", I said. "Next."

The next one was a sort of swooping sound that repeated just once.

There were two more after that, the first one a steady hum, and the second a clicking sound.

"That's excellent, Tina. How do you want to be paid — cash or invoice?"

"Cash. A hundred and twenty will cover it."

I pulled out my wallet, counted off six twenties, and passed them over to her. I was genuinely pleased. I smiled, we shook hands, then Dan and I left. We were able to grab a cab almost immediately. On the way back to my place, I told Dan what it was that we had heard.

We sat in my smallish living room and talked about things in general. Dan had a number of questions, and as usual they were evidence of a mind right on the ball.

At quarter past four, I left to make my way to the hotel to get set up for the meet with Phillips. Dan would follow about half an hour later.

We were on, but it was now all in the hands of the gods.

Chapter Thirty

I knew the layout of the InterContinental fairly well, but I looked it over carefully anyway, wanting to make no false steps. There were several possible locations giving good sightlines, but it would depend on where Dan chose to sit, and that would depend on where people were sitting when she arrived. There were just six or eight people scattered around the lobby, and I guessed that Dan would choose the couch at the back and to the left, nicely slotted into a corner, no mirrors behind it, no large armchairs anywhere near, and a large, low table in front. Once two people had seated themselves there, it wasn't easy to see how anyone could park within hearing. To keep an eye on that location, I chose a spot on the mezzanine. But I identified three other spots in the lobby that Dan might pick, and three corresponding locations on the mezzanine, each one having a good view of one of those lobby locations. There was nothing to do now but wait.

At twenty-five to six, Dan walked in. She looked around as if expecting to see someone, then chose the couch at the back and to the left, the spot I had considered best. She picked up a magazine that was lying on the low table and began flipping through it. Every five or six minutes, she looked up, scanned the lobby, then returned to her magazine.

Six o'clock came and went. Dan remained completely relaxed, showed no anxiety or agitation. From where I sat I could see about two-thirds of the lobby, and I scanned it regularly.

Nothing.

Six fifteen came and went. We continued our waiting game. Dan must have read the entire magazine three times by now, but at regular intervals she gave the impression of encountering an ad or an article that caught her interest.

Six thirty.

We had agreed that if Phillips hadn't shown up by seven thirty, we'd call it a bust and leave.

Six forty-five.

Keep cool, I told myself. Phillips had a lot riding on this. He would play it how he saw it.

Six fifty.

I saw Dan look up. There was recognition on her face but no smile. She raised her right hand. Following her gaze, I traced across the lobby, but whoever she saw was out of my range. But then someone was walking toward her. Not quickly. Not slowly. Not flicking glances around. Looking exactly as would someone who was meeting another person they knew only slightly and wanted to make sure of the identification.

It had to be Phillips. He was wearing a long-sleeved shirt, and his right arm was oddly rigid.

The cast. Or at least the immobilization device.

Dan rose. I could see them speaking. Phillips moved around behind the low table and sat about three feet from Dan. They both sat, their backs to the wall so they could see anyone who might approach long before they came anywhere near.

They began speaking. Almost immediately, Phillips started to shake his head. Dan turned on the seat so she was half facing him. Her hand motions were smooth and downbeat. She was reassuring Phillips about something.

They talked for about ten minutes. Phillips stopped shaking his head, and it seemed he was doing most of the listening and Dan was doing most of the talking.

They broke off for a moment and just sat there eyeing one another.

Then Phillips pointed to his chest. His actions became slightly more vigorous. Dan spoke to him again and nodded. Once again they sat looking at one another. Then Dan ran her left hand through her hair. That was the signal.

It took me less than three minutes.

Phillips looked up in alarm at my approach, but I stopped about three metres away from him.

"You said you would come alone!" he said accusingly to Dan.

"This isn't an ambush", I said. "Far from it. I'm sure you recognize me, and the thing I want to say to you right away is that I have nothing against you. In fact, I would like your help. And in exchange for that I will help you. Dan has already explained some of this. But you need to hear it from me. May I sit down?"

Phillips looked from one to the other of us, and apparently he came to a decision, waving his hand at a large chair about five metres away. I walked over to the chair, dragged it across, and sat facing them on the opposite side of the low table.

"Let me tell you in straightforward terms what I want", I began. "First of all, I'm seriously out of pocket, and I think the person to blame is the guy who hired you. He's after something, he seems to think that I know where that something is, and I don't trust him not to turn violent. So, I want my expenses back. Not from you. From him. Second, I want him out of my hair for good. With your help, I think I can achieve both those objectives. So let me explain in some more detail please."

I then walked him through the history, since it was quite certain that he had not been told the whole picture. I told him about the body in my bookshop, the missing book and its mysterious return, and the surveillance on me. I told him about retaining Dan, and said that I had done my own digging, but without going into details.

"The police were involved in the body in my bookshop, inevitably, and I'm not sure where their inquiries have got to." I told him about McGrath being the body, and what the coroner's service had discovered. I also told him about Reynolds and the collector Greer.

"I think these events are all related. I don't know how you figure in all this."

Phillips bristled right away.

"Look, I haven't been involved in anything other than surveillance."

"I know that you were watching my hotel in Halifax. I don't know why, and I don't know what you might have done if things had worked out in any other way than they did."

"My job was just to report."

"Okay, let's just say that I believe you for the time being. Can we talk about how we can help each other?"

"I doubt that I can help you. And I can see no way you can help me."

I looked at him for a moment.

"All right, Mr. Phillips. I'll come clean. I have information. That information relates to what was clearly an execution, and what looks like a murder. The simplest course open to me is just to turn over to the police everything I have and let things take their course. If someone gets hurt — someone like you, for example — well, that would be too bad. But I think that would rid me of my problem."

Phillips looked at Dan, who remained completely po-faced, and then looked back at me. I detected a hint of worry in his face.

"On the other hand, if you tell me everything you know, then I think I can isolate the guy who hired you."

"You don't know who he is", Phillips said, a bit too confidently.

"That's where you're wrong, Mr. Phillips. I do know who he is. I know quite a bit about him. But forget him. We're talking about you now. And you need to decide. Are you going to work with me, or do I just leave you to your fate?"

I sat there looking directly at him, hoping he would conclude that I had finished talking, that it was the end of the line.

"Can I think about it?" he said after a pause of almost a minute.

"Yes. But you need to do all your thinking here. When you leave here, either you're working with me, or you're on your own."

He was now beyond trying to show a bluff of confidence. He rubbed his hands up and down on his jeans. He looked from me to Dan and back again. He looked at the floor. He looked at the ceiling.

"If I decide to—"

"No ifs, Mr. Phillips. I want a clear and unambiguous decision."

"Okay", he said quietly after another thirty-second delay.

"Okay what?"

"Okay. I'll work with you."

"Good", I said, and smiled mirthlessly.

"What happens next?"

"One of us will contact you tomorrow morning. We'll make all the arrangements then. So, please give us your contact details, telephone and email." Saying this, I drew a notebook and pen from my pocket and waited, pen poised.

He gave me the details.

"Good. Would you prefer to leave first, or would you rather that we leave first?"

"I'll leave first."

He hesitated, looked from one to the other of us again, seeming to wonder just what had happened. Then he nodded once, rose, and walked out into Bloor Street.

Chapter Thirty-One

My reception in M&B Resto was as hearty as ever. Michelle was there emitting her distinctive laugh, the lugubrious Hinge was working magic in the kitchen, and in general the place seemed to be running on its own form of adrenaline.

I did all the usual things I do after being away for a while. I spent time with everyone. They really are a genuine bunch, and, let's face it, provide a fair proportion of my bread and butter. I had a monologue with Hinge. Everything was all right there. I squinted at the wine cellar. That was an urgent job for tomorrow. Apart from a few items, food stocks seemed to be good.

"Hey, Rolls! When will you make bread again?"

"Just as soon as I can, Rory."

A cheer went up, and I took a hammy bow.

Ginger seemed to have a lot to say, so I spent a good ten minutes with her. The others spent their time, variously, either chattering like sparrows in a shrub or doing the lone artist thing, gazing into a swirling conceptual haze from which they hoped to pluck their masterpiece. For some of them, it was important to be talking. For others, it was important to be listening. For the rest, it was enough for them just to be around.

There remained the one important piece of business. The Colonel was sitting in his usual booth, reading what looked like a journal article. I walked over and sat across from him.

"Hello, Rolls. To what do I owe this?"

"We haven't spoken for a while. I know that you're different from most of the regulars here, but I thought it was time for a chat."

He closed the paper and looked at me, a pleasant expression on his face. The volume of noise in the room was adequate for what I had in mind.

"I want to talk about Robert Greer, Tim Reynolds, and Roger Phillips."

If I hadn't been looking closely for it, I would have missed the slight flicker in his expression. But the set of his face didn't change apart from a gradual but masterly shift from pleasant expectation to one of unexpected puzzlement.

He smiled and shook his head slightly.

"Sorry, Rolls. You're three steps ahead of me. You need to slow down a bit for an old guy."

I kept my expression as neutral as possible.

"I don't want to joust with you, Stanley. Oh yes. I know that you are Stanley Rattray, that you were a colonel in the Canadian Forces, but your discharge was labelled "with disgrace for misconduct", and that your background since then has been, let's say, checkered. I've spent a lot of time and effort lately trying to work out who's been dogging me. I've recently proved to myself that it's been you."

He managed a very convincing chuckle.

"Where are you getting all this stuff, Rolls?", his smile fading gradually as he spoke.

I lifted my laptop from its temporary spot between my feet, opened it on the table between us, and pressed a few keys. The voice came over clearly.

"This is my third attempt to reach you. Where are you? Get back to me as soon as you pick this up. No excuses."

I was watching him closely. The flicker passed over his features again.

"And what is that, Rolls?" The amused note was gone from his voice now.

"That's you, Stanley. I got that from a message recorded on Roger Phillips' cellphone."

"Roger Phillips? Who's Roger Phillips? I know nobody of that name."

"That's odd, Stanley, because he certainly knows you. And that's because you hired him."

Rattray's expression was harder now.

"You know, Rolls, I think you must be losing it."

"You can stop the tap dancing, Stanley."

I pressed three more keys on my laptop. The double swishing sound played. I turned and followed Michelle's passage down the restaurant and into the kitchen. She entered, and as the swing door closed behind her, it made exactly the same double swish.

I looked again at Rattray, more sternly this time, and pressed three more keys. About six seconds of repeated cyclic squeaking came from the laptop's speakers.

"That's the sound of the wheels on the dumb waiter over there."

I looked down at the keyboard and pressed three more keys. The sound of a woman's infectious descending tone laughter was heard.

"Recognize that? That's Michelle." And as if on cue, Michelle's laugh rippled across the room.

"Those three sound clips were all parts of the background noise in your recorded message to Phillips. You sent that message from this room, probably from this booth. But you never expected me, or anyone other than Phillips, to hear it."

"So, what do you think you've got here, Rolls. Huh?" Rattray's expression was now hard and cold.

"I know exactly what I've got here. It's part of a case against you. This, along with the evidence from one of Reynolds' old partners in crime, and the proof that it was you who hired McGrath to be a live-in spy in Greer's place, all that will be quite enough for the police to take a close second look at you and everything you've been doing for the past few years."

Rattray just sat there looking at me. His expression was unreadable.

"Of course", I began, "there is another way."

The flicker appeared again.

Rattray said nothing, but inclined his head slightly, an indication that I should continue. I looked at him for a long moment.

"You can repay me my out-of-pocket expenses — the costs I incurred trying to figure out who was dogging my every step and what risk I was at. That's a total of just over sixteen thousand dollars. Of course, it's all itemized."

"You enjoy being a blackmailer?"

"Call it what you will, but I have no interest in playing games with you any longer. You have a choice. Reimburse me or I send the entire package to the police."

"Well. I think you're bluffing. But just for the sake of entertainment, let's suppose that you're not. If I agree to your alternative, then I get all the material you claim to have."

"No. You don't. That stays with me."

"That's no deal."

"It's the only one on the table."

His expression had now gone flat, emotionless. He sat there, looking at something.

"I'll give you my answer in the morning."

"You'll give me your answer now, then we'll go to the bank and you'll make out a cheque for this amount and have it certified", and, saying that, I laid on the table next to my laptop an envelope. He looked at it, opened it, and drew out my typescript sheet, showing tabulated expenses, and receipts stapled to it.

Rattray gave a nasty, humourless laugh.

"This is all amateur stuff, Rolls. Sixteen thousand dollars. What's that?"

"Don't be obtuse. The sixteen thousand dollars just means that I won't be out of pocket. But what I really want is for you to be out of my life, permanently. You're not so stupid that you can't see that. I know that you're after a prize. You can pursue that all you want, as long as it doesn't involve me. If any of your activities crosses my path ever again, the package I have goes to the police."

We sat looking at each other.

"What's your answer Stanley? The clock's run out."

He picked up my sheet of tabulated expenses and looked at it again dismissively.

"I won't give you a certified cheque. I'll give you the cash now." Saying that, he reached into his jacket pocket, pulled out a thick billfold, counted out a hundred and sixty hundred-dollar notes, slipped them into the envelope, and slid it across the table to me. I have to admit that I was amazed. And as he was counting, Dan's comment came to mind again. "A planner who looked after everything, in great detail. Somebody who left no possibility unassessed." Why was he carrying all that money? Was there some contingency that he…? Shit! Had I just been lucky…?

"Are we done?"

"Almost", I said. "I just want to remind you that if anything happens to me that can be attributed to you, even remotely, I've left with a lawyer my package of material and detailed instructions on what he is to do. Are you completely clear on that?"

"Crystal."

"Good. I suggest that you leave now. I fully expect that I'll never see or hear from you again."

Rattray nodded once, expressionlessly, rose, and left M&B Resto.

I pulled out my cellphone. My hand was shaking as I found the contact.

"Hello, Dan?"

"Yes. It's me. What happened?"

"He agreed. He gave me cash. And now he's gone."

"Good. Can we meet?"

"Yes. Give me a chance to stop at the bank. My place? Half an hour?"

"See you there."

All the way to the bank, and from the bank to my place, I had a surreal feeling. It seemed as though there was somebody, or something, following me, shadowing me. It was hard to believe that the whole thing was finished, but then I reflected that I had become involved in something very dangerous, had no idea just how dangerous, that I had got in way over my head, and only time would tell whether it really was finished. In fact, I realized that I was deathly afraid. I reached my place, and Dan was waiting at the door, ready with a somewhat unexpected, but greatly appreciated, long hug.

We went inside and sat. We talked for a while. Dan excused herself at one point and walked into the next room to take a telephone call — obviously business. Then we talked some more.

"What will you do now?" she asked.

"I want to get my life back to normal. Almost the first thing is to go back to the bookshop, get the feel of book dust on my hands, collect a few paper cuts, all the normal shit."

Dan smiled.

"Almost the first thing?" she asked.

I walked over to my small liquor cabinet and pulled out a bottle of brandy and two glasses, inclining my head at Dan.

"Yes, please."

I poured us two generous measures.

We clinked glasses lightly and took a sip.

"Mmmm!" Dan looked at the bottle, then at me.

"Metaxa. Is that Marielle?"

I must have blushed. Dan broke into a full belly laugh.

"Yes … it is … ahh…Do you … mind?"

"No. Not at all." And then she laughed again.

***

Life came back to normal much more quickly that I had expected. There was a story to be passed around the Resto to explain the absence of The Colonel.

The picture I painted for everyone who asked, and almost everyone *did* ask, was, "He explained to me that he had some offshore business to attend to". Nobody seemed to question that, but then The Colonel had not really mixed with the Resto crowd. Only I knew the reason why that was so.

Inexplicably, the body in my bookshop remained a topic of active interest for weeks. It certainly didn't hurt business, and my competitors seemed to be dying to know just what I was doing to keep all this ghoulish interest alive. Well, fuck 'em. The customers want what the customers want.

It took me some time to extract an invoice from Fairley Investigations, and when it did come I argued with her that it was too thin. She added seventy-five dollars to it, but wouldn't budge beyond that. I paid, with thanks. She got busy with other things, and although I tried to speak to her every second day or so, I had the feeling that we were drifting apart. That feeling made me uncomfortable and anxious.

A little less than three weeks after my final chat with Rattray, Dan called me.

"How about lunch?" she asked.

"Sure", I said.

"Any preference where?" she asked.

"The Isherwood, for old times' sake", I said without hesitation. At just after eleven that day, I struck out for the pub.

Fully expecting to be there first, I was surprised to see Dan sitting at a corner table on the back patio when I arrived. I strode toward her and could feel the smile on my face. She rose and gave me a hug. She wasn't smiling.

What's this? I thought, apprehensively.

"I just heard this morning", she said, sounding a bit too businesslike.

"Heard what?"

"They found Rattray last night. Shot dead."

I didn't say anything in response, just looked at Dan uncomprehendingly.

"Phillips turned himself in to the police this morning. Said he had done it."

"Phillips?" I exclaimed. "Do you believe that?"

"Yes. I do. I think he feared for his life."

We talked about it for a few minutes. It wasn't a great way to begin a lunch, and even though it was significant news, it isn't my habit to celebrate death.

Dan took turns rolling the beer mat back and forth on the table and fiddling with the top button on her shirt. It looked as though she had just been with or soon would be with a client, because she was wearing a stunning blue pantsuit, a very pale blue, high-quality blouse, and a pin on her lapel that pulled all the colour and style together.

She smiled briefly, and I kicked myself for being, yet again, a transparent bumpkin.

"In almost every way, this isn't a good thing", Dan said. "But it does lift a cloud from your life."

I had to agree. Nodded. Said nothing.

We ordered, ate, drank modestly, and the lunch was a success ultimately.

I paid, and we left together. Outside on the street, we chatted vaguely about our work.

"Will you be home tonight?" Dan asked.

"Yes. Why?"

"Oh. Thought I might give you a call."

"In that case, why don't you come for dinner. Six o'clock?"

"I'd love that." Her smile was back.

Back at the Resto, I worked hard for a couple of hours. At three o'clock, I dropped by the bookshop, and was delighted to see that Rice had everything in hand. I left almost immediately, picked up what I needed to make a beef goulash for the evening meal, then went home and got the meal preparations started.

Dan turned up at ten past six, dressed down in jeans, sneakers, and a denim shirt. I let her precede me down the hall toward the kitchen, but before we were halfway there, she turned, put her arms around my neck, and gave me a passionate kiss.

"Wow!" I said softly.

She beamed a huge smile, then resumed her way toward the kitchen.

"What can I do?" she asked over her shoulder.

"Well … er … I think … no, everything's ready."

"Glass of wine?" she asked, heading for my wine cooler.

We stood in the kitchen, the rich aroma of beef goulash filling the air, water ready to be heated for pasta, the elements of a salad sitting to one side. I sipped my Sauvignon Blanc, wondering to myself what had just happened. Dan sipped her wine, looking as though she knew.

As we sat down to dinner, we changed gears. Conversation flowed. We laughed. The meal was very good, but that was according to Dan.

"Maybe I should go into the restaurant business", I muttered.

I carried our plates to the sink.

"What's for dessert?" Dan asked.

"Tarte au sucre."

"Ah! Did you make it?"

"No. It fell off the back of a truck."

I served our dessert. We lingered over it.

"Digestif?" I asked.

"No thanks", Dan said.

The look on her face registered.

"In that case", I said, "come with me."

Chapter Thirty-Two

The bedclothes were warm. Muffled traffic noise gave that odd sensation of being enfolded within a living, friendly city. Our dinner, now several hours in the past, rested easily, and the flavours of the voluptuous gamay that had washed it down continued to tickle my mouth and tongue. I lay on my back, looking at nothing at all on the ceiling.

I turned my head toward Dan, our eyes met, and we smiled at each other conspiratorially. It was now mid-September, almost five months since the discovery of the body in my bookshop, since I hired Dan, and lying next to her in bed was just about the last thing on my mind back then. Well, almost the last thing.

"What do your friends know about me?" Dan asked.

"Oh, not much. Only that you wear your combat boots to bed in case of a terrorist attack."

She shifted her hips in the bed, giving me a vigorous butt from one side. Even that was enough, and a tent began forming almost immediately.

"Now look what you've done!"

"Relax", she said. "There's a little known jiu-jitsu move that can handle situations like this."

I was about to offer a reply that I thought would hobble this discussion, but just then my cellphone on the night table buzzed.

Dan gave me a who-can-that-be look, then said "No, don't answer it" as I reached for the phone.

"Not really an option. It's likely for you, and if nobody answers, the anti-terrorist squad will come crashing through the door in thirty seconds.

"Rolls here."

"Salut, Roule! C'est moi. Yvon."[23]

"Who's that?" Dan whispered, but not softly enough.

"Comment ça? Qui ça, Roule? Est-ce que je te dérange?"[24]

"Non. Pas du tout. Tu ne me déranges pas."[25]

Dan looked at me and mouthed a question I didn't catch.

It was clear to Yvon, from what was developing into a stop-and-go conversation with him, that there was indeed a *someone else* present.

"Ahh ... Roule ... Je m'excuse! Je m'excuse!"[26]

"Yvon! C'est formidable! Tu me rappelles Émile Zola! Je m'excuse! Je m'excuse!"[27]

Despite himself, Yvon began to chuckle, and once his sense of humour was primed, he broke into a full, uproarious, infectious laugh. I recalled that laugh from our time in his airplane. I smiled. I couldn't help it. Then I started to laugh. And it was only a matter of seconds before all three of us were laughing.

He could likely guess that we were in bed, and I decided it was only fair, in the spirit of the Gallic frankness I knew he would understand right away, to put him in the picture.

"Yvon. Je te présente Dan."[28]

His laughing stopped abruptly, as though he had been unplugged.

"Mais ça veut dire Daniella" [29], I clarified.

Immediately someone plugged him in again, and they also turned up the juice. *"Tu me tues, Roule!"*[30] Yvon managed to say just before he broke out laughing once more, now almost out of control.

"Est-ce qu'elle..."[31], Yvon began but could get no further, his laughter had taken over again.

---

23 "Hey Rolls! It's me. Yvon."
24 "What? Who's that, Rolls? Am I disturbing you?"
25 "No. Not at all. You're not disturbing me."
26 "Ahh ... Rolls ... My apologies! My apologies!"
27 "Yvon! That's terrific! It reminds me of Emile Zola. J'accuse! J'accuse!"
28 "Yvon. Let me introduce Dan."
29 "But I mean to say Daniella."
30 "You kill me, Rolls!"
31 "Is she...?"

"Non. Elle ne porte pas ses rangers."[32]

Rangers? Dan mouthed at me.

Combat boots, I mouthed back.

An elbow dug me in the ribs. There was more laughter. I asked him why he had called, and Yvon managed to utter a few words, broken up by outbursts of laughter.

"Ta visite prochaine ... ici ... à la baie des Chaleurs ... mais ... je vais te rappeler... demain...Tu me tues Roule!"[33]

I eventually said goodbye to Yvon and his infectious laughter, hung up, and had my attention diverted almost right away by the need to do something about the tent. Some time later, Dan murmured and snuggled up.

"What if I take another job working for you?" she asked.

"I guess I'll need to lock my bedroom door."

"Why? Everything that happens in here is covered by investigator–client confidentiality."

"Maybe. But I wouldn't want your views, your ability to make judgments, your independence, to be compromised."

"Hmmm!" Dan said, a smile in her voice, and then she looked at me through a smile that was only partially scrutable. "I'm afraid that I was compromised almost as soon as I met you."

"Well, in that case, I guess I'll need to line up another PI. Just in case."

"A male PI, of course."

"Well now, I don't know. I don't have much experience with men in bed. I think I work better with women."

A grip was taken on some sensitive body parts, as a warning. Then we just lay there a while, thinking about things. How it was that our present had developed. What the future might look like.

We talked for quite a while. About odd aspects of the case, and Dan said how she was still surprised at the way something that started out as what seemed a routine job to detect surveillance became so complex. And so interesting. And having such an outcome...Her hand found mine.

---

32 "No. She's not wearing her rangers."

33 "On your next visit ... here ... to la baie des Chaleurs ... but ... I'll call you back... tomorrow... You kill me Rolls!"

She also asked about strange little odds and ends.

"Especially that page in the book where the letters o had been filled in everywhere. What was that?"

"No idea", I said. "Must have been just doodling."

But mostly we talked about the future.

Our view of the future was a common one. Sure, we had different interests, but there were many things in common. We asked ourselves whether this body-in-a-bookshop project, this unusual recent experience, our involvement at an unaccustomed and hectic level, had painted a pseudo-reality for us, something exciting but just short-term, and as a result something illusory rather than solid and sustainable. We looked at it from many angles, but regardless of the perspective it seemed to both of us that, in many areas, we were of one mind.

Having explored that notion, we then spent some more time being of one body.

I had no idea what time it was. Didn't care. Tomorrow was too far away to worry about. But *tomorrow* is always implacable, and it would roll around sooner rather than later. That signalled the need to bend my mind to more practical considerations, or at least to thoughts of a vertical sort. I tried to line up at least some of the big pieces for the coming days.

Then I turned my head to look at Dan. She wore a pensive look. I had a sudden feeling. And then, somehow, I knew it was sitting there in the background, somewhere. It took a long time to surface, but eventually the question was in the air.

"What would Marielle think about all this?" Dan asked.

Although somewhat oblique, it was a serious question, and I took my time answering, since the answer could point only in one direction to be acceptable.

"She would be proud of me. And I'm pretty sure of that."

I didn't expect a follow-up question, and there wasn't one. But after a few minutes, Dan asked about something altogether different.

"What about la baie des Chaleurs?"

"What about it?"

"You're going back there. Aren't you?"

"I hope that it's you and me who are going back."

"But I sense that it means something to you."

There was a long delay while I thought about this.

"You know that I'm big on history."

A nod.

"I've always had some sort of sympathy for the Acadians, a kind of visceral connection. When I met Yvon down there, he and I clicked right away. It seemed to me that there was history in his bones, in his blood. And he was just bursting to show me things, to explain things. I have to go back, Dan. I'm not at all sure what it is. But I need to spend time there. I need to have Yvon show me things, explain things. And I really would like you to be there with me."

I could sense Dan looking at me, waiting to see if I had something more to say.

"I think there's something more to it than that though."

"Yes", I said. "There is. The big thing is the history. But the history is just a thread. The driver for all that is the Acadians themselves past and present, their tenacity, their love for l'Acadie, and now their resurgence, the literature they're producing ... there's just something electric about the place."

"But...?" Dan prompted, after I had lain silent for too long.

"It's more an *and* than a *but*. The Seven Years War swept across Atlantic Canada. A lot of people died. There was great displacement and hardship. But the way we learn all this is ridiculous. In the history books, it was all just a sideshow to the bigger drama involving England and France. England won, and we eventually became the Dominion of Canada. And that's where things stopped. For us, the great European show was over. Everything that happened here after that was just inconsequential local shuffling. Well, when you look at it on the ground, when you see the physical markers of history, when you get to know some of the resurgence taking place there, today, it's ... well, it's almost like getting to know the Acadians all over again. And not just the Acadians."

After another longish pause, Dan stirred beside me.

"There's something else, isn't there?"

Her intuition was impressive.

"Yes. But let me say right away that I'm not trying to keep things from you. I'm working all this out in my own head as I go."

Dan waited for me to continue.

"I'm convinced that there is a prize down there. And now that Rattray is out of the picture, there's one less threat involved."

"But there must be others who would be just as determined as Rattray was."

"Yes. Probably. But I have to think that I've got the jump on them. I came clean with Armstrong at the Maritime Museum, and I know that I have a friend there, someone who has great respect for the region's historical patrimony. We've had our long chat with Angus Conway, and I think we can be pretty sure he's a straight arrow. He's not short of cash, so I think he would be happy to join in just for the thrill of the hunt."

"And the prize itself...The more I hear about this, the more curious I become."

I smiled. In anticipation.

"I'm pretty sure it involves the *Machault*. And there will be physical artefacts, I'm sure."

"Artefacts? More than one?"

"Possibly. Maybe even probably. But the real prize, for me, is the human story behind it all. There are real people in that story. They did what they did more than two hundred and fifty years ago. The people within the flow of events back then, the people who did the real suffering, they don't appear in the history books. But they're part of what I like to think of as the actual stuff of history. Their stories, when we understand them, against the backdrop of the times back then, and the real interest they raise for us today, well, for me those stories are dynamite stuff. They're stories that are begging to be told."

"And the artefacts themselves. Do you know what they are?"

I smiled at Dan.

"I have suspicions, and I think I know where to start looking. But artefacts are just physical things. Let's take it slowly. Remember. It's not so much the destination as it is the journey..."

Dan smiled.

I looked at her for quite a while. Here was an unusual woman. A woman of real substance. A woman who was capable and determined. And a woman who now had my full emotional engagement.

Capable and determined.

Somewhere, way at the back of my consciousness, a voice was asking things, about what role Dan might have had in the way things turned out…

I suppressed that voice.

"Where were we?" I said. "Ah yes. The journey…"

But there was more than one journey here.

I looked closely at Dan again.

There was something irresistible in her eyes.

Our hands spoke.

Their message was crystal clear.

www.ingramcontent.com/pod-product-compliance
Lightning Source LLC
Chambersburg PA
CBHW031101020726
47495CB00007B/1986